Being
Miss Nobody

Being Miss Nobody

TAMSIN WINTER

USBORNE

This book is dedicated to anyone who has ever found it difficult

to speak up. And to my son, for helping me find my voice.

First published in the UK in 2017 by Usborne Publishing Ltd., Usborne House,
83-85 Saffron Hill, London EC1N 8RT, England. www.usborne.com

Text copyright © Tamsin Winter, 2017

The right of Tamsin Winter to be identified as the author of this work has been asserted
by her in accordance with the Copyright, Designs and Patents Act, 1988.

Page 206 Quote from *The Twits* by Roald Dahl, published 1980

Cover and inside illustrations by Emma Trithart © Usborne Publishing, 2017

The name Usborne and the devices ♀ 🎈 are Trade Marks of Usborne Publishing Ltd.

A CIP catalogue record for this book is available from the British Library.

JFMAM JASOND/17 ISBN 9781474927277 04335/3

Printed in the UK.

#prologue

Before I start, here are some things you should know about me:

1. I have not been a very nice person. You are probably not going to like me very much.
2. I have done some bad things. Some really bad things.
3. I have lied to a lot of people I know. In fact, everyone I know.
4. All of the above I have done pretty much deliberately.
5. I am Miss Nobody.

1

#awkward silence

I was first diagnosed as Officially Weird two years ago, when I was nine years old. But actually, I had been Unofficially Weird for a long time before that. My parents must have suspected it too, because we were all in Dr Langley's surgery and everyone was staring at me. Dr Langley said, "I would just like you to say your name," which I thought was extremely weird considering she had been our family doctor since like for ever, and if she didn't know my name by now then who did she think it was showing up to my appointments?

So Dr Langley was staring at me and my parents were staring at me too and even though I can speak, something always happens to the words in my head in Certain Situations Like This One, which is sometimes they Disappear Completely, so what I can say is this:

Or too many words come into my head at once and they get into a Massive Muddle so I can't say any of them, like this:

ignored lie weird ignored
nobody ignored
nobody ignored
weird ignored scared
ignored scared
ignored lie
scared
weird
lie weird scared
nobody

Or sometimes I know exactly what I want to say, but the words get stuck somewhere and I can't get them out, like this:

And when it's Really Bad, it feels like my lips have actually been superglued together.

So when these things happen (and they happen a lot) I can't speak. Not even one word.

And that's what happened in the doctor's with everybody staring at me, but also it happens when I'm around people I don't know (and a lot of the people I *do* know) even if they aren't all staring at me. And up until this appointment with Dr Langley, my parents thought I was just Painfully Shy and would grow out of it. In fact, that's what everyone thought.

(Apart from me.)

Because I had known for a long time – pretty much my whole life actually – that if I can only speak normally to about four people in the whole entire world, that's not being Painfully Shy, that's being Something Else.

So there I was, nine years old, feeling like I must be

from another planet or something because I wanted to tell Dr Langley everything, but I couldn't say even one word. And everything I wanted to tell her got stuck inside my head. Like how I'd never spoken normally in front of anyone apart from my parents and my little brother and our next-door neighbour Mrs Quinney. And how much I hated school because I couldn't speak to anyone, apart from sometimes very quietly to the teaching assistant Mrs Palmer (but only if no one else was there). And how my teacher Mrs Long used to roll her eyes whenever I couldn't get my words out. And how she would put a big list of questions on the board and go round the class one by one, and before she even said my name a massive ball of panic would rise up from my tummy to my throat to inside my head. How she would point at me and say, "What's the answer to number three, please?" And even though I knew the answer, I could never say it because it was like someone had taken a pair of scissors from the wooden block on the window sill and chopped my voice out. So I would sit there, petrified, looking at the floor, with Mrs Long repeating my name and clicking her fingers saying, "I *know* you know the answer! Just say it!" And I wished there was some way for me to disappear like Alice down the rabbit hole. But classrooms don't have rabbit holes, so I had to sit there with the ball of panic inside my head, wondering why I can't be like everybody else and Just Say It.

Whenever my parents went into school, all my teachers would say the exact same thing: "I'm afraid she is just so *Painfully* Shy!" But then Mrs Long retired and we got Miss Castillo. On her first day she took the register, and when she called my name Phillip Day shouted out, "She doesn't speak, Miss," like it was The Most Normal Weird Thing in our class ever. Only clearly Miss Castillo didn't think so, because she called my parents in for a special meeting. And after that they took me to see Dr Langley.

So that's why I was sitting in her room not able to say anything, not even an easy thing like my own name. (Which is Rosalind, by the way, but obviously everyone already knew that.) And my little brother, Seb, kept wandering around pulling his pants down and up (which I thought was a much weirder thing to do in front of people than not speak). But Mum said nothing about that and said, "Why is she so shy, doctor? Why won't she speak to people?"

And everyone stared at me again, puzzled, like they were sharing the room with some kind of alien species. I just went bright red and stared at my shoes. (I do this a lot.)

So it was me who got the "I'm afraid there is Definitely

Something Wrong With Her" diagnosis, and my little brother who got the *I'm Brave!* sticker. It turns out that if you can't even say your own name in front of Dr Langley then you haven't been brave enough to get a sticker, but repeatedly flashing your six-year-old bare bum at everyone seems to nail it. If Dr Langley had *I'm Weird!* stickers, she would probably have given me one of those. But considering I already felt like I'd been wearing one my whole life, I didn't exactly need it.

She didn't say what was wrong with me, only that it wasn't Painful Shyness and if I was going to grow out of it I would have done it already. A bit like Seb always talking about dinosaurs and poo (which he's never grown out of actually, but Dad said that's more of a personality issue). My weirdness is more serious, apparently.

So we left Dr Langley's room that day in a Totally Awkward Silence, and maybe all a bit disappointed that she didn't have some kind of special medicine to make my voice appear whenever I wanted it to. But Dad held my hand, and I carried on staring at my shoes the whole way out.

In the car on the way home Seb was going on about the biggest-ever dinosaur fossil that had just been discovered in Argentina. It had a special name but I can't remember what it was. I was too busy worrying about other words I'd heard for the first time that morning that I didn't understand, like *disorder* and *hyper-sensitivity* and *psychologist* and *anxiety*. They flickered in my head as trees and houses and pavements scrolled past the window, and big raindrops ran down distorting everything. And I wondered, if I'm not Just Painfully Shy, or Totally Weird, or An Actual Alien –

What am I?

2

#brickwall

A few weeks later, I had my first appointment with a psychologist. I didn't even know what a psychologist was, so when Dad told me it was a special doctor for your brain, I pictured someone chopping the top of my head off and peering inside, or poking a tiny camera into my ear hole, or searching for my voice somewhere inside my brain with a special microscope. And I was Totally Terrified about it.

Dad suggested looking up psychologist in the encyclopedia, which is like a way slower, really heavy, old-fashioned book version of Google that he's addicted to making us read. Like if you say you need to google something he points to it and says, "This was googling stuff before googling stuff was even invented!" or "This is Google without the adverts!" or something else that makes the *Encyclopedia Britannica* sound much better than Google, when actually it totally isn't. And no matter how many times I tell him not letting me just google something is So Weird And Annoying, he always says, "You will thank me later!" Which I definitely won't because looking anything up always takes so much longer than it's supposed to.

The encyclopedia said a psychologist is someone who studies the human mind and uses therapy to help people with their problems, which sounded okay, but when I looked up therapy and it said it involves people *talking* about their problems, I actually felt sick. I didn't tell Mum and Dad, but I knew therapy was something I wouldn't be able to do. Even the thought of it made my throat feel weird, like it does when no words will come out of it. So all the way there I prayed for God to make me temporarily disappear. And when we got there I felt like I kind of had.

The therapy room was like an office on one side, with a wooden desk and black leather chairs, but the other side looked like a mini version of this soft-play area called The Fun Zone (which I never liked going to when I was little because it was always too crowded and too noisy). There were red and yellow cushions on a big blue sofa, different toy boxes all stacked up, and black-framed pictures of jumbled up shapes. The only thing I liked was the big white rug on the floor in the shape of a cloud, which was good because I spent a lot of time staring at it.

When I first walked in the psychologist made this joke which was, "I'm Dr Peak, so don't ask me to play hide-and-seek!" Which I didn't understand at first because obviously I couldn't ask him to play hide-and-seek otherwise I wouldn't have been there in the first place. Then I realized he was making one of those jokes that adults make when they are trying to let you know they are Not Like Other Normal Adults because they are fun and understand kids, but to me it just made him seem Even More Scary And Weird. Plus it was a doubly stupid joke because his name was spelled Peak not Peek, but obviously I couldn't tell him that.

I sat down and he switched on this little grey box which he said was going to record everything. And that's when I knew for one hundred per cent sure I was going to say Nothing At All Ever to Dr Peak Not Peek. I was already scared of talking to him, but getting my voice recorded was A Million Times Worse than anything I had imagined. (I would have preferred having a camera poked in my ear.) I must have been staring at it because he said, "Oh, don't worry about that, just try to ignore it." Which for Someone Like Me is a bit like someone putting a hungry lion in your bedroom and saying, "Just try to ignore it!"

Dr Peak Not Peek tøld me to think of the first time I could remember not being able to speak. He gave me a yellow notebook with my name on, which was good because I like written projects, and I wrote about the first birthday party I ever went to when I was about five.

Lauren's Party

It was Lauren's birthday and she told everyone in our class she was having a magician. I really didn't want to go because I always feel very nervous and scared if I have to go anywhere there will be lots of people (like basically everywhere). Also because the day before my dad had told me that sometimes magicians chop people in half. I cried a lot when we got there so Mum said I could stay next to her. But when the magician got there we all had to go and sit down on the floor to watch the magic. He said, "HELLO, BOYS AND GIRLS! I'M MAGIC ANDY!"

in the loudest voice ever. Then he made everyone shout "HELLO, MAGIC ANDY!" at him again and again, louder and louder, only I couldn't open my mouth to say anything so I couldn't join in. And then he told us to shout "ABRACADABRA!" at him. I can remember not wanting anyone to hear my voice.

Then Magic Andy said, "NOW, WHO WOULD LIKE TO BE MY SPECIAL MAGICAL ASSISTANT?" And straight away I thought, Not Me. I don't like standing up in front of people, I don't like anyone looking at me, and I had decided by then that I didn't like magicians very much either. So everyone put their hands up apart from me and this boy called Charlie Hooper, who at that exact moment had his fingers up his nostrils. And it was a bit like being in An Actual Nightmare because Magic Andy (which is a very un-magical sounding name anyway) did something I thought was against the law — he picked me to be his volunteer. The only person without their hand up who really did not want to be his volunteer. (I'm still not sure about Charlie because of the nose picking.)

Everyone turned and stared, and I felt like they were playing a trick on me or something, because I had accidentally volunteered myself by Definitely Not

17

Volunteering. I felt hot and dizzy and I couldn't move my head to see if Mum was behind me. I was frozen to the spot but someone helped me up to the front and everyone was clapping.

I couldn't say my name when Magic Andy asked me, then I couldn't say the magic word and I looked for my mum but I couldn't see her. I started crying so Lauren's mum came up and put her arm around me and took me to sit in the kitchen and I heard Lauren's gran say, "It doesn't pay to be sensitive in this world!" Then Mum came in and took me home.

After that I didn't want to go to any more birthday parties in case it happened again. Dad would always try to make me, but I would get upset so Mum would say I didn't have to go. Then after a while people stopped inviting me anyway.

After I'd finished writing, Dr Peak Not Peek read it, then asked me some questions I couldn't answer because my words got in a Massive Muddle and my throat was closed up. Then he said, "Okay," and wrote down loads of stuff on his clipboard.

And that is what Dr Peak Not Peek's monthly therapy sessions were like. With the little grey box on his desk recording me not saying anything. Not even one word.

Just long Awkward Silences where my voice should have been.

I wished it could record the Massive Muddle of words in my head, or the words stuck in my throat, or how hard I was trying, or how bad I felt about not answering his questions. Because then maybe he could have seen how much I wanted him to help me. But little grey boxes don't record stuff like that. So I spent every therapy session not answering his questions, writing about Other Awkward Silence Scenarios in my yellow notebook, looking down at the white cloud rug wishing it would turn into a real cloud and float me away.

The only thing I liked about Dr Peak Not Peek was that he told me the name for my condition, which is Selective Mutism (SM for short). And I liked having an Official Name for it, because it meant that clearly I wasn't The Only Person In The World who had this particular type of weirdness, even though it feels like that sometimes.

Dad said out of all the Possible Weirdness Scenarios he rated it 7/10 weird, which to be honest I was completely disappointed with. I think it rates at least 9/10 just for the Awkward Silence factor alone. But Dad said he thought Tourette's syndrome was a worse thing to have and if I wanted my weirdness rating to be higher then I'd better hurry up and get something else because he suspected Seb might overtake me on the weirdness scale pretty soon. Anytime I get upset about it now he always says, "Rozzie, whatever weirdness you have, it is still one hundred per cent better than being Completely Normal." But that's my dad for you. And he wouldn't say that if he was the one who had to go to my school.

Because the main problem about having my type of weirdness is that for as long as I can remember, I have never had any friends. (Brothers don't count.) Some people (I see them all the time) can go up to someone and say "Hi!" then the other person says "Hi!" and they start talking and everything is just normal. But if you go up to people and say nothing most people will tell you to go away, or that speaking to you is like Speaking To A Brick Wall. And I have found that in general people do not want to be friends with a brick wall.

If you feel sorry for me at this point then you probably shouldn't. You see, it is all my own fault. It's like Mrs Long always used to say, "You can't expect to have any friends if you won't speak to people!" And unfortunately she was right. But to me, being in a situation where I'm expected to speak to someone is actually less appealing than sticking my head down the toilet. Even after Seb's done one of his "poosplosions".

Anyway, it wasn't long after my first therapy session with Dr Peak Not Peek that we found out Seb had The Illness, so my parents kind of left me to it. And that was two years ago now. It turns out that if you're not exactly dying of something in my house, then you're not exactly The Main Priority. Even if sometimes maybe you wish you could be.

#tellmeabout yourself

After a year and a half of saying Nothing At All Ever to Dr Peak Not Peek, he decided that he couldn't help me any more, and he referred me to a different therapist. And I was half Massively Relieved I wouldn't have to sit in his office surrounded by the Awkward Silence any more, and half Totally Scared about meeting someone new. He told me to write something about myself and my family for my new therapist while he had a meeting with my parents. So I sat on a plastic chair outside his office and opened my yellow notebook for the last time.

My house is number 3 Byron Hill. All the streets in

my area are named after famous poets. There's Rossetti Drive, Shelley Close, Tennyson Street, Coleridge Avenue and Clare Street. Our area is an okay area for the town where we live. Which means it could be a lot better, but it could also be a lot worse.

The Main News at my house isn't me, it's Seb. He's my brilliant little brother and he's dying. He's not dying quickly like what happens if you get certain diseases, he's dying really slowly. Because we found out ages ago, and he's had four rounds of chemotherapy now but he's still not getting better. I can't be very good at therapy either, because I've had seventeen sessions with Dr Peak and I'm still only speaking to about 0.0000000001% of the world's population.

When we first found out Seb was ill, Mum wanted to move house. She said she wanted us to live somewhere nicer where trees are planted in the pavements and people say "Hello!" to you when you walk past. But when I asked Dad if we were going to move he said, "The problem is we had children the wrong side of the financial crisis." And when I looked confused he said, "Put it this way — if we moved somewhere more expensive we would have to start cutting back on luxuries such as wearing clothes and eating food."

Mum always says, "Even though Seb's really poorly, there's Still Every Reason To Hope he will get better." But last week I overheard Dad say, "We have to Prepare For The Worst." So I'm not exactly sure what to think. Some days Seb seems okay and some days he's too ill to do anything apart from sleep, and some days he's like a normal eight-year-old boy (apart from his personality). Anyway, whatever happens, I'm massively glad I don't have strangers saying "Hello!" to me all the time.

Seb doesn't go to school any more because of all the germs, but he's still brainier than anyone I know. He has a special tutor called Brian, but Seb calls him Brain because he is really clever but also because it's an anagram. Brain tested Seb's IQ when he first started tutoring him and said it was a lot higher than normal. One of Dad's all-time favourite sayings since then is This Family Just Doesn't Do Normal, which I agree must be true, but I'm still not sure if that's a good thing or a bad thing.

As well as being able to memorize really hard things like the names of loads of astronauts, star constellations and every dinosaur that existed, Seb's obsessed with poo. He kind of already was, but when his medicine started giving him diarrhoea all the time, he called himself a pooperhero and since then he makes at least one poo joke a day. It's like even though he is way cleverer than normal, the age part of his brain is way younger than normal. He's also way happier than normal too. He never seems to get sad, even though he's dying, which is kind of the Exact Opposite to me because I definitely feel sad a lot of the time and I hardly ever get ill.

Even though I can speak normally at home, I have to be careful around Seb not to mention his illness. He knows he is ill but I'm not supposed to bring it up in conversation unless he does. Once I asked Mum if she would have another baby if Seb dies and she got really upset and I wished and wished I hadn't said it, because she didn't stop crying for ages. Since then I try not to mention it. If Seb dies I will be an only child, then I really will have no friends.

We don't have much extra money because Mum quit her job to look after Seb, but we're saving up to go on a family holiday. We are going to Egypt because seeing the pyramids would be Seb's Dream Come True. He's a little bit obsessed with pharaohs and last time he was in hospital he asked the nurses for bandages so he could mummify his toy dinosaurs. He made a wig out of tinfoil and makes everyone call him Pharaoh Poopookhamun anytime he wears it, which is a lot.

Ages ago Mum wrote to this charity that gives you a Dream Come True if you're dying, but they can't afford to give everyone a Dream Come True, so we can't count on it. That's why all our spare money goes into Seb's holiday fund and that's the reason I don't get pocket money because I want it to go to Seb's dream. I'm looking forward to going to a country where everyone speaks a different language, because no one will expect me to talk to them.

Since we found out Seb's got The Illness, our house is only happy at certain times, like when Seb's around, then at other times everyone gets really upset, like last week when Seb had to stay in hospital again and Mum wouldn't stop crying. And other times I feel like something bad is happening but my parents kind of pretend it isn't. But I know it is definitely happening because the silence feels weird. If my house had to be a colour, sometimes it would be sunshine orange and sometimes it would be rain-cloud grey.

That's why I like going next door to Mrs Quinney's, because although her house isn't exactly really happy, it's always the same no matter what.

And the silence in her house isn't the scary kind.

What with Seb's hospital visits, and Dad working extra hours, I end up going to Mrs Quinney's house a lot. One of the reasons I love Mrs Quinney is because she is one of The Few People On Planet Earth I've always been able to speak to. She's half-battleaxe, half-fruitcake according to my dad, and she lets her cats, Mary and Bernard, launch their bum rockets in our garden according to Seb. But Mum appreciates what she calls "Mrs Quinney's Victorian Finishing School". (Mrs Quinney calls it etiquette.) She's taught me how to correctly lay a table, how to sew people's initials onto a handkerchief, and I can balance three books on my head and walk around her living room, which is called posture and it's important in case you ever want to get married.

Dad wishes I didn't have to go there so much because last Christmas he asked me what I wanted from Santa and I said, "Peace on earth." Then Dad said he was going to have a word with Mrs Quinney about brainwashing me.

But Mum said, "She can speak normally there. And Mrs Quinney loves her. I'm sure she must get lonely. It won't do Rozzie any harm to learn a little bit about God."

And Dad said, "Fine, but when she comes back wanting to become a nun, I'll blame you."

For the record, I only ever wanted to become a nun for about two days when Mrs Quinney told me they can take a vow of silence and then they don't have to speak to anyone. But when I looked it up in the encyclopedia and found out they have to get up really early and do loads of chores and praying, I changed my mind. Anyway, if I was a nun I don't think God would like me very much because what I really want more than anything is the Exact Opposite of a vow of silence — to be able to say whatever I want to everyone. But unfortunately, that's not the sort of Dream Come True you can save up your pocket money for.

One of the best ever things Mrs Quinney taught me is calligraphy, which is like a special type of handwriting that is actually a form of art. The word calligraphy comes from the Greek language, meaning beautiful writing. I looked it up. Mrs Quinney has the most perfect handwriting I have ever seen, but her hands are old now and she says her writing was even better when she was younger.

The first thing Mrs Quinney taught me was how to do swirly letters. You start by practising the alphabet which takes Literally Ages, then you can move on to short, joined-up phrases like this:

Hello, friend!

I love doing calligraphy because whatever is happening with words in my head, I can always write some down on paper. And since doing calligraphy, I can make them look nice, which is not how they feel in my head most of the time. When I feel worried (which is a lot) I do calligraphy and it helps the panic in my head go away a bit.

Anyway, I'm writing all this because Dr Peak said you are an expert in helping people like me. And I'm really hoping that's true. I need someone to help stop words from getting stuck in my head when I try to speak to people. Because even though my dad says being Completely Normal isn't very good, it still sounds A Million Times Better than being me.

4

#whatif

Even though I never actually spoke to Dr Peak Not Peek, things got a bit better for me at my primary school after they found out I had SM. I never said anything in class, but Miss Castillo gave me special cards to hold up – a red one for if I needed five minutes outside the classroom on my own, a pink one for if I needed to go to the toilet (which was a massive relief), a green card if I knew the answer, and a special whiteboard to write things down on. I even spoke to her quietly after class when no one else was around. Everyone agreed I was Definitely A Lot Better. And even though I still didn't have anyone who could be classed as An Actual Friend, no one called me weird or a brick wall any more.

But then Year Six finished, and I had to start a whole new school where I didn't know anyone. In their special meeting, Dr Peak Not Peek told my parents it would be better for me to start at a secondary school where no one from my primary school would be going, so I could have a Totally Fresh Start. He thought it would help me be able to speak normally, to "break my pattern" of being totally silent. Only I didn't exactly understand what that meant. Anyway, what happens if you're Someone Like Me is your parents listen to the expert (which wasn't me unfortunately). So everyone from my class went to Stanthorpe Academy, and I had to go across town to Manor High.

And I suppose that's when this whole thing kind of started.

Going to a new school felt a bit like there was this massive train coming towards me, and I couldn't get out of the way because I was tied to the tracks. All these questions were flying around in my head like bats, conjuring up Awkward Silence Scenarios like: *What if I can't speak to my new teachers? What if I can't say my name? What if I get ignored again? What if everyone at my new school thinks I'm weird? What if no one likes me?* And the main one:

**What if
I can't actually
speak
at all?**

And all the words jumbled up into a Massive Muddle of

what if what if what if what if what if what if what if what if what if what if what if what if what if what if what if what if what if

Because even though I had spent literally the whole summer wishing my SM would magically disappear before my first day at Manor High, I was seriously worried that, actually, it might get worse.

And it turned out I was right.

Which just proves that no matter how many times you wish for something, getting a Dream Come True when you are Someone Like Me is probably the closest you can get to impossible.

5

#badintro

It was the start of September, and my first day at Manor High. Seb was going through a bad patch so he was in bed. I'd heard him being sick in the night. Dad was obsessively cleaning everything like he always did when Seb got bad, and Mum was at the kitchen table reading her book about alternative medicines. Seb called them Mum's Miracle Cures, but they weren't like real miracles because they never seemed to work. I was wearing my new uniform and trying my best to hide the Massive Silent Panic I was having about going to my new school (because I knew for sure Mum didn't have a Miracle Cure for that).

When Mum saw me she got up from the table, gave me a hug, tucked in my shirt, did up my top button and said, "There. You look great! Are you sure you don't want Dad to go into school with you? He could help you find your class and just, you know, make sure you're okay."

I said, "No, I'll be okay. I'm actually Totally Fine. I'm sort of looking forward to it!" Which was a Massive Lie because a) I would rather have walked barefoot across the bum-rocket rose bushes than go to a new school, and b) I really did want Dad to come with me, but even I know if there's a way to look like a Complete Weirdo on your first day at a new school, it's taking my dad with you. Especially when he's wearing his **I HUG PUGS** T-shirt.

Dad gave me a hug, being careful not to touch me with the bubbly washing-up gloves he was wearing and said, "You'll be fine, Rozzie. Totally Fresh Start, hey?"

I smiled, trying to make it look as convincing as possible even though the words

What if I actually get killed?

bubbled up in my head.

"Seb made you a card," Dad said, and pointed to the table.

The card said GOOD LUCK, ROZZIE! on the front and I hope your first day at school goes with a BANG! inside, next to a picture of a school exploding, which I hoped was his way of telling me he knew I didn't want to go to Manor High and not some secret terrorism fantasy.

"And me and Dad got you this," Mum said and gave me a red-and-white striped parcel. Inside was a new notebook and pen and on the first page it said:

I'm Rosalind Banks.

Sometimes I find it hard to speak.

Dad said, "We're sure you'll be fine. Your new teachers know about…you know. This is just in case."

Then a million little grey clouds inside my head started raining the words

STAY AT HOME

But I said, "I'll be okay. I probably won't even need this," because it looked like Mum was about to cry. Then I said, "By the way, I'm definitely not the one you need to worry about," and showed them Seb's exploding school picture.

"Honestly, I don't know where he gets it from!" Dad said, pointing at Mum.

So I spent that morning the same way I'd spent the entire summer: telling my parents I felt Totally Fine about starting my new school and, unfortunately, they believed me. Which is annoying, because the truth was I felt Totally Like I Was About To Do A Bungee Jump Off A Massive Cliff With No Rope Attached. And not telling my parents that was probably my first Major Mistake.

Letting Mum tuck in my school shirt so tightly, do up my top button and send me to Manor High with a notebook and pen in my hands was Major Mistake Number Two.

The first Traumatic Experience Of The Day was catching the school bus. To me, catching a bus filled with people I don't know, when I might not be able to say a word, is like asking someone to get into a tank full of hungry sharks wearing a seal costume.

The sound of everyone's voices over the rumbling engine made it really noisy. People shouted things across me as I got on and the whole time I wished Dad had taken me to school (or let me be homeschooled by Brain for the rest of my life actually). A girl wearing blue-rimmed glasses sat next to me and said, "Hey, I'm Ella, is it your first day too?" I tried my best to say "Hi!" but all my words Disappeared Completely and I couldn't even move my head properly to nod. She must have thought I was being rude because she said, "Okay, whatever! Don't speak to me then!" and leaned forward to speak to the girl in front. I looked down at my new shoes, feeling like there was some kind of giant spotlight on me showing everyone on the bus how Totally Silent And Friendless I was.

The bus stopped just outside the school gates and I waited until everyone had got off. I tried to say something, anything, just whisper a word quickly to myself like Dr Peak Not Peek had told me to, but it seemed like there were millions of people outside rushing and shouting and the bus driver was telling me to "HURRY UP!" so my lips wouldn't move at all.

I got off the bus and gazed up at the grey buildings casting their enormous shadows over me like massive storm clouds. Everything and everyone was so much bigger than primary school. There weren't any teachers telling people to line up, and everything was noisier and more crowded than I'd expected. I'd missed the Year Seven Orientation

Day because that day Seb had been rushed into hospital with a really high temperature, so it seemed like everyone knew where they had to go apart from me. I took out the blurred map the school had sent me, wondering if there was any place on it I might be able to speak.

My new form tutor was called Mr Bryant and my form room was E14, which stood for English 14, which meant I had to somehow find the English block from where I was standing. When I'd shown Seb the map, he'd said that even Christopher Columbus would find following it a challenge, so for me with Literally No Sense Of Direction and in the middle of a Massive Silent Panic, it felt impossible.

I waited for a gap in the crowds that looked Unlikely To Result In Me Getting Crushed To Death, put my head down and walked in what I hoped was the right direction. Suddenly a tall boy with dark messy hair stood right in front of me blocking my path. He leaned down really close so his nose was practically touching mine and he was half standing on my foot. He shouted, "Geek!" and I felt his hot breath on my face. He ran off laughing and my cheeks burned red.

So that was my Welcome To Manor High. The bell hadn't even rung and my chances of speaking to Anyone At All Ever went crashing down from Not Exactly Likely to a

Massive Zero. My hands were shaking and the tears stinging my eyes made everything look blurry, which I suppose at least made the map more accurate. A surge of people moved behind me and I got carried along in the crowd, feeling like a tiny spider being washed down the plughole.

I spotted the word *English* on a building to my left, so I headed towards it, thinking if I could just get away from all these people, maybe I'd be okay. But when I got inside, most of the classrooms were missing their numbers and everyone looked too scary to ask them anything in my notebook. So I walked up and down the graffitied corridors doing emergency prayers to God to let me find E14 before I was late. And maybe God was listening, or maybe He has a strange sense of humour, because I found the classroom, but waiting for me inside was something that made me wish I was late: The Introduce Yourself Game.

Introducing yourself to people is literally impossible when all your words have Disappeared Completely. It's not like you can just put your hand up and say, "Sorry, everyone, I'm Rosalind but I can't play because I can't even say my own name right now." I wonder who even invented this game, because sitting in a circle so everyone can see you, looking at the condensation on the window wishing there was some way you could turn into water vapour before it's your turn, doesn't exactly seem like very much fun to me.

Clearly Mr Bryant didn't realize this because he said, "It's just a bit of fun to break the ice, and a great way of getting to know each other!" Which isn't true because when it was my turn to say my name and three facts about myself I literally said this:

All my new classmates were staring at me, whispering, "Why isn't she saying anything?" and the girl wearing blue glasses called Ella whispered, "She wouldn't speak to me on the bus either!" So it felt like actually, a massive wall of ice had been built around me and no one wanted to get to know me at all.

Mr Bryant must have finally realized who I was because he got really flustered and said, "Right! Hold on! Yes, of course! Sorry!" and looked at the register and said, "Rosalind?" I managed to nod my head, then he told the next person to go.

I could hear people whispering, "Can't she speak English?" and "Why didn't she speak?" and "She didn't even say anything!" And I sat there feeling like a Totally Silent Failure, wondering if Literally Dying Of Humiliation could be any worse than this.

After the bell went, Mr Bryant asked me to stay behind. He said he was sorry and that he'd thought I might be able to join in a little bit. But when your voice has completely disappeared, the best joining in you can do is not running out of the fire exit (unfortunately I couldn't tell him that). He told me the Special Educational Needs lady, Mrs Kingsley, wanted to see me at lunchtime, and put a tiny circle on my map where her office was.

I looked at my timetable. I had a different teacher for every subject, not like primary school where Mrs Long and Miss Castillo just knew everything. The first lesson was history with Mr Dean. I hurried along the corridor, then out across the concrete quad to the humanities block, hoping the fresh air would cool my burning cheeks. Everyone was already sitting down when I got there, and they stared at me as I walked in. I sat at the only empty desk and heard a few people whispering, "She's bright red!" I sank as low as I could into my seat, wishing it had some kind of ejector button.

Mr Dean came in and said, "Good morning, everyone!" in a gruff voice, and his grey moustache wiggled. He handed out exercise books and told us to write a page about a memorable part of history. One of the projects we had done at primary school was about the Second World War. It stuck in my mind because Miss Castillo told us about how the evacuees had to wear name tags, which sounded like a really good idea to me because then no one would have to ask me who I was.

I started writing and finally felt the massive lump that had been in my throat since the bus journey fading away. Because when I try to speak my words get all frozen up, but it never seems to happen when I write. I put the title *Blitz Britain* and before I knew it I had written four pages. Which was okay until Mr Dean saw it and said, "Well done! That's one for the Manor High record books!" and a few people laughed. I felt my face go bright red again and the lump in my throat came back.

When I met Mrs Kingsley at lunchtime I was so nervous all I could do was stare at her gold glasses chain that kept getting caught in her hair as she spoke. She took out a big red file with my name on the front, and handed me a pack of word cards saying, "I've made you these, so have a look through them and let me know if you need any more, although I can see you've brought a notebook, which is good." She put her glasses on and looked at some papers for a few minutes. "Now, I'm sure I read somewhere that you love reading, is that right?" I nodded and she said, "Ah good! There's only one place for you then!" And when I looked at her blankly she took off her glasses and said, "The library!"

The library at Manor High was much bigger than the one we had at primary school. The shelves of books were higher up and it had round wooden tables, a row of computers, and the carpet had big colourful dots on it. Along the back wall in big swirly letters it said:

Lose yourself in a book!

And I thought, if there was one big enough to hide in I would totally do that right now.

A lady with curly brown hair was sitting at a table by the back windows talking to three students who all looked older than me. Mrs Kingsley took me over and said, "Mrs Goodacre – this is Rosalind, the Year Seven girl I emailed you about. This is Mrs Goodacre, our librarian. Now, I have to go and meet some other students, but if you need anything, you know where I am. I'll see you again Friday lunchtime." And then she left.

Mrs Goodacre smiled warmly at me and said, "Oh, wonderful! We were hoping you would make it. Sit down. This is my library committee!" I looked at the three new faces, trying my best to smile, thinking, if I'm going to fit in anywhere at Manor High, this is probably my best chance (and if I could only get my lips to move I might be able to stop the whole day – and my entire life – from being A Massive Disaster).

The boy sitting next to Mrs Goodacre stood up and said, "Nice to meet you, I'm Rajit. I'm in Year Nine so I'm in charge of the library squad here. I'll take you on a quick tour, then we can start the interview."

And before I actually fainted Mrs Goodacre said, "Rajit, I have told you enough times now, we are a library *committee*, not a squad, and we certainly don't conduct interviews. It's not like we're inundated with applicants, is it?" She smiled at me again. "We are, however, in the middle of a meeting."

Rajit smiled awkwardly, said, "Sorry, Mrs G. My bad," and sat down.

Mrs Goodacre introduced me to the rest of the committee: Suzi and William who were both in Year Eight. (When Mrs Goodacre said she wasn't exactly inundated with applicants, she was In No Way Exaggerating.) "Now, I know it's a little way off, but I'd like to start advertising the half-term read-a-thon a bit sooner this year. Who would like to make the flyers?"

Immediately Rajit put up his hand. "Already on it, Mrs G."

"Right, but I want to see them before you hand them out this time, please. We don't want a repeat of last year's fiasco. The prize is a ten-pound book token and everyone who reads three books or more gets a certificate."

"That's what I put last year, Mrs G."

"Well, some people misinterpreted the words 'large cash prize'. Put 'book token' this time, and I want pictures of *books* on the flyer. The dollar bills you used last year just added to the confusion."

After the meeting Mrs Goodacre and Suzi showed me around the library and told me about the different jobs the library monitors do. I got a library card with my name on it and chose a book to take out. Before I left, Mrs Goodacre gave me a tiny green badge in the shape of a book to pin on my blazer.

"You're part of the library squad now," Suzi said, and William gave me a double thumbs up from behind the *Guinness World Records* book. And for the first time since I arrived at Manor High, I felt like my brain wasn't on red alert, which was a bit like finally reaching the ground after spending all morning on a high wire.

The library already felt like the one place in the entire school I could go where I didn't feel like I had Some Kind Of Social Leprosy. Unfortunately, it also happened to be the one hang-out that confirmed to others I Definitely Was Suffering From Some Kind Of Social Leprosy. But considering I would rather stick my head in a toilet than be in a situation where I'm expected to speak to people, that wasn't such a Major Issue. Not then, anyway.

The first lesson after lunch was English with Miss Carter. As we walked in she said, "Welcome, everybody!" in a smiley voice, then fiddled around with her computer. I emergency-prayed she wouldn't ask me to say anything. The screen flickered on and we had to copy down *Miss Carter's Rules and Expectations!* that beamed out. While we were writing she came round to each desk to tick off the register, which I liked because it meant no one paid attention to me when I pointed to my name on her list instead of saying it.

On the wall there was a poster about the different clubs you could join, like brass band and drama club and chess club. But to join clubs like that you really need to have a Special Talent like acting, or playing an instrument or being really clever. I'm sure you are not surprised to hear that I have Exactly None of these Special Talents, which is annoying because going to clubs like that is a good way of finding The Holy Grail Of Friendships: A Friend For Life. The only thing I am any good at is calligraphy.

At the end of the lesson Miss Carter held up my book to the class as a good example of handwriting and general neatness. But unfortunately, being good at handwriting and general neatness will not win you any friends at my school, believe me.

# #

When I got home Seb was feeling better because he was in the living room with Mum. When I walked in he said, "Look what we made, Rozzie!" and pointed to a cake which was luminous green.

"Wow, Seb! Is it supposed to be green?"

"It's not snot!" he shouted, then laughed until he was out of breath.

"Seb, please take it easy! What did the nurse tell you today? It's *avocado* cake," Mum said, and before I could say anything she cut me a slice, saying, "It's really healthy!" Which is what Mum always says when she knows something is going to taste bad. "So, tell us all about your first day!"

And luckily I had already prepared my answer on the

way home. Which wasn't about the scary bus journey or The Boy Who Shouted Geek or The Introduce Yourself Game Fail or being Totally Silent all day or people whispering about me. Instead, I showed them my library monitor badge and told them about Mrs Goodacre and the library committee, about Mrs Kingsley and Mr Bryant and how I didn't need to use my notebook all day. It wasn't even hard because I wasn't Technically Lying. Apart from maybe when I said the cake tasted nice.

Later, when I went next door to show Mrs Quinney my English book and tell her what Miss Carter said about my handwriting, she said it was good, but I was not to be too pleased with myself. Being too pleased with yourself leads to terrible things.

6

#voicemail

The next morning, I stood on my own in the quad wondering where I had to go for assembly. I'd tried to follow Ella, but lost sight of her in the squash of people getting off the bus. I didn't like that everyone could probably see how red my face was because my hair was blowing all over the place. I scanned the groups of people, and finally spotted a tall boy called Adrian, who was carrying a trumpet case and walking with another boy from my class, so I followed them across the quad and into a big grey building with stone steps.

Inside there were loads of people crowding in a long corridor. Some people were standing in lines, some were messing about. The ceiling was really high and it felt like it was full right up to the top with A Million Different Voices except mine.

Mr Bryant was at the other end of the corridor near some big double doors and when I got there he was telling everyone to line up in alphabetical order. My surname is Banks which means I have to go near the front, which I don't like. People were asking each other their names and a boy said, "I'm Michael Bell," and kept asking me who I was. I stood there with my throat closed up and my words hidden in some kind of brain-vacuum, feeling like I might just faint right there, in probably the wrong place alphabetically. Mr Bryant came over and said, "Okay, go in." And Michael kept saying, "Go!" in my ear and tapping me until I finally managed to get my feet to walk forward, which wasn't easy when they actually wanted to run A Million Miles in the opposite direction.

Inside the hall was a sort of hushed quiet. People were whispering and teachers were saying "Shh!" A man wearing glasses and a brown suit was standing at the front with his arms folded. Light was gleaming through the big windows onto my face like a big spotlight, and it felt as if hundreds of eyes were looking at me. My shoes squeaked on the wooden floor and my hands were sweating. I felt a bit like how I imagine a pirate must feel being forced to walk the plank, only instead of shark-infested waters it was an enormous sea of The Totally Unknown that I might drown in. My heart was beating so fast I thought everyone must be able hear it.

Our class had to sit in the front row because we are class 7A, and the brown-suit man, who turned out to be the principal, Mr Endeby, walked up and down right in front of us. The question

What if he picks on me to say something?

echoed in my head, like someone coughing in the hall, but getting louder and louder and louder, which did not feel like A Wonderful Start To A New Academic Year, no matter how many times Mr Endeby said it.

I relaxed a little bit when he started talking about a girl in Year Eight called Jenny Baker who was on TV over the summer in this maths challenge quiz thing where you had to do hard sums really fast. He showed a clip of it on the screen and spent ages talking about her even though she didn't win the quiz. He said, "Fifth place out of everyone in the country is A Tremendous Achievement and everyone in the school should feel very proud!" I remembered what Mrs Quinney had told me and made sure I didn't feel too proud of Jenny.

On the way out of the hall I heard some people sniggering and Ella poked me in the arm and said, "Why are you bright red?" All my words got tangled up in a big knot in my head. I shrugged. She turned to her friends Katie and Maisy and said, "See?" Then they laughed until a teacher shushed them.

I walked as quickly as I could up the stairs to maths, feeling like my cheeks were on fire. I took a seat near the back next to the window. The rest of my class came in noisily, all taking seats that weren't the one next to mine. A boy called Connor Mould sat in the one directly behind me and said, "God, stop being so loud!"

Then his friend Vinnie said, "Yeah, stop talking so much!"

For the entire maths lesson, whenever Mr Pearson was at the other side of the room, Connor and Vinnie would say things like, "Stop distracting us!" and "Stop talking!"

And every time Mr Pearson would say, "Try to keep the noise down over there, young lady!"

And it reminded me of the things my Uncle Pete used to say.

Even though I had known Uncle Pete and Auntie Marie for like ever, whenever they came to our house I felt this Massive Sense Of Dread come over me like a tidal wave. (I feel like this a lot.) I could never say anything the whole time they were there, only nod or shake my head. Auntie Marie was always nice to me about it, but Uncle Pete used to make jokes like, "Hello, Little Miss Chatterbox!" and "Stop being so noisy, Rosalind!" and "No one can get a word in edgeways with you around!" Then when they were leaving he would always say, "You can't spend your whole life not speaking to me, you know!" Which I did actually, because they got divorced and I haven't seen him since. I don't think even Auntie Marie speaks to him any more.

I spent most of my lessons that day trying to hide my face in my new exercise books. It was only my second day at Manor High, but already I had become The Weird Girl Who Can't Speak. And the chair next to me was Permanently Empty.

After lunch, instead of going to double sport, I stayed in the library for half an hour because I was leaving school early. I had to meet Octavia Welland, my new therapist who was a specialist in speech therapy, which was another of Dr Peak Not Peek's Brilliant Ideas (only I was secretly quite pleased about this one). I just hoped my heart rate would be back to normal by then. I tidied up the books on the display, then went to reception and signed out.

Dad was waiting for me just outside the school gates. When I opened the car door he said in a robot voice, "Get. In. The. Car. Subject. 57035893." And when I got in he said, "Prepare. For. Your. Normalness. Therapy." I laughed a tiny bit. He said, "Was school okay?" and I smiled and nodded. Which only felt like a Fifty Per Cent Lie because I wasn't totally sure if nodding counted or not.

The therapy building was next to the hospital but not actually in the hospital, which I liked. It had a blue sign with white letters saying *Sternberg Speech and Language Centre* and there were little rows of perfectly round plants outside. When we parked, Dad said, "Want me to come in with you, Rozzie?" Only I said no because having Dad with me in a place where I might not be able to speak to him feels Massively Weird. It's one of the reasons we hardly ever go out anywhere as a family (and because Dad's obsessed with keeping Seb away from germs). Anyway, I wasn't too scared of meeting Octavia because of the message she'd left me on Mum's phone the week before telling me about the centre and that I didn't have to speak to her in therapy. Her voice was warm and went up and down so much it sounded musical, like one of those big xylophones, and when she said bye she said,

"Bye-eee!" so that it went up at the end.

I went through the doors and signed in on the special computer Octavia had explained about. I tapped the screen then typed in my date of birth. My name came on the screen with the words *Please Take A Seat* and a picture of a big smiley face. I liked this a lot because it meant I didn't have to speak to anyone. Everyone who goes to the centre has some kind of issue with speaking so they have a good understanding of what it must be like to be Someone Like Me, which is a nice feeling.

I sat in the waiting room and after a few minutes I heard the floor creaking, so I looked up and saw a lady with a big yellow scarf wrapped around her hair and kind eyes and a big half-moon smile. She was wearing keys on a string around her neck and a big beaded necklace, and a pair of glasses were hanging around her neck too, so every time she moved she clinked and jingled and jangled.

She said, "Hello, Rosalind, I'm Octavia. I'm so pleased to meet you! My room is back this way, so if you're ready come along." Her voice sounded even nicer than it did on the voicemail; it filled the room with warmth and music and I thought, already this is way better than Dr Peak Not Peek, and not just because she didn't make any stupid jokes.

In her room there were certificates in frames that said things like *Direct Speech Management, Neuro-Linguistic*

Programming and *Realizing The Potential of Children Who Stammer*. I liked it that she had these because I also like getting certificates. I only got two from primary school and I keep them in a special folder at home that Mum bought me. They are: *Super Speller* and *Reading Award*, both from Year Six. I seriously doubted I would get any from Manor High, unless they gave out certificates for Being Weird and Having No Friends, in which case I would probably fill my folder by the end of term.

The next thing I thought was how much Dad would hate this room because it was seriously messy. It was filled up almost to the ceiling with books; there were too many on the shelves and piles and piles of them on the floor. Octavia stood at her desk rummaging around and the whole time she sang a made-up song going, *"Where are your notes, Mrs O O O?"* I think she must have become a speech therapist because she is the Exact Opposite of me in that she literally cannot stop talking.

She pulled out some crumpled papers from one of the drawers then reminded me she didn't expect me to say anything. "The main thing we will work on is Not Feeling Afraid when you need to speak." She wrote it on a big bit of paper which I liked (because that is sort of how it feels, although I thought she should maybe change it to Not Feeling Like I Want To Spontaneously Combust).

She told me how she was going to help me and gave me a questionnaire to fill in while she hummed and sang and spoke about books I might like and told me about some charity websites and blogs about SM I could visit. There wasn't an Awkward Silence like there used to be with Dr Peak Not Peek and the room felt safe because she didn't have a grey recording box, or ask me any questions, so I knew for sure she meant it when she said I didn't have to speak, which isn't what therapy used to feel like. At the end when I was leaving I said, "Thank you," really quietly. And Octavia smiled like she understood exactly how much I meant it.

On the way out of the centre I was still smiling because I felt like Octavia's therapy was going to be Totally Different (In A Good Way). But Dad was on his phone leaning against the side of the car saying, "Okay, don't worry, we'll come straight home." And when he saw me he hung up, then smiled even though I could tell something was wrong.

Once we were in the car he said, "So, what was Octodoc like?" which was what Seb called Octavia when he heard her name on Mum's answerphone.

I said, "She's really nice. I think she's going to be able to help me. I said thank you to her at the end."

Dad looked surprised and said, "Wow! Really proud of

you, Rozzie! Mum will be thrilled. That will really cheer her up." Tears formed in his eyes but he blinked them away, then he started the engine and said in the robot voice, "Normalness. Therapy. Working. Very. Good."

So I left feeling like maybe I was one per cent Less Weird and wondering if Octavia might be one of those people Mrs Quinney had told me about, who is not exactly an angel, but not exactly a normal person either. Because being able to say thank you to her when I'd only just met her felt like something resembling An Actual Miracle.

When I got home Seb was in his room and Mum looked like she'd been crying even though she was smiling. Dad went straight upstairs and Mum started talking in the really cheerful voice she uses sometimes when she's trying not to cry: "So, how did you get on with Octavia?"

Half of me told her about therapy while the other half of me wondered what was happening with Seb. And when she asked me about school I said it was good, which was a bit of a Massive Lie, but it felt easier than telling her what it was really like, which was bad. And later when I asked if Seb was okay, Mum said, "Yes, he's absolutely fine, just tired!"

Which proves I wasn't the only one being Not Exactly Truthful About Stuff in my family.

7

#whatdid yousay

With all the million new faces and classrooms and bells ringing and crowds pushing, and never-ending rainy days, and disappearing words, I spent most of my time at school wishing I had one thing: A Friend. But when you can't speak, friends can be rarer than unicorns. What weren't rarer than unicorns, however, were people who wanted to make me feel worse than I did already.

Because if you spend the first two weeks at a new school not speaking to anyone, some people think you are doing it on purpose, and that you're being rude. Or you don't want to join in. Or you don't like them. Or you are Totally Weird. And some people think you don't have anything to say at all, like you're just an empty person with no words and no thoughts. Like some kind of walking blank page of nothing. A Nobody.

And nobody wants to be friends with a Nobody.

That Friday lunchtime Mrs Kingsley peered at me over the red file and asked if I had used my word cards yet. I shook my head. "Well, do try to use them next week, Rosalind! It says in here that using cards helped you at primary school." I tried to say okay, but it got jammed in my throat. So I just stared at the carpet and nodded.

That weekend two different doctors came to visit Seb, and both times Mum and Dad were being Awkwardly Silent when they left. The house filled up with the rain-cloud grey feeling like it always did when Seb was bad. He slept practically the whole weekend, and I was only allowed to go in to see him if I promised not to get him excited. So on Sunday I read him a really long poem from the Victorian times that Miss Carter had given us to read for homework, until Seb sat bolt upright and said, "Rozzie, are you trying to put me into a coma?"

On Monday I sat in my usual place in form time, second row from the back, next to the wall with the Genres of Literature poster. Mr Bryant hadn't arrived yet, so I was looking through my word cards, deciding which one I could maybe use first, when a girl called Maisy Love came over to me. She stood looking at me for a few moments, then asked me The Most Impossible Question To Answer Ever: "Why can't you talk?"

The Silent Panic started building, first in my tummy, then in my head. I looked down and shrugged, but she carried on, "Isn't it weird though? Can you say *anything*? Can your parents talk?" And I didn't know at first if she was being mean or if she was actually interested in whether you get SM from your parents like eye colour or something. But then she said, "They must be well weird if they had you!" And she laughed and walked back to her seat. I didn't dare look up in case she said something else, but I heard other people laughing too. I hid my word cards inside my planner, and blinked away the silent tears that were forming in my eyes.

In history we were learning about the witch trials that happened because this king ages ago was scared of witches. Loads of people were burned on bonfires or got drowned in lakes because everyone said that they were definitely a witch, even though they actually probably weren't. When Mr Dean was explaining about this special seat for the drowning test called a dunking stool, Maisy turned around, pointed at me and whispered, "Maybe she's a witch!" and I could hear people giggling.

Then Connor Mould shouted, "Put her on the dunking stool, mate!"

Mr Dean stopped what he was saying and said, "What was that, Connor?"

But he said, "Nothing, sir."

Mr Dean said, "Perhaps you'd better come back at lunchtime to tell me then, *mate*." And everyone apart from me and Connor laughed. Mr Dean went back to talking about how you could only prove you weren't a real witch by actually dying. Which didn't even seem that bad to me at that point.

I could feel myself starting to cry even though I didn't want to. And that was when I put the word cards back inside my bag. Whatever happened to me at Manor High, being The Weird Girl Who Can't Speak was bad enough, without being The Weird Girl Who Can't Speak And Uses Flash Cards.

Things got worse the next day in music. Mr Coles said, "Where's Rosalind?" in front of everybody, which made the inside of my head go weird, and all of my words vanished into nothing. He said, "Don't worry – I know you can't sing, so you can play this instead!" and smiled at me wide-eyed, nodding, as if he had just solved my entire life's problems by handing me a triangle.

My hands were shaking when I took it from him, then

Maisy said loudly, "Why does she get special treatment? Why can't I have an instrument?" Other people started joining in, so Mr Coles handed out musical instruments to practically the entire class. Which at least meant I wasn't the only one, but I did end up wishing I had some earplugs.

The next day in geography, Ms Bhatt was doing a Powerpoint about earthquakes and in the middle of one of the slides Maisy shouted out, "What film is that from?"

Ms Bhatt looked confused and said, "These photographs are from the earthquake that happened in Nepal. Your case study."

Maisy said, "I've never seen it, Miss."

Ms Bhatt said, "It's not a film, Maisy. These photographs are from a real earthquake. Nepal is a country in Asia. It's from the case study. I've been talking about it since the start of term!"

And Maisy said, "Oh my actual God! Are you saying earthquakes happen in real life?"

Then suddenly Connor stood up and shouted, "Boom! This just got real!" and started pretending we were in a real live earthquake, which basically involved him knocking all of my stuff onto the floor. Ms Bhatt told him to sit down, but he ignored her and ran over to Adrian, who looked terrified. Connor grabbed his trumpet case, shouted,

"Earthquake rules!" and before Ms Bhatt could stop him, he threw it out of the window. Ms Bhatt made Connor go and fetch it, then kept him in at break time. Luckily it landed on grass, so Adrian's trumpet was okay, but Connor was still laughing about it later.

And lots of lessons were a bit like that. I felt scared in class a lot. I was scared of being noticed and scared of being silent. I went home that day wondering if being in an actual earthquake could be any worse. Primary school seemed like a faraway dream, because even though my words got stuck there, at Manor High it felt like they had packed up and gone on a permanent holiday. That night I went to sleep with tears soaking into my pillow and too many words I wished I could say in my head.

The next morning, Mum said Seb had to go to the hospital for some tests, so asked me to wake him up. I went into his bedroom quietly, but he was sitting up in bed playing on his Xbox wearing a Yoda mask. He said, "Want to help me destroy the Death Star?" And it was the first time I laughed all week.

When I had a meeting with Mrs Kingsley at lunchtime she said it was Totally Normal for Someone Like Me to take a while to settle in, and that in a few more weeks I would feel much more relaxed. I couldn't say anything because the door was still open a little bit and I could hear someone talking outside, and it made everything I wanted to say get in a Massive Muddle. So I nodded and she said, "And before you know it, it will be half-term and by then you'll be so settled in you probably won't even want a week off!"

Which kind of proves Mrs Kingsley doesn't know anything.

#tinysound

The October leaves were falling and getting stuck to my shoes. And I was doing whatever is the Exact Opposite of settling in at Manor High. But for Some Reason so far undiscovered by speech therapy, whenever Mum and Dad asked how it was going, I always said, "It's okay," when what I really wanted to do was beg them to let me be homeschooled by Brain and also never make me leave the house ever again.

But when your little brother's really sick, and your mum keeps saying she needs something from her bedroom but you can tell she's about to cry, and Dad's doing a massive clean every night when he gets back from work, and they are both being weirdly quiet, there never seems to be a good time to bring up the fact that actually, things at school are Definitely The Exact Opposite Of Okay, and that your words are more trapped than ever. And that Dr Peak Not Peek's Brilliant Plan of me talking normally and making some friends at Manor High had sort of Massively Backfired.

Because if there was one thing Massively Obvious to everybody at Manor High (including me) it's that I was a Total Nobody. And being a Nobody at Manor High means you're basically part of the school subspecies, so it's against the rules for anyone to be friends with you. (Not the normal rules, I'm talking about The Unwritten Rules which, it turns out, are way more important than any rules the teachers put up on the walls or talk about in assembly.)

And one morning on the bus I heard Ella say, "Do you know that girl can't actually speak?" to someone behind me, and suddenly it was like I'd replaced the boy with red hair and a girl who apparently smelled as The New Person To Bully. And every day this boy called Lucas Merry would shout from the back seat, "Will it speak today? Place your bets!"

And each time he did it I would sit there, watching the familiar streets go by, wishing for An Actual Miracle to happen so I could get my voice to come out instead of trembling silently in my head.

# #

Later that week in maths Mr Pearson was running late, and I was sitting there totally scared with my words all in a Massive Muddle because I knew Connor was going to say something to me. (He'd been pushing my stuff off my desk at every opportunity since the pretend earthquake.) He brushed past my desk, knocking my pencil case onto the floor, then said, "Sorry, weirdo!" and Vinnie laughed.

Then Maisy said, "She's like one of those dolls they have in shop windows! What are they called?"

And someone else said, "She's a dummy!"

And I tried my hardest to get a word out, any word, just to prove to them that I could speak, but all my words were so muddled up, the only one I could hear was **DUMMY**, and I kept hearing it again and again and again.

Mr Pearson must have come in then because he said, "What's going on over there? Get to your seats, please!"

And Connor said, "Sorry, sir. I was just picking up her pencil case for her."

Mr Pearson said, "How chivalrous of you, Connor.

Now I wonder if you can apply that heroic attitude to these equations."

And he started writing $6b =$ something on the board, but I couldn't read it properly because my eyes were blurry with tears. I could see a few faces across the room looking in my direction, so I put my head down and a tear blobbed onto my exercise book. I stared at it slowly soaking into the paper, thinking about Maisy and Lucas and Connor, and then another thought came into my head. It was really quiet at first, but then so loud it was practically pounding out of my ears...

I've got to find a way to speak.

In therapy, Octavia gave me a big smile as she walked me to her room. Once the door was closed I said, "Hi," and tried my best not to look down at my shoes when I said it.

She said, "Hi, Rosalind." And smiled at me even bigger. "I'm not going to ask you to say any words today, but I'm going to show you some breathing and vocal exercises, and if you can join in then do, if not, don't worry – you can practise them at home."

And I don't exactly know how it happened, but it was like my brain put her messy room full of books into some kind of Place That Is Safe To Speak category, because after that I didn't feel so worried about Octavia hearing my voice, and my words didn't disappear there. I could blow out my breath really slowly like she showed me, then really quickly, and I coughed and hummed with her, and because she hummed like she was in some kind of opera, I laughed and she did too.

And that's when I told her I hadn't spoken at all at Manor High in all the weeks I'd been there.

But instead of her saying this was Very Bad News That Probably Meant My Entire Life Was Ruined (which is kind of what it felt like at that point) she said, "You haven't spoken one word at Manor High *yet*." Then she smiled her half-moon smile and said, "Small steps, Rosalind. Small steps. How about starting with just a sound?"

So the next day at break time, I went straight to the library and hid myself amongst the tall shelves of books by the back wall and breathed a long breath out slowly, then quickly. I double-checked no one was around, then let out a tiny cough. And my smile went almost as big as Octavia's.

The next day at lunchtime I went back to the library and did the same thing, only this time I coughed in front of Mrs Goodacre, and it can't have been a tiny one because she said, "Oh dear, I hope you're not getting ill!" And William's hand popped out from behind the *Guinness World Records* book holding a cough sweet.

That weekend Seb was feeling a bit better. The sickness had stopped but he still wasn't allowed outside, so I sat with him doing some calligraphy while he played on his Xbox. I told him Octavia had set me a target of speaking to the librarian next week. He said I should treat it like a secret mission. "Just pretend you're a superhero like Batgirl and the library lady is The Target. Only instead of punching her brains out, you have to speak to her. And once you've done it you've saved the entire school from her evil plan. And you'd better do it soon, Rozzie, because otherwise your head will get so filled up with words it might actually explode."

But that's my little brother for you.

#answerme

So it was The Week To Say One Word at Manor High, and Mrs Goodacre was in her office. By this point, the voice inside me was screaming to get out. (And I was technically stalking Mrs Goodacre.) I told myself, if I could just say one word today, then I wasn't a Total Failure, doomed to spend the rest of my life not speaking to anyone ever at Manor High, possibly ending with my head exploding in the library.

I did what Seb suggested and imagined I was a superhero on a secret mission, only instead of saving the entire school (which I probably wouldn't do even if I was a real superhero considering I daydreamed about it disappearing on a daily basis) I was saving myself. I watched The Target typing on her computer and looked around. There was no one else in the library; it was a randomly sunny day, the first time it hadn't rained for ages, and everyone was outside apart from me.

Octavia had told me it might help if I planned what to say before I said it, so I'd decided to say the word *okay*. Okay was easy. I said okay at home all the time when I didn't even mean it. I could say okay to anything Mrs Goodacre said, because she always asked me to do stuff, like tidy up the books, or empty the recycling box, or fill up the printer tray and, whatever it was, I was ready.

I took a deep breath and hummed quietly to get my voice ready like Octavia had taught me. Only Mrs Goodacre heard me and said, "Ah, Rosemary!" (Mrs Goodacre always calls me Rosemary, and because I can't tell her my name is actually Rosalind I have no choice but to just carry on acting like my name is Rosemary for ever.) My heart was beating really fast, but I kept humming quietly.

Then Mrs Goodacre said, "Would you mind going outside and handing out these read-a-thon flyers for me?"

And my mind was suddenly backtracking and saying

NO NO NO NO NO NO NO NO NO NO!

But it was too late.

"Okay."

I had already said it. The word had escaped and I felt like it was hovering right in front of me.

Mrs Goodacre did a double take, like she had heard a voice from beyond the grave (which was nothing compared to how I was feeling) and said, "Oh! Great! Thank you! They were supposed to go out in form time last week but I had to get Rajit to make some changes and you know how slow that photocopier is!" She plonked a pile of flyers in my hands and must have noticed me looking at them like they were on fire because she added, "You'll be fine doing that, won't you?" But instead of handing them back to her and saying, actually no, I would rather get slowly squashed to death in the library photocopier than hand out these flyers, I smiled and nodded.

So I hit my speaking target, and simultaneously discovered it was physically impossible for me to say no to

Mrs Goodacre. She said, "Great! I'm going to send Mrs Kingsley and Mr Bryant an email telling them how marvellously helpful you are!" Which was annoying because I'd actually just tried my hardest not to be.

Even though Manor High is technically a school, it really isn't somewhere to be seen with a book (unless you're tearing it up, throwing it out of a window or drawing rude pictures in it). People do not like books. Or the library. Or library monitors. And now I had to go outside and promote the read-a-thon. On my own. On the sunniest day all month when there were hundreds of people outside. Maybe Mrs Goodacre had an evil plan after all.

So before I even knew what I was doing, I was standing in the middle of the quad holding a pile of bright-red flyers saying THE READ-A-THON ROCKS! WIN BIG BOOK TOKEN!

I tried to tell myself to just keep calm and hand out the flyers like a Normal Person, only I seemed to have frozen to the spot. It felt like there were thousands of people all around and the spotlight was on me again, beaming down so everyone could see I was stuck there, like a statue of A Totally Petrified Girl, wishing I could somehow sink into the concrete. And every word in my head evaporated into the October sunshine.

Then a group of girls came over to me.

A few of them went behind me and some went in front so I was trapped. A girl with bleached hair started firing questions at me so quickly it was like being shot by verbal bullets: "What are you standing here for?" and "What are you doing?" and "What year are you in?" and "Are you in Year Seven?" and "Do you have any money?" and "What bus do you get?" and "Why aren't you answering me?" and "Why aren't you saying anything?"

Then she saw the flyers and said, "What are they?" She pushed me and I dropped some of them and she said, "What are they?" again and "What does this even say?" and "What is wrong with you?" and "Don't you know who I am?"

I stared at the ground feeling like I had actually become a statue, when I heard a different voice that I recognized laughing and saying, "Oh My God, Crystal! She's in my class! She is Really Weird!" and "There's no point talking to her because she can't even speak!" and then "Oh My God! She probably has these because literally her best friend is the librarian."

And that voice belonged to Maisy Love.

My throat was totally closed up and my chest felt so tight I could hardly breathe. And that feeling got worse and worse as Bleached Hair Girl carried on with her verbal-bullet attack, ending with a massive, "WEIRD-A-THON!" when the bell went.

I stood there not making a sound, with tears running down my face, and read-a-thon flyers scattering over the quad like fallen leaves.

But something felt different.

My tears didn't feel like the sadness tears I was used to. These tears felt angry. And angry tears hurt more.

Suddenly the answers to all of her questions started pouring into my head.

No, I don't have any money because we are saving up for Seb's dream and, yes, technically there is something wrong with me and I'm trying my best to get better, but people like you aren't helping, and, yes, my best friend probably is the librarian who doesn't even know my actual name, but she's still way nicer than anyone else in this entire school.

And then: *no, Bleached Hair Girl, I don't know who you are. But I hate you. And I hate Maisy Love.*

Once the quad was almost empty, I walked back to the library and heard someone shout, "Rosie!" I turned and saw William walking towards me picking up flyers on his way and putting them inside the *Guinness World Records* he was carrying. He shouted, "Are you okay?" and I nodded, but as I did I felt something inside me sort of snap.

And it was a Really Weird Feeling, but not a totally bad one. Because I walked through the library doors and before they even closed behind me, one word untangled itself from the rest that were tumbling around in my head. And I said it out loud to myself.

"No."

And that was probably the Exact Moment things started to change.

10

#whisperit

When I got home from school, Seb was on the sofa watching a film. His face was puffy, which happened sometimes because of his medicine. I asked what he was watching and he said, "*The Secret Garden.*" And when I looked confused he said, "It was Mum. She said I had to watch this or she'd read it to me again."

Mum is Totally Obsessed with *The Secret Garden*. It was her favourite story when she was little so she always used to read it to us, especially Seb (Dad said because he's a captive audience). And whenever we went out somewhere to do with nature like a forest or went on a walk or something, which wasn't exactly often, Mum always used to say, "Oh, it's just like *The Secret Garden*!" And we would all groan as if we were sick of it because she said it so much, but really I liked it when she was happy like that.

Mum poked her head round the door. "Rozzie, he practically forced me to put it on." Seb shook his head, but I noticed he didn't actually take his eyes off the screen.

I took off my coat, tucked myself under the blanket next to him and said, "I guess it can't be any worse than the book. Has Colin seen the garden yet?"

And Seb said, "He's just about to!"

Mum said, "Let me get my phone. I want to send a picture of this to Dad. He won't believe it!" And even though I totally hate having my photo taken, Mum actually looked excited, which she hadn't done for a long time, so I pretended I didn't mind.

"Tell him I spoke at school today too if you want."

Mum practically squealed with excitement. "This is a cause for celebration!" And five minutes later she came out of the kitchen with glasses of organic apple juice and a plate of beetroot brownies (which is apparently my mum's idea of a celebration).

When Dad came home later he bear-hugged me and said, "I know we're not supposed to make a big deal about it, but I'm so proud of you! It's great you're settling in so well at school." Which definitely doesn't count as a Total Lie because it wasn't me who said it.

# #

The next day in assembly Mrs Goodacre was making an announcement about the half-term read-a-thon. And the whole time she was speaking Maisy was kicking the back of my chair. Only instead of my words getting muddled or disappearing like they usually did, the word

STOP!

came into my head at full volume. My cheeks burned and it got all tangled up in my throat, and I couldn't concentrate on what Mrs Goodacre was saying.

Anyway, she must have said something good about it because that lunchtime the library was busier than usual. Not many people go into the library at lunchtimes usually, and the ones who do aren't scary, which is why I like going there so much. Most people spend lunch walking about in big groups, which I don't like, or they play football on the field even though there are no nets in the goalposts, and some people go into the art block because the teachers don't mind you eating in there. Others sit on the concrete benches in the quad. But to go to those places you really need someone who is your friend.

Sometimes I wish I could have started late in the year because you get given a special buddy to hang around with for the week and everyone in the class has to be kind to you because you're new. Personally I think that is a really good way of getting a friend because although it is kind of by force, no one minds.

Or sometimes I wish I could be funny in class because then maybe people would like me. And that's the thing with my school. Even if you get into trouble a lot like Connor, people will still like you. The same if you have a cool phone. (Which I didn't because my parents wouldn't even get me a not-cool one.) Sometimes even if people are scared of you they will still like you. Needless to say, not being able to speak to anyone apart from the librarian has the Exact Opposite effect.

That week Lucas and Maisy and Connor carried on saying mean stuff to me. But although my heart pounded and I felt my cheeks go bright red and hot tears stung my eyes, it didn't feel exactly the same as before. Because my head filled up with words like **GO AWAY** and **LEAVE ME ALONE** that sounded so loud I was actually amazed no one else could hear them.

Then it was finally half-term. I woke up the first morning feeling a massive sense of relief, like I'd been holding my breath for weeks, and now I could finally let it out. A whole week of no school stretched out ahead of me; the only homework I had was writing a poem for Miss Carter about Something Important and reading three books so I could get a certificate from Mrs Goodacre. (I didn't want to win because Suzi told me last year she had to collect the book token in front of everyone in assembly.) Plus, I hoped to convince Seb that wearing a towel as a skirt and Mum's necklaces and carrying a plastic shield did not make him look in any way fierce, even if it was what pharaohs used to wear.

He must have been feeling better, because he burst into my room asking if I wanted to help him make a chariot. "I'm going to use Mrs Quinney's cats for the horses," he said, peering over a massive piece of cardboard.

"Have they agreed to that?"

"They don't have to. They're my slaves," he said, a wide grin spreading across his face. "I need you to make me a spear, Rozzie. Dad says there's some bamboo in the shed, and erm, get some pots and things for when you come to worship me. Come on!" I heard him go downstairs, then thirty seconds later shout, "Dad! We need more loo roll!"

Dad called back, "I don't think the Egyptians used to mummify pot plants."

It was the first time for ages that I actually had a smile on my face (and meant it). Maybe for some people spending a whole week at home over half-term would be boring in the extreme, but for me, it meant I wouldn't be on the verge of a Massive Silent Panic, or that my head was about to explode. And that was a really nice way to feel. For a whole week I wouldn't have to be The Weird Girl Who Can't Speak, I could just be normal me, in my normal house, with my normal family, celebrating the life of Poopookhamun in the back garden with tinfoil and loo roll.

On Monday Dad was off work so we had a family day out. (Even though he had Major Reservations about taking Seb anywhere there might be germs.) Seb really wanted to visit the National Space Centre, and we hadn't heard anything from the Dream Come True charity, so Dad didn't take that much convincing. It was a long journey and I wanted to get my homework done for Miss Carter, so I put a notebook and pen in my bag, and hoped I would find some inspiration at some point. Surely there must be Something Important at an actual space centre, even if all Seb was talking about was how astronauts pee in space.

We hadn't been out anywhere as a family for ages because of Seb's illness (and my SM) so in the car on the way there I was feeling a bit nervous. I don't like going anywhere I might not be able to speak to Mum, Dad or Seb, which basically means anywhere outside of our house. But Seb's excitement must have been contagious or something, because by the time we parked I was actually looking forward to seeing a moon rock. Anyway, it had to be more exciting than the six-hour reenactment of the Battle of Naseby Dad had taken us to once.

The first thing Seb wanted to see was the rocket tower. He grabbed my hand and dragged me there even though Mum told him to slow down. And while we were standing there and Seb was talking about liquid hydrogen and aerodynamic resistance and escape velocity, I could see strangers looking at him, only not because he looked ill, but because they were impressed. Dad put his hand on Seb's shoulder and said to Mum, "I keep telling you, that encyclopedia is the best thing I ever bought these kids."

And later, when Seb gazed up at the stars in the planetarium, the light shone on his wide eyes and his huge smile, and words flooded into my brain – I had my inspiration. So in the car on the way home, while Seb slept, and Mum kept her hand on Dad's knee, and the street lights glowed, and wispy clouds hid the real stars, I wrote (in my best handwriting possible while the car was moving) my poem for Miss Carter, about Something Important.

I write this in a whisper,
So I don't wake him up,
Because being his sister,
Is a job I can't mess up.
I can't hug him too tight,
Or tickle him too quick,
Or keep him awake at night,
It might make him more sick.
My little brother's super,
In so many different ways,
He's amazing on a computer,
Could talk dinosaurs for days.
He thinks stars are totally brill,
He loves to watch the night sky,
And though he's really ill,
You'll never see him cry.
He's the best little brother ever,
I don't mind when he's being gross,
I wish he could stay for ever,
Because he's the thing that matters most.

#

Maybe it was all the talking Seb did about stars, but half-term went by at the speed of light. And before I knew it, it was the night before I had to go back to school. As it got closer to bedtime, worries clouded my mind. I prayed for some kind of Divine Intervention, like maybe Manor High could accidentally be crushed by a giant meteor. Seb must have noticed I'd been quiet, because he came into my room and asked me, "Why don't you want to go back to school, Rozzie?"

And I have this thing with Seb, which is that I basically can't lie to him. (Plus I was already a bit worried about all the lying about school I'd done to Mum and Dad that week.) So I said, "You remember what I was like at primary school, right?"

"You mean, when you couldn't speak?"

I nodded. "Well, most people at Manor High think that makes me some kind of Massive Weirdo." Seb's usual smile dropped. "So I haven't exactly made any friends, that's all. And people at school can be a bit mean sometimes." I told him about The Boy Who Shouted Geek and Bleached Hair Girl and Maisy and Connor and Lucas Merry, and how I wished Manor High would be struck by a giant meteor that night. (Actual chance of it happening according to Seb: less than one in a trillion.)

"You know what, Rozzie," he said. "Your school really needs a superhero."

And I said, "Well, don't look at me. If I was a superhero my special power would probably be Being Weird."

His eyes opened really wide and he said, "Mine would be a superpower that makes your wee come out like a tornado!" Then he spun around a few times pretending to blast his tornado wee at imaginary bullies. He could be really gross sometimes.

I said, "It actually amazes me that I'm the one in therapy."

He suddenly stopped and said, "Hang on a minute. I've had a Brilliant Idea."

Five minutes later he came back into my room wearing his dressing gown like a cape saying, "I'm Seb the Pooperhero!" He made me sit cross-legged on the floor and said, "I'm going to surround you with a special pooperhero forcefield of protection." Then he built a circle of Lego around me while he said words I recognized from *Star Wars*. Afterwards he made me touch his bottle of anti-diarrhoea medicine and say he was The All-Time King Of Pooperheros and Tornado Wees. (Which he admitted later was not really part of the forcefield ceremony, then laughed hysterically saying, "LOLcano!")

So I started back at school with Major Doubts about

Seb's Forcefield Of Protection, but a strange new determination that if Seb could start and end every day with such a massive amount of happiness, then I could make it to the end of term without crying.

And I actually almost did it.

11

#speakup

The next morning as I was getting ready to leave for school, Seb came downstairs in his dinosaur pyjamas and gave me a hug. Mum said he was looking so much better (despite what the doctors said) so I focused on that thought, and felt it wrap around me.

And it lasted about ten seconds.

As soon as I walked inside the English block I heard someone shouting, "Hey! Please! I need it today! Give it back! Please!" and some other voices laughing. The panic feeling started in my tummy, and my skin felt prickly, and I could feel my cheeks going red. Adrian was at the bottom of the stairs trying to get his trumpet off a group of boys.

One was dangling it in front of him and they were laughing as Adrian tried to grab it. Suddenly they pushed past, almost knocking into me, and ran out of the door laughing. Adrian sat down on a step, looking at his empty trumpet case like he was about to cry. He said, "Do you know who that was?"

And as usual my voice ran to hide, but I didn't look at the floor. I shook my head.

He said, "My mum's going to kill me. It's the second time they've taken it. They said they'll beat me up if I tell anyone." He wiped a tear on his coat sleeve. "I'll just tell my mum I lost it again. I wish they would leave me alone. They always hassle us at band practice too."

He looked at me with tears in his eyes. I wished my hardest that I could say something to make him feel better, to tell him I knew how it felt. But all the words in my head were locked inside a Massive Muddle. And I couldn't say any of them. I looked down at my shoes. Not speaking up to bullies like Connor and Maisy felt bad, but being Totally Silent while Adrian was crying felt even worse somehow. (But he did smile at me later, when I saw him fishing his trumpet out of the biology pond.)

The next day at lunchtime, as I was getting my calligraphy book out of my locker, one of the trumpet thieves walked past me. I definitely didn't mean to stare at him, but my head just moved in his direction. "What are you staring at?" he said, and my throat immediately felt like it had been double bolted and padlocked. "Don't stare!" he shouted, and grabbed the book out of my hands.

Suddenly I heard a voice shout, "Craig Bull! I saw that! Come here!"

But Craig Bull dropped my book, ran down the corridor and disappeared out of sight. A teacher I don't know said, "Are you all right?" and I nodded, then he asked my name but it couldn't come out because of my throat being padlocked. I mouthed *Rosalind* but he said, "Speak up, girl! I can't hear you!" And I tried again but I couldn't even move my lips after that. He sighed really loudly and walked off saying, "Never mind! I'm late for a meeting. I'll catch up with Craig Bull later."

Only whatever that teacher said to him actually made it worse somehow, because the lockers became Craig Bull's new hang-out.

He emptied out bags, pushed books out of hands, chucked people's stuff around. And it turned out Craig didn't just steal trumpets; he also stole lunches. A lot of them. He only actually stole mine once, which wasn't that much of a surprise to me, considering it was on the day of Mum's avocado, blueberry and peanut butter sandwich experiment. But bullies like Craig Bull obviously prefer not having avocado in everything, because other people had their lunches stolen a lot.

Only no matter what Craig did, no one spoke up. My SM kept me silent, but it seemed like fear was keeping everyone else silent about it too.

That Friday Miss Carter gave us back the Something Important poems we had written over half-term. She said, "If your poem has a star sticker on it, it means your poem was fantastic, so come up to the front and read out your poem to the class. If you didn't hand in your homework, I'm afraid you're writing a poem over lunchtime in detention entitled, *Homework Is Something Important.*" Connor and Vinnie let out simultaneous groans.

My heart was pounding. I wanted Miss Carter to like my poem, but the last thing I wanted to see on it was a star sticker. She smiled at me as she put my poem on the desk. At the bottom of the page she had drawn three little stars, and next to them she had written: *This poem is beautiful! It really touched my heart. I hope you are able to read it to me one day.* And even though my face was frozen, I felt my heart kind of smile.

In our meeting that lunchtime Mrs Kingsley said, "I'm getting very good reports back from your teachers, Rosalind. They tell me you are working very hard. The librarian says you've been helping her out every lunchtime." I smiled and felt my cheeks glow red. "I'm still a little concerned about the word cards." I looked at my shoes. "And I've spoken to Mr Bryant and we would like you to have a go at spending a couple of lunchtimes a week *not* in the library." I swallowed the lump that was forming in my throat. "Try to get yourself around the school a little bit. You might even make some friends!"

So in the weeks that followed, I did what she said and did a few quick laps of the school at lunchtime. And almost everywhere I went, I saw people – other nobodies like me, in corridors, around corners and all the other hidden places teachers never go – being called names, having their stuff thrown about, getting pushed out of the way like they didn't matter. And it seemed to make my SM worse. Every time I tried to speak up, the words got jammed in my throat. It hung over me like a curse, making it impossible for me to say any words at all, no matter how desperately I wanted to shout them. But there was nothing I could do about it.

And then one day, when everyone was watching their breath escape in little white puffs except me, and everyone was talking about when it would snow except me, and everyone was saying what they were getting for Christmas except me, I got home and overheard Dad say to Mum, "We've got to face the possibility it might be Seb's last Christmas."

And those words stuck like a massive piece of ice in my heart that wouldn't melt, making me feel colder than I had in any December.

12

#say
something

There was lots to do at school as the Christmas holidays got closer. Everyone was getting more and more excited and time seemed to rush past, even with Connor and Maisy calling me a Total Weirdo on practically a daily basis. I spent every day with the words SEB'S LAST CHRISTMAS pounding around in my head the whole time, and almost every bus journey Lucas slapped his gloves against the back of my neck, chanting, "Speak, freak, speak, freak!" over and over again. And every day I would shout

LEAVE ME ALONE LEAVE ME ALONE LEAVE ME
ALONE LEAVE ME ALONE LEAVE ME ALONE

(but only in my own head).

The only part of school I liked was being in the library, and leaving early to see Octavia, and not just because that meant I got to miss double sport once every two weeks. (I hated trampolining. Miss Johnson has a rule that everybody has to stand around the trampoline in case you fall off and they all just stare at you.) I looked forward to leaving early because I actually liked my sessions with Octavia, even though it was technically therapy.

In history Mr Dean had moved us into a seating plan, which maybe was some kind of social experiment because he put me, The Weird Girl Who Can't Speak, right at the front of the class next to Maisy, The Mean Girl Who Seems To Hate Me. I don't like sitting at the front and Maisy was whispering horrible things to me. I couldn't concentrate on what Mr Dean told us to do, and I accidentally turned to the wrong page in the textbook. So instead of learning about the Norman Conquest, to prepare for our trip to Cardiff Castle next term (which was Another Reason To Not Be Cheerful), I wrote out three pages of notes on the Tudors. Only that meant so did Maisy.

For the whole lesson she was saying things under her breath to me like, "Why don't you just say something?" and "What is wrong with you?" and "You are so weird!"

and "No one even likes you by the way!" and "You literally have no friends!" like maybe I hadn't realized or something. When Mr Dean wasn't looking she turned to Ella and said, "Why do I have to sit next to The Weirdo?" The words **GO AWAY** kept bubbling up into my throat. And it isn't exactly easy to absorb information on the wrong historical period or notice Maisy is copying every word you write while that is happening, believe me.

Then, towards the end of the lesson, Mr Dean said, "So, who can tell me the answer to question one: Who won the Battle of Hastings?"

Maisy put her hand up and said, "Anne of Cleves."

And everyone laughed. Apart from me. Because my heart practically stopped beating. She was going to think this was all my fault.

After the lesson I put my books in my locker and Maisy bumped into me on purpose. I wasn't shocked or anything because I was expecting it. So I did what I usually did: pretended it didn't happen and tried to walk off. But Maisy said, "SAY SORRY THEN, WEIRDO!" really loudly so everyone around us stopped and looked at me. I felt my cheeks go bright red and my arm was hurting from where she barged me, then I looked down at my shoes.

I wished so badly I could just say sorry like she told me to, but my throat completely closed up. And I knew some words were there because I could feel them practically choking me. Only what everyone else saw was Total Silence.

And that is So Not The Ideal Response when somebody like Maisy Love tells you to say sorry.

She pushed me again, harder this time, and shouted, "SAY SORRY!" Someone behind her said I looked like I was going to wet myself (which I definitely was *not* about to do – if wetting myself was something I still had to worry about as well as not being able to speak, I don't think I would ever leave my house). Maisy pushed me again so hard I fell backwards onto the floor and said, "Why don't you just SPEAK? You are so WEIRD!"

I got up as quickly as I could and ran all the way to the one place I knew I would be safe: the library.

I didn't want Mrs Goodacre to see me crying so I ran into the library toilets but actually, this turned out to be The Biggest Mistake Ever, because in there were three girls doing their make-up. When I burst in one of them looked at me in the mirror, did a massive tut and said, "Oh my God! You just made me smudge my eyeliner!" I looked at her reflection and I did kind of recognize her so I thought maybe she got my bus or something. I wanted to say I was sorry and that I was running away from Maisy because she had pushed me. But no words would come out.

I wished I could have Just Said It because it would have made my day (and probably my entire life) a lot better. But for some reason my brain works against me in this kind of Massively Awkward Scenario. Literally, someone could have a gun pointed at my head threatening to kill me if I didn't say something and I still couldn't make any words come out.

And this moment is a good example of why being Completely Normal is one hundred per cent better than being Someone Like Me. Because what happened was this:

The Girl With The Smudged Eyeliner grabbed me by both shoulders and pushed me into one of the toilet cubicles. She punched me in the stomach so hard it winded me and I felt like my chest was going to collapse. I really couldn't breathe at all. I felt tears coming out of my eyes even though I didn't mean them to, then she hit me again on the side of my head. I could hear her friends laughing and then she pushed me and I hit the back of my head on the toilet. I thought, she is actually going to kill me, right here in the library toilets. All because I can't speak. Then I thought about Seb and how shocked my parents would be about me dying before him.

But then she stopped and said, "Tissue." And I thought she was offering me one at first because although no sound was coming out I was crying quite a lot, but she meant for me to give her some tissue to clean up her eyeliner. I gave her some tissue even though my hand was shaking really badly. She went to the mirror, wiped her eyeliner and then the three of them left.

I couldn't move, so I stayed there crying in complete silence with too many words hammering inside my head, like this:

sorry stop please please help me help me sorry help me please help me leave me alone please stop leave me alone please stop leave me alone please help me alone leave me alone please help me sorry stop help me I can't breathe help me please help me help me please leave me alone please so unfair leave me alone please stop stop so unfair leave me alone sorry stop sorry stop please stop

because they wanted so badly to be spoken.

The bell rang for the end of lunch, but I stayed sitting there. I didn't want to be late for my lesson, but I couldn't stand up because my head felt so dizzy. I wished really hard for Mrs Goodacre to come in and find me, but she didn't.

I waited until the storm of words in my head had calmed down and I could stand up without feeling like I would fall over. Then I went into the library office and told a Massive White Lie to Mrs Goodacre without actually speaking any words, which is kind of an achievement for me.

She said, "Rosemary, you look dreadful!" Then asked if I had been sent down here to work, which is what happens sometimes if you're ill and no one is home to pick you up and the school nurse isn't there, so I nodded.

She got me a cup of water and said I could stay in the office but I mustn't try to do any work because, "Frankly, Rosemary, you look like death warmed up!" which I thought was a bit harsh but was exactly what I felt like anyway, apart from the warm part. Then she gave me a book to read (which is Mrs Goodacre's Miracle Cure for everything).

I was only a tiny bit worried about being caught because Madame Laurent never took a register and anyway, like a lot of my teachers, she barely knew I existed. I didn't care that much because I don't like French anyway. I have enough problems not being able to speak in English without learning how not to speak in other languages.

By the end of the day I had stared at the same page of *Jane Eyre* for what felt like hours, with just two words from it staring right back at me – *remain silent* – and all I wanted to do was tear them right out of the book. Because if there was one thing I definitely did *not* want to do for ever, it was remain silent. I had A Million Things I wanted to say to people at Manor High, but they were all trapped inside my head.

On the way out I managed a quiet, "Thank you," to Mrs Goodacre.

She smiled and said, "Now, you go home and get some rest!"

I didn't take the bus as I was worried The Girl With The Smudged Eyeliner might be on it, so I put on my hat and gloves and walked the two miles home. Cold air was stinging my face, and so many words were bunched up in my head I could feel them pounding with every step.

When I got home I didn't want to speak to anyone, so I called to Mum that the bus had been late and I had some reading to do in my room. I went straight upstairs before she saw me and looked in the mirror in my bedroom. My cheeks were flushed from walking so far in the cold and my eyes were red from crying. I stood there and thought about all the things people couldn't see on the outside, but I could feel inside my heart. How invisible they were to everyone. Just like all the words I wanted to say but couldn't.

That evening I sat on my bed, leaned my head against the wall and listened to Seb playing on his Xbox with Dad, and laughing, which he always did. I wondered how Seb could have so much happiness in his heart, but so much badness in his body. In a weird way I wished I could be like him that night. He was protected, always checked on, tucked in at night, cuddled, loved by everyone. He didn't have to go to Manor High. No one would ever beat him up in the library toilets for smudging their eyeliner. He was Super Seb. Not even one person at school knew or cared who I was. And that's exactly how I felt: like a Total Nobody.

I tried telling myself that I had Reasons To Be Cheerful, like Mrs Quinney was always going on about, like my family, having enough food, not living in squalor and poverty or having flies feast on my wounds like some of the people she had seen when she worked for God. But that night I didn't feel like I had any Reasons To Be Cheerful at all.

I was totally exhausted but I could hardly sleep. The sick feeling that came after being hit by The Girl With The Smudged Eyeliner never really went away. It just stayed there, like a bad dream you can't wake up from. And school loomed in the distance.

13

#callinsick

The next day I did such an excellent job of faking sickness I could have joined the school drama club: I whined, I clutched my stomach, I moaned, I made exaggerated sick noises in the bathroom. Eventually, Mum bundled me up in a blanket and took me next door. She apologized so many times when Mrs Quinney eventually answered the door I actually felt a little bit insulted. Mum explained she had to take Seb to the hospital and couldn't risk me contaminating him, and could I stay with her for a couple of days? I was immediately overjoyed at this prospect. Mrs Quinney was Definitely Not.

Mum said she would pop in to see me later and gave

me a quick kiss. Mrs Quinney took me up to her spare room (I had never been upstairs in her house before so already I was feeling excited; staying at Mrs Quinney's would be like some kind of exotic holiday compared to school). She put me into bed and brought me a jigsaw, a hot lemon drink and a yellow handkerchief, all on a large tray which had a picture of a cat on it. And it wasn't long before her cats Mary and Bernard joined me.

Of course, I had to mask my excitement as I was Officially Sick, but after such a horrible experience at school the day before, being looked after by Mrs Quinney felt like exactly the kind of therapy I needed. I didn't even feel bad lying to everyone about being ill, although when Mrs Quinney prayed for me to get better soon, I did an emergency prayer to apologize when she left the room.

I was slowly completing the jigsaw, looking as weak and in pain as possible, when Mrs Quinney set up a chair in the corner of the room and began one of her Instructions For Leading A Wholesome Life Unlike The People At Number 17 talks. Mrs Quinney knows a lot about how to live a good life, how to become a person of substance, how to avoid accidentally slipping into the devil's clutches, and she bakes really nice currant buns. I'm not exactly sure how old she is but Dad said she is somewhere between Extremely Ancient and Tutankhamun. I don't care that she is really old because her house smells of cakes and she actually used to work directly for God, which is definitely better than Dad, who designs washing machines and never prays.

Mrs Quinney held the Bible open on her lap while she talked, but she only looked down a couple of times because she has most of it memorized. She said, "*Thanks be to God, who in Christ always leads us in triumphal procession, and through us spreads the fragrance of the knowledge of Him everywhere.*" And I thought if Seb heard that he would totally make a joke about Jesus having a farting problem. I hoped Mrs Quinney wouldn't notice me trying to not laugh.

By the end of the talk I had completed the jigsaw (which had 250 pieces so that shows you how long it took). Then Mrs Quinney told me, "Sickness is an excellent time for moral and spiritual cleansing," and, "Along with the contents of one's stomach, one can purge the corruption of one's soul!" I didn't exactly understand how it worked, but I think she meant that if you pray really hard when you are ill, sometimes when you puke up some of the badness in your soul comes out.

I don't think any badness came out of my soul while I was pretending to puke up in Mrs Quinney's bathroom. If anything, I think some new badness probably went in there.

The next day I carried on refusing food; obviously I didn't want to appear to be getting better too quickly. Needless to say, I was starving, but the dread of going back to school was stronger than my hunger, so I said no to Mrs Quinney's offer of toast and tomato soup, even though it felt like I was Dying A Slow And Painful Death By Starvation And Jigsaws.

While Mrs Quinney was telling me about the time Jesus cooked lunch for about a million people (which made me even more hungry), I started counting all the bad things that had happened to me since I started at Manor High. And by the time Mrs Quinney got to the good bit in the story when An Actual Miracle happened and they had loads of food left over when they didn't have enough to begin with, I'd lost count.

And maybe Someone Like Me – a library monitor who can't say anything back – is a bit of an easy target. But what about all the other Nobodies I had seen being pushed around at the hands of Manor High's Ruling Class? What had any of us actually done to deserve it? I started daydreaming about all the things I would say to the people at school if only I could somehow get my words to escape from the prison inside my head.

Mrs Quinney coughed, like she could tell I wasn't concentrating. She read me another passage from the

Bible while I nodded and occasionally looked up towards heaven in a I'm-grateful-to-God kind of way I hoped Mrs Quinney would approve of. Then she told Bernard and Mary to behave themselves and told me to sleep.

Only I wasn't tired, and I couldn't get Mrs Quinney's words out of my head. The bit she'd read was about how we should be grateful for our suffering because it will make us into better people. I wondered if this was why Seb was such a good person – because he suffered so much.

Later Mum came to see me and said Seb had some special medicine to make sure he didn't feel any pain but it made him drowsy so he needed lots of rest. She said, "He's doing really well!" But recently he hadn't looked very well to me at all. Even though he would still laugh and do disgusting jokes like coming out of the bathroom saying, "I got poo-kaemia!"

I wondered if my suffering by being beaten up in the library toilets by The Girl With The Smudged Eyeliner had made me into a better person. Considering I had lied to Mrs Goodacre, my parents and Mrs Quinney about being ill and was also technically truanting school, I somehow doubted it. I eventually fell asleep with Mary and Bernard lying either side of me like warm, fluffy bodyguards.

The next day was Friday, so I felt it was safe for me to start acting like I was feeling better. I wouldn't have to face school until Monday, and then there was only a week left before we broke up for Christmas. Anyway, I wasn't sure how many more nights I could deal with Bernard sleeping on my head and Mary acting like my toes were made of mice.

After breakfast Mrs Quinney let me use her best calligraphy pens to practise all morning. She even said I was becoming a talented calligrapher! I wrote that down a few times but then hid it in my bag in case Mrs Quinney thought I was becoming too pleased with myself.

That afternoon we drank sweet tea from her special teacups from Austria which she keeps in a wooden cabinet in the living room. They have hand-painted pictures of tiny goats jumping on them and Mrs Quinney knows they are my favourite. They are also the only things in her entire house which don't have pictures of cats on. And then she showed me her diary from when she was working for God in Africa, which is probably the oldest thing I have ever seen up close in real life, apart from Mrs Quinney.

It was a brown leather diary marked *1962* in gold letters. And she was Totally Right about her handwriting being even better when she was younger. All of her letters were perfectly lined up and the full stops were exact circles. She let me hold it and I read this:

My calling from God is getting ever stronger.

I am certain He knows I am doing His good work and treading the right path.

I asked her what she meant by treading the right path, and she said, "Each of us has something we can contribute to the world, and if we are moving in the right direction, God will give us little signs to show he is pleased." But she couldn't tell me what the signs looked like because they are too mysterious. Then she said, "A wonderful way of recording your contributions, and improving your character, is writing a diary like this."

I thought I probably did need to improve my character, but not as much as some of the people at my school. I carried on reading:

Henry is continuing to build the school for the orphanage, despite some opposition from the sponsors. It is a blessing and a privilege to work beside him, and I pray that God keeps him safe and beside me always.

I wondered what she looked like in those days and who Henry was, as she had never mentioned him before. She must have read my mind because she said, "Oh, Henry O'Kelly!" and stared into space for a while. Then she said, "I have some old photographs somewhere if you're interested?"

Maybe it was all the boring Bible talks and jigsaws,

because I said, "Yes please!" possibly a bit too enthusiastically for a recovering patient.

But she stared into space again and said, "I think I shall save them for another time when you're feeling better." Then she switched on the TV for *Antique Treasure Hunt*.

And the strange thing was, it was the second time I'd been told to keep a diary recently. In my last therapy session with Octavia she had suggested it too, as a good way of getting my feelings out. And what with Mrs Quinney telling me to look out for signs from God and everything, I wondered if He was telling me I should start writing a diary. But what was the point in recording all the horrible things that happened to me at Manor High, when I'd be the only one to read it?

I looked out of the window to see if God would give me a sign that keeping a diary was a good idea, but all I could see was a person smoking behind my neighbour's bin. And I know that God moves in mysterious ways but I didn't think He used people smoking behind bins as signs. So I decided to think about it, and just look for Signs From God along the way.

Which actually turned out to be an Exceptionally Bad Idea.

14

#tune

The last week of term is probably okay for most people. But for me, when lessons sort of stop and teachers do Things Normal People Probably Consider Fun instead, like team quizzes and games and working in pairs to write a winter-themed song, every lesson becomes Massively Scary. Because the only thing that makes these kind of lessons fun is a friend. And if you don't have a friend then what you absolutely must have is a voice. And if you are like me and you don't have either of those, then the week before the Christmas holidays can feel Lonelier And Scarier and more Massively Silent And Awkward than ever.

Octavia had set me a target to speak in class before Christmas, but every time I tried it was like all the words I knew got stuck in a massive snowstorm in my head.

Or I knew what I wanted to say but it got frozen in my throat.

Or sometimes, like when Mr Dean did a history quiz and put me in a group with Adrian and his friends who were nice to me, my words still got lost in a thick fog and I couldn't hear the questions because it was like I was miles away hiding from everyone.

And it was annoying because I was speaking to Octavia normally, and in my last session before Christmas she said I made A Huge Step Forward because I read to her with the door open. And though I only read really quietly, and lost my breath a little bit, and stumbled over the words a lot, and had my back to the door the whole time, she said it still counted.

She told me to set a speaking target for the holidays, so I decided I would try to say one or two words to someone I didn't know. And it was a Huge Target for me because I had literally never done that before.

When I was about to leave she said, "Oh, I almost forgot!" And she opened and closed her desk drawers, then looked in her bag, singing, "*Where did you put it, Mrs O O O?*" Then she said, "Aha!" and the *ha!* went really high and she handed me a parcel. "Don't open it until Christmas Day!" Then she told me The Best News Ever, which was she was going to come out and speak to my dad about letting me go on the computer more so I could look up stuff about SM. I was a bit worried Dad would tell her I could use the *Encyclopedia Britannica* but he didn't.

While they were talking in the freezing cold car park I watched the frost sparkling like tiny jewels in the sun, and for the first time started feeling excited about Christmas. Octavia said, "Writing is really good for her," and told Dad about my speaking target. When she said it Dad put his hand on my shoulder and that's when I realized he had polar-bear-paw gloves on. I squeezed his arm which was my emergency signal that I wanted to leave because I was feeling anxious, but actually it was mostly because of the gloves.

Dad said, "Right, well, we'd better get going. Thank you for everything you've done so far with Roz." And as we were walking off he put up a paw and called, "Merry Christmas!"

Octavia said, "Merry Christmas!" back, and her voice sounded like bells.

#

On the last day of term we had a special Christmas assembly. I sat in the front row with Maisy and her friends behind me tapping my back and spelling out F-R-E-A-K in whispers, only they kept getting it wrong and saying "F-R-E-E-K", and Mr Bryant kept shushing them every few minutes. So I had the wrong spelling of freak going through my head, and wanted more than anything to turn around and say something not very Christmassy to Maisy Love, until Mr Bryant made her move to sit next to him.

Mr Endeby's speech about the major Manor High achievements of the year didn't last long, and he spent most of it talking about the TV maths quiz legend Jenny Baker again. He showed us some solar-powered Christmas lights made by someone in Year Nine, which was a good demonstration until he turned off the main lights and they stopped working. Some people on the back row booed, and Mr Endeby warned them that Father Christmas doesn't visit naughty children and they laughed.

Mrs Goodacre announced that Suzi was the winner of the read-a-thon, and she blushed as she collected her prize. Over the clapping I could hear some people laughing and a boy shouted, "Geek!" really loudly. Mr Endeby told him to go and wait outside his office, and everyone stopped clapping after that.

Then he said, "And now for Another Great Achievement at Manor High: our wonderful brass band will play us a festive song to get us all in the mood for a very merry Christmas!"

The band started playing something sort of resembling "We Wish You A Merry Christmas" only they all started at different times, and the flute player's music stand fell over. A boy in the back row stood up and shouted, "TUNE!" and practically the whole back row started dancing like they were in some kind of rave. So the whole thing got ruined anyway.

Mr Endeby said, "Some people in the back row need to get some manners over the holidays!" and I thought, there is about Zero Chance of that happening. It would probably be more likely for a meteor to strike. I pictured a meteor obliterating the people on the back row, then Maisy Love, then The Girl With The Smudged Eyeliner, and The Boy Who Shouted Geek, and Connor Mould, and Bleached Hair Girl and her gang that all looked like her, and Craig Bull, and every single other bully at Manor High.

I turned my head a tiny bit and looked at the rows of faces gazing up at Mr Endeby. And I looked at the ones staring down at their shoes. I wondered if they were wishing for a meteor strike too. If only there was some way I could speak to them, to tell them they weren't the only Nobodies wishing for a Manor High Miracle.

Mr Endeby started talking about what to do in case of heavy snow next term. A not very quiet murmur of excitement started going round the hall as he told everyone to calm down. "In the *extremely* unlikely event the school is closed, we will put an announcement on the website."

And when he said that, something in my mind started stirring, like my brain was trying to tell me something, but I didn't exactly know what. As if somewhere above my head, a tiny light bulb was starting to flicker.

15

#whitelie

Since Seb got The Illness, Mum and Dad have made a massive effort to make any kind of celebration as over the top as possible. And this Christmas was no exception. Dad spent the weekend making our house look like the Blackpool Illuminations. Fairy lights covered every window, a huge Santa face hung on the front door, and he put giant inflatable snowmen in our tiny front garden that bopped around so much it seemed like they were leaping out at people as they walked past. And, as if that wasn't embarrassing enough, Dad wore reindeer antlers and the polar-bear-paw gloves for most of the holidays. There must be something in my dad's DNA that prevents him from feeling any kind of social embarrassment whatsoever. I feel the Exact Opposite to that pretty much all the time.

I wanted to do Octavia's speaking target as soon as possible. So I decided that speaking to A Random Person who works at a supermarket miles away from our house that I would Definitely Never See Again might not be such an impossible thing to do (if Dad didn't wear the antlers). Mum gave us a list of enough food to feed our family for about three years and off we went, on a mission to say One Or Two Words To A Total Stranger.

"I have a target in my sights," Dad whispered to me over the bulging trolley. "Friendly-looking checkout lady spotted at till five." (This was my dad Not Making A Big Deal About It apparently.)

Octavia had told me not to pile too much pressure on myself, so before I thought about it too much (and before Dad made any more spy jokes) I walked over to Friendly Checkout Lady. Waiting in the queue felt like An Actual Eternity, but I focused on the two hours of computer time Dad had promised me if I spoke, or as he put it, if it was Mission Accomplished. He had offered me unlimited computer access for the whole of the holidays if I wore flashing antlers, but literally nothing in the entire universe could make me do that, apart from maybe a visit from the Archangel Gabriel with a message from God saying He would take away my SM for ever, which so far didn't look very likely.

Friendly Checkout Lady smiled at us and said, "Hello!"

I took a deep breath, hummed a little bit and said, "Hi!" only it came out really loud and a few people turned around and I felt like the entire world was staring at me and that any moment Friendly Checkout Lady would ring her bell and announce over the tannoy, "Weirdly Loud Voice Girl at till five!"

Dad tapped my shoulder and said, "Start packing then!" and handed me the bags, which was for once the Exact Thing I needed him to do because he made it feel like I'd just done The Most Normal Thing Ever.

While I was packing jars of mincemeat and bags of satsumas and the most cleaning products ever, I couldn't help smiling because Dad was trying to act normal but he had tears in his eyes that he was trying to blink away and he looked like he had just won the lottery or something.

In the car on the way home he said, "Good job, Rozzie. Want to call Mum and tell her?"

"That we couldn't find any marzipan?"

Dad laughed and said, "Yes, exactly. Just tell her that we couldn't find any marzipan, but we do seem to have got ourselves a brave little daughter."

"Little? Dad, I'm eleven."

He handed me his phone and said, "Okay, that we have a medium-sized daughter incapable of finding marzipan but can greet friendly checkout ladies in busy supermarkets even when she is scared of doing so."

And actually, that felt like a pretty nice thing to be able to say about me.

#

On Christmas Eve Mum told me to invite Mrs Quinney over for dinner, "To say thank you for being a brilliant neighbour and looking after our wonderful and brave daughter."

Dad added, "And for all the wonderful brown gifts her cats keep on giving to my rose bushes, even when it's not Christmas." And Seb laughed so much he snorted apple juice through his nose.

Mum said, "Can we all try to just act normal when she arrives, please?"

Dad dangled baubles from his ears and said, "Sorry, This Family Just Doesn't Do Normal." And even more apple juice came out of Seb's nose.

Mrs Quinney is what Dad calls Jesus's Biggest Fan, but I'm not sure she enjoyed the dinner as much as I thought she would. She jumped out of her chair when we pulled the crackers and wouldn't even try the UFO-shaped mince pies me and Seb had made. Dad said later she was Brandy's Biggest Fan, which I suppose might explain why she dropped a roast potato in my orange squash. But Mum said it was lovely when Mrs Quinney said grace, and at least she fell asleep before Seb's charade of Jesus Christ Pooperstar.

On Christmas morning, Seb was literally shaking with excitement as he unwrapped a telescope, and I was speechless (which believe me was an Extremely Rare Thing at home) because Mum and Dad had got me a phone (maybe it was the million times I had asked them, or maybe they had finally realized leaving your daughter handwritten notes taped to the front door is only what people from the olden days do). Then Dad asked Mum, "What time is Auntie Marie arriving?"

And I had what can only be described as A Major Emotional Meltdown On A Colossal Scale.

It was like an enormous Auntie-Marie-shaped bombshell had just been dropped on me and totally demolished Christmas. And everything in my head all came pouring out in a massive word tsunami.

it's not fair won't be able to speak in real time won't wonder to say my -focus grace it's not fair for me to have a totally special grace silent christmas

I cried and shouted at Mum saying I wouldn't be able to speak for the entire time Auntie Marie was there, and how it wasn't fair for me to have a Totally Silent Christmas. Mum started crying saying she was sorry and that she thought Dad had told me, and it was too late to cancel because it was Christmas Day and Marie would already be driving, and she'd only invited her because it was her first Christmas without Uncle Pete. I shouted why couldn't she just go to the place Mrs Quinney goes to have Christmas dinner, but Dad said, "Marie isn't part of the mad old biddy brigade." And that made Seb laugh but I still couldn't stop crying. And I shouted, "Now I won't be able to say the special grace I've written for Seb! It will just have to stay in my pocket being totally unspoken for ever, just like everything I try to say at school!"

I stopped speaking, and we all sat there, surrounded by tinsel and twinkling fairy lights and shredded wrapping paper and empty boxes and all of the words I had just said.

Mum sat next to me on the sofa and hugged me. She stroked my hair and rocked me like a baby and said over and over again in her softest voice, "It's okay, it's okay, it's okay." And I felt like there were no words in my head because they had all just accidentally spilled out onto the carpet.

Then Seb said, "It *is* going to be okay, Rozzie, because I've just had a Brilliant Idea."

So later, we all sat at the table, and listened to the grace I had recorded in my bedroom on my brand-new phone, which turned out to be The Best Present Ever and not A Slippery Slope To Becoming Addicted To Google like Dad said it would be (but maybe only because it didn't have 3G).

"*Dear God, you probably have lots of people talking to you today to say thank you, so I hope you can hear me say this. Because I have a very big Thank You to say. You've probably noticed, there aren't many places on your earth I can speak, so thank you for giving me a home where I can. But mostly, I want to say Thank You for giving me the best little brother in the world. He makes every day feel special. And please, please let us have lots more Christmases together. Amen.*"

Mum cried because she said it was the nicest grace she'd ever heard and Auntie Marie cried because she'd never heard my voice before and she said it was lovely, and Dad cried a bit later because he said he'd had too much of Mum's sherry trifle. Seb told us the jokes he would put in crackers, which were all really disgusting, then sang "Happy Birthday To Jesus" when Dad lit the Christmas pudding.

After dinner, even though it was freezing, we all went outside and looked at the stars through Seb's new telescope. He told us the different constellations we could see and that they were always there even though we can only see them at night. And I didn't feel so much like I had ruined Christmas after that.

When Auntie Marie had gone home, and Seb had gone to sleep, I was reading in my bedroom when Mum came in. "Rozzie, can I have a Serious Talk with you about earlier, about what you said about not being able to speak at school?"

And my heart sank, because I felt back to normal by then, and I hate Serious Talks, so I said, "It's okay, Mum. I can handle it."

"But it's clearly upsetting you a lot, Rozzie. Me and your dad feel awful we've only just found out. We thought you'd been doing so well. Meeting your speaking targets, and speaking in the supermarket. Why didn't you tell us you couldn't speak in class?"

I shrugged. "You always seem upset and I didn't want to make things worse. Anyway, it's not like you or Dad can do anything about it. No wonder people think I'm weird."

Dad popped his antlers round the door and said, "You're not weird to us."

I put the duvet over my head. I didn't want to tell them how bad things actually were at school, because the nice orangey-sunshine feeling had come back in our house and I didn't want it to turn grey again.

"Look, Rozzie, if you want, I could drive you into school, and pick you up whenever I can, that way you'd maybe feel less worried. And we'll speak to Mr Bryant about some things your teachers can do to make you feel a bit more comfortable."

I came out from under the duvet and said, "Honestly, Dad, you don't need to speak to Mr Bryant. If you could just drive me into school that would make it so much better. It's the bus journey that's the worst thing. It's so noisy, it gets me off on a bad start. The rest I can work on with Mrs Kingsley." And that definitely wasn't a Massive Lie.

Dad took a deep breath and looked at Mum, who nodded. He said, "Okay. But I want you to be honest with us this time. If you're finding it difficult. And if people are calling you weird or whatever about it, I'll go in and speak to Mrs Kingsley and Mr Bryant myself."

So it turned out to be an okay Serious Talk because Dad was going to drive me to school every morning and Mum promised she would try not to cry so much. (Only that must have been a White Lie because when she hugged me I could feel her tears on my cheek.)

I went to bed that night feeling like I'd run a Christmas Day marathon or something because I was so tired I don't even remember trying to fall asleep. I woke up in the morning to Mum bringing me breakfast in bed and on the tray was a rectangular present. She said, "I found this under the tree. We must have missed it!"

And it was my present from Octavia.

I opened it to see a diary. It was coral-pink and said *Top Secret* in dark blue letters. On the inside cover Octavia had written:

If you are always trying to be normal, you will never know how amazing you can be.

– Maya Angelou

I read it over and over again, and each time that light bulb above my head that had been flickering came on full blast. And that's when a thought as clear as water came into my head, and it was a thought that changed everything:

What if I could be more than just a Nobody?

16

#serioustalk

The next morning, while my parents were recovering from too much sherry trifle, and Seb was being visited by one of his nurses, I was in my bedroom planning my Brilliant Idea: How To Speak Up At Manor High When You're A Total Nobody Who Can't Speak, also known as Getting A Metaphorical Meteor To Land On Manor High.

I drew it all out in my new diary using my best calligraphy pens, then after Seb's nurse had gone downstairs, I went into his room to get him to help me. I called it my new contribution to school. Seb called it Project Meteor.

While Mum and Dad were talking to the nurse in the kitchen, me and Seb made use of the unlimited computer time Dad gave us for not disturbing them. Seb did all the coding so it looked the way I wanted it to, but I got him to show me how to do it myself. Seb drew an image which we uploaded, then I chose the font and layout so it looked exactly the way I wanted. And just before we launched Project Meteor, I had my own Serious Talk with Seb.

"Listen, you can't mention anything to Mum and Dad about this, okay? It has to be Top Secret. Promise me."

"I won't say anything, I promise. It's a secret mission because you're going to be a superhero!" He thought for a moment then said, "It won't take *that* much to buy my silence."

So I agreed to let him play on my new phone for the rest of the day, and he immediately started referring to Mum and Dad as The Enemy.

And there it was: my new diary. Only this was nothing like Mrs Quinney's diary that had been locked up in a cupboard for a million years. Or like the one Octavia had given me which said Top Secret on the front.

My diary would be the Exact Opposite of Top Secret – it would be online for *everyone* to read.

I was finally going to have a voice at school. The voice I wanted so badly. A voice loud enough to speak up for myself and all the other Nobodies silently suffering at Manor High. This voice would tell everyone exactly what I wanted to say but couldn't.

I got Seb to check it was all anonymous. I set up a new email under the name Project Meteor, so no one would be able to trace it back to me. So, thanks to my super little brother, Miss Nobody was protected with a shield of anonymity, like a real superhero with a mask to protect my identity. Only mine was written in computer coding.

Small, unimportant Nobodies like me who got picked on every day of their lives needed someone to speak up.

And Miss Nobody was the girl to do it.

EXPOSING BULLYING AT MANOR HIGH

I AM MISS NOBODY

Geeks. Weirdos. Dorks. Bookworms. Freaks. Brainiacs. Loners. Nobodies.

I think it's about time we Spoke Up.

School can feel like a lonely place. Especially in a school where we, the Quiet Ones, are made to feel Totally Invisible. Or worse.

How many of us have been victims of violence, just for being ourselves? How many of us go to school knowing our packed lunch will end up in somebody else's stomach? That our musical instrument might end up in the biology pond? That our favourite book might get graffitied? Or that our chess pieces might end up plummeting out of a second-floor window?

How many of us have been picked on just for being different?

And how many of us have spoken up about it?

(No, me neither.)

At Manor High stupidity and spitefulness are celebrated. Popular people strike fear into the hearts of us Nobodies. It seems like to be a Somebody you have to hurt a Nobody.

And we're all too scared to speak up.

But I think it's about time that changed.

I'm starting this blog to Speak Out against the Brutal Bullies and the Vanity Squads who make our lives a Living Hell.

I'm here to Speak Up for all of you out there who know they don't sell pi in the canteen, that Carbon Dating isn't a new TV show, and that the Mona Lisa isn't a selfie.

But mainly this blog is for People Like Us to join forces and maybe (hopefully) help each other.

If you are being bullied at Manor High then you are Definitely Not Alone. Because it's been happening to me for what feels like a long time now.

And I don't know about you, but I'm pretty sick of keeping quiet.

Manor High School desperately needs a makeover and (with your help) I'm the girl who's going to do it.

So bullies of Manor High, you'd better Listen Up – because I'm not going to Keep Quiet any more. I'm going to tell you exactly what I think.

I hope some of you Nobodies out there want to join me.

Speaking Out Against Bullying at Manor High School.

I am Miss Nobody.

And then all I had to do was tap Publish.

#alittlebirdie
toldme

On New Year's Eve Mum and Dad let me and Seb stay up late to watch the fireworks. Because we live on a hill, you can see them going off in different places across town from our back garden. I don't like all the bangs, so Mum put her fluffy earmuffs on me, and we watched the colourful fizzes bursting in the sky, then we spelled out our names with sparklers. And while Mum, Dad and Seb were spelling out a massive triple *Super Seb*, and wishing for a lucky new year, I twirled mine into a tiny twinkling *Miss Nobody*.

The next morning Seb gave me the idea for making a poster. He said there are over a billion websites in existence so it would be extremely unlucky, maybe actually impossible for Mum and Dad to come across my blog, particularly considering they both found it difficult just checking their emails. I told him that they can't be as bad as Mrs Quinney, who I know for a fact has never been on the internet.

It was no good writing a blog to speak to people at school if I was the only one who ever read it. It would be like a crime-fighting superhero just making sure they didn't commit any crimes themselves. No, if I was going to make a real difference to any of the Nobodies at Manor High, then I needed *everyone* to read it. And there was only one way to get that to happen: advertising.

I couldn't exactly take out an advert in the school newsletter, and I couldn't use our printer because it had been broken since, like, for ever, but I definitely could take advantage of my position as library monitor. One of the few perks of the job was almost total unauthorized access to the library photocopier. I mean, we were obviously supposed to ask Mrs Goodacre first, but I was sure she wouldn't mind me breaking this one tiny library rule for such an important project.

Seb agreed to draw another picture to use on the poster if I promoted him to chief designer and programmer. I also had to make him a badge with his job title on. I told him, "When you're on a top secret mission it is not a good idea to wear a badge telling everyone about it," but he said he would only wear it during secret meetings and by this point I had no choice but to agree to his terms. He also made me give him the rest of my Christmas chocolate to sweeten the deal. So I spent the last few days of the holidays perfecting my calligraphy for the poster and wondering how my little brother became such a hustler.

Because of Miss Nobody, I didn't feel like going back to school would be such a Total Disaster – in fact, in a strange way I was looking forward to it. Now I didn't need to worry so much about not speaking, because Miss Nobody would be able to say everything for me.

Even though Dad was driving me in, I still couldn't relax on the journey to school. All I could think about was the poster hidden in my art folder. I was more than a little bit worried about Craig Bull tipping the entire contents of my folder on the floor, but part of me also felt excited. I said bye to Dad, put my head down and focused on the job I had to do: tell as many people as possible about Miss Nobody without saying a word.

One good thing about the first day back for Someone Like Me is that everyone is so excited to see their friends, they forget about hassling us Nobodies. (The bad thing is sometimes that makes you feel just as Unimportant And Friendless.) I made it to lunchtime without my poster being discovered, and I took managing to completely avoid Craig Bull at the lockers as the first Sign From God that I must definitely be on The Right Path.

Mrs Goodacre's lunchtime meeting seemed to drag on. We sat at the round tables by the windows and ate our lunch while she talked to us, which I liked because it meant I didn't have to eat lunch by myself. But it was obvious to me that even though I'd managed to avoid Craig that morning, he had definitely got to the other library monitors, unless Suzi had only packed a squashed banana for lunch and William dropped the *Guinness World Records* on his sandwiches.

Mrs Goodacre talked about the main thing coming up at the library this term, which was Book Week. This was the library equivalent of the Oscars only less glamorous and with a much smaller budget. Rajit was allowed to be in charge of it because he was in Year Nine and also because he patted Mrs Goodacre's hand and said, "I got this, Mrs G."

Suzi said Book Week was the only time the library ever got busy at lunchtime, and Mrs Goodacre said, "It gets the whole school buzzing about reading!" which I found hard to believe. The only thing that got the whole school buzzing, in my experience, was someone getting beaten up on the field.

Mrs Goodacre asked if I could help with the decorations because, "A little birdie told me you have beautiful handwriting!"

I felt my cheeks glowing red underneath my hands, but I whispered a tiny, "Okay." And, because it was the first time I had spoken in front of the library monitors, my heart practically bumped out of my chest, but none of them said anything. Dad said later it was probably because the library monitors had their own social problems to deal with. Considering Rajit spent most lunch breaks timing himself doing sudoku, I thought that was probably true.

Rajit said he wouldn't be able to help with decorating the library because he had something called Repetitive Strain Injury, which you get from playing too much World of Warcraft. He was wearing special elastic bandages on his wrists so he wasn't allowed to use his arms for the whole term and his parents had banned him from gaming. He said, "So, Mrs G, I need to use your computer to catch up because games are blocked on the normal ones."

Mrs Goodacre said, "Rajit, why don't you read a book?" (Which is what she says to everything.) I couldn't even imagine Dad letting me use the computer for long enough to get Repetitive Strain Injury.

Once the meeting was over, I waited until everyone

had left and Mrs Goodacre had popped out to get a coffee. I double-checked no one was around and then sneaked into the office where the photocopier was. It didn't take long to do the copies I needed, but it was noisy and really slow and I was petrified Mrs Goodacre would catch me. If she did catch me, my plan was to Deny All Knowledge by looking innocently at the noticeboard. I doubted I would be her top suspect anyway. And that was one of the best things about this whole Brilliant Idea. Literally no one would suspect me of writing a blog. Most people thought my brain was as silent as my tongue and even though that is So Not The Case, being the quietest person in school was The Perfect Alibi.

The photocopier eventually spat out the final copy, so I put them in my folder and put Mrs Goodacre's staple gun and Blu-tack in my pocket. Then I spotted the stack of Book Week posters Mrs Goodacre had told us needed putting up around school – another Sign From God! Two in one day! I took the pile, left a note for Mrs Goodacre saying I would put the posters up for her, and for the first time ever made my way out of the library feeling confident, which was sort of a totally new feeling to me.

Putting the posters up without being seen wouldn't be easy for just anybody, but being a Nobody like me is about as close to having actual invisibility as you can get.

And now I had the Book Week posters, no one would suspect a thing.

I started in the arts block. There was music coming from the dance studio and a few Year Nines hanging around outside the art classrooms, but no one took any notice of me. I put up the Book Week poster next to the display board decorated with little pictures of ballerinas, which would have looked really nice if someone hadn't drawn boobs on them in felt tip. After checking no one was looking my way, I stapled up a Miss Nobody poster.

It took me the rest of lunchtime to put posters up in all the places I could without being noticed and I still had some left. The bell went, but I wanted to finish my secret advertising campaign. I would have to be late for PSHE, but I could write a note for Mr Bryant saying I was helping Mrs Goodacre, which was Sort Of Another White Lie, but I had no choice. Anyway the good thing about Mr Bryant was he never checked up about anything. (This was also the bad thing about him.)

So, armed with the rest of my posters, and with what I was certain must be God smiling down on me (despite my very small criminal acts involving stationery) I went back to the library, put a folded-up poster in as many of the books on display as I could, and hoped it wouldn't be long before my new voice was heard loud and clear.

Afterwards, I walked out of the library doors and felt some words fizzing in my throat. I opened my mouth and felt them wrap around me like a cloak of invincibility as I whispered them into the cold wind.

"I

    am

        Miss

            Nobody."

18

#sayalittle prayer

The next day Dad woke me up really early. Mum had taken Seb to the hospital in the middle of the night and I would have to miss school because we had to see him, and Dad wanted to miss the traffic. I got dressed in a massive panic because Dad was telling me, "PLEASE, ROZ, HURRY UP!" I just had time to brush my teeth and grab my writing stuff.

In the car on the way to the hospital, Dad said, "Maybe all the excitement over Christmas wore him out. Maybe we should have made him rest more. His temperature's sky high again." I thought about what I had made Seb do over Christmas. Maybe making him my chief designer and programmer and getting him to work for ages on the computer had made him more poorly. Mum had even warned me a few times not to tire him out. I wouldn't be a very good online superhero if I had accidentally made my little brother even more sick.

Mrs Quinney keeps telling me that God always listens, so I prayed over and over again to say I was sorry and please don't let Seb die from making my blog. I closed my eyes really tight, prayed as hard as I could, and tried to stop myself looking out of the window for a Sign From God because the only signs I could see were for closing down sales.

God, I don't ask for your help very often, but please make Seb get better. Please don't let him die. I will do anything, just please make my little brother be okay.

When we arrived at the hospital Dad knew exactly where to go. Seb was in the Children's Special Care Unit, which meant that it was worse than the last time I went to visit him in hospital. In a hospital, special means bad.

Dad typed in a code which opened the door to the Special Care Unit and I looked out for Mandy, because she is the nurse who knows me the best. She doesn't ask me questions or anything, and says I can help myself to the juice they keep in the fridge (which I only did once because it tasted weird).

They have tried to make the hospital not look like a hospital by painting a big jungle scene on the walls, but some of the animals aren't right. Like there is a tiger hugging a penguin, which of course wouldn't exactly happen in real life anyway because a) penguins don't live in the jungle, but also b) the tiger would totally just eat it. When I said this to Dad ages ago he said, "Poorly children don't want to see pictures of animals eating each other when they are trying to get better." And when I asked Seb he said he would, but Dad said he's "probably not representative".

Dad quietly opened the door and I saw Seb linked up to lots of machines. One was monitoring his heart rate, and one was like a drip but had three different liquids going into the back of his hand, and he had an oxygen tube going into his nose. I was allowed to go in and see him, but he was asleep. Mum hugged me really close and I could feel her tears on my cheek.

I couldn't say anything because different doctors kept coming in to talk to Mum and Dad about a new treatment, and even when they went out no one shut the door properly so my words got stuck in my throat. All the things I wanted to say to Seb started forming in my head, like tiny clouds, but they were just out of reach.

If Seb was awake he would probably have pretended the tubes were full of some kind of super-power juice and made out like they were just making his brain get bigger or something, but I'm not good at jokes like him, so I just held his hand and tapped his arm gently, which was my way of telling him I loved him when I couldn't speak at the hospital.

What I really wanted to say was that I felt like a really terrible sister and a really, really terrible person. Because all this time I had just been worrying about myself, and I had only prayed for Seb that one time in the car on the way to the hospital. Maybe Seb had got extra poorly because he'd worked so hard making Miss Nobody. Maybe it had taken the energy he needed to get better. Whether I liked it or not, I had directly or indirectly caused my brother's illness to get worse. Only I didn't have a tapping code for that. And here I was, getting hugs from my parents, who knew nothing about any of it.

It was late when me and Dad drove home. Street lights passed by the car window in a blur and I felt more silent than I had for a long time. Being silent at school felt like nothing compared to not being able to talk to Seb. Dad squeezed my hand when we pulled up outside the house. "He'll be okay; he's in the best place." And I thought, only that best place is where I can't tell him I'm sorry.

When we went in I went to my room, got into bed and decided that it would probably be best for the whole world, including my immediate family, if I never came out.

19

#quickword

The next morning I came downstairs and overheard Dad on the phone saying I wouldn't be coming into school again today. And usually my heart would have leaped at the prospect of a day off, but it just sank because it meant Seb definitely wasn't better. I stood at the kitchen window looking out at the frosty garden; the sky was foggy, like all the clouds had fallen to the ground, but I could just make out Bernard creeping into the rose bushes.

When Dad put the phone down I said, "Is Seb going to get better if they do the new treatment the doctor said about?"

He put his arm around me and said, "I hope so, Rozzie,

I really hope so. It's a brand-new treatment, and he's had a bad reaction to some of the treatments they tried before, so…" And he left the sentence just hanging there unfinished.

And that was kind of how I felt all that morning, hanging around at the hospital, uncertain what was happening, or if I would get a chance to see Seb without any doctors being there so I could say how much I loved him.

But that afternoon Seb's temperature was back to almost normal, and he was awake and sitting up in bed. Dr Freestone checked him over and wrote loads of stuff down, then said, "Could I have a quick word with Mum and Dad?" and they stayed outside the room talking for ages, so I went over and closed the door. Mum caught my eye through the window and smiled.

And the words that had been hiding somewhere in my brain all started to appear. I leaned over to Seb and said quietly, "Sorry if doing Miss Nobody made you more poorly. I wish I could make you magically better so you could come home."

And Seb said, "My blood makes me poorly, not blogs! Anyway, I'm okay. Mandy said she'll let me play on her iPad later if I eat my dinner. I just hope it's not the stuff that looks like squashed bugs again." And he did a sick noise then said, "Did anyone read Miss Nobody yet?"

I shrugged. "I haven't had a chance to check it yet. Dad was hurrying me this morning and my phone can only go on the Wi-Fi at home. Anyway, Mum made me switch my phone off."

"But you could write another one now in your notepad and upload it at home later? This time tell the bullies you've been drinking this!" He held up a page in the magazine Dad had been reading, which was an advert for a special muscle-gain formula. Then he said, "Maybe you could drink double the amount so your muscles get ginormous and everyone's scared of you, then you would be as strong as Batman and you could change the name of your blog to Miss Hardcore Body!" I didn't tell him why that probably wasn't such a good idea.

Later that afternoon, when Mum went home to freshen up, and Seb slept, and Dad kept dozing off in the uncomfortable chair, I got out my notebook and started writing.

STUPID RULES AT MANOR HIGH

School is supposed to be all about education. But it seems like there are so many stupid people at ours.

I bit my lip. Was I actually ready to start naming

names? I thought back to everything that had happened to me since I started at Manor High. The teasing, the name-calling, the laughter, being pushed around, the Million Silent Panics. All the times I hadn't been able to say anything back. I looked up at Seb sleeping next to the soft beeping machines. This was our project. Project Meteor. I carried on writing.

Practically every day at lunchtime, three Year Nine boys (who you might recognize from the matching bleached patches in their hair and their Amazing Ability to communicate in grunts) attempt to squash as many Year Sevens into the art cupboard as physically possible. Are they attempting a new Guinness World Record? Is it a new form of art? Are they actually trying to collect Year Sevens? No, it is bullying-meets-kidnapping and it is about time it stopped.

Equally stupid is Craig Bull, the bully who thinks it is okay to Totally Terrorize people half his size, which, let's face it, is pretty much everyone considering his head alone must weigh more than the school minibus. Which is probably why he uses it to barge people out of his way in the lunch queue, even though he spends the morning stealing our food. Listen, Craig — if you aren't going to change your thieving ways, then at least use the proceeds to buy a belt. We really don't like seeing your Spider-Man pants when we're being put in a headlock for our sandwiches.

Answering Back to the bullies at Manor High School.

I am Miss

"What's that you're writing?"

I jumped and the notebook and pen dropped to the floor. "Nobody. I mean, nothing." I quickly picked them up and closed my notebook. "Just some calligraphy."

"Can I see?" Dad reached out his hand.

My heart was racing. "Um, it's not finished yet. I'm actually quite hungry."

"Hmmm. Okay, me too. Fancy leaving Sleeping Beauty for a minute and getting a snack then?"

I nodded. And in my head I wrote a mental note: *It is possible to distract Dad with food.*

When we were at home later I said I needed an early night, so Dad gave me a kiss and said, "I'll take you to school in the morning, but take your phone, okay? You might have to go to Mrs Quinney's after school, but I'll text you. And if you need to…you know, if you have any problems…if you want me to come in and speak to…"

And suddenly it was Dad who couldn't get his words out.

"It's okay, Dad. I'll be fine. I really want to speak up for myself. It's my New Year's resolution." And that was Definitely Not A Total Lie.

I went upstairs, switched on my phone and clicked on the link to my blog. Then it was me who needed an oxygen tube, because I could hardly breathe.

56 New Visitors

I sat there for a minute letting it sink in, with my heart pounding in my chest, thinking, *fifty-six* people have actually seen it! I clicked on Add New Post and typed out what I had written at the hospital. My finger trembled over the Publish button for a little while as I thought about seeing Craig Bull in his daily locker barge. But then I reminded myself – *I'm* scared of Craig Bull, but Miss Nobody isn't. So I smiled and tapped Publish.

Suddenly Dad opened my bedroom door. "Hey, I thought you'd be asleep by now. Five minutes then…" I dropped my phone onto my lap, but its glow seemed to beam straight into Dad's eyes. "Rozzie, I think it's a bit late for screen times."

I tried to act as normal as possible, which isn't very easy when it feels like your heart just leaped out of your mouth.

"Okay. And it's called screen *time*, by the way."

"Whatever it's called, I'm sure the little pokebots can wait until tomorrow. You're back at school in the morning."

I rolled my eyes and quickly switched off my phone, for once actually thankful Dad knows literally nothing about technology (washing machines don't count). "When will Seb be coming home?"

Dad was quiet for a moment so I already knew the answer before he said, "He's got to stay at the hospital while they try this new treatment. You'll be able to visit him again at the weekend. The doctors…" Then he shook his head a tiny bit and said, "Nothing." He leaned down and kissed me on the head. "Try to get some sleep."

I got into bed, closed my eyes, and felt the house slowly fill up with the weird grey silence again.

20

#tellme aboutit

The next day I got into school early because Dad wanted to get to the hospital. No one else was around, which I liked, so I put my stuff in my locker, and got to my form class without seeing anyone apart from a few teachers. I sat in my usual seat and started looking through the calligraphy book I always take to school. I didn't really feel like doing any, so I went over some of the letters with my finger and tried not to think about Seb, which was Literally Impossible.

I heard some voices coming and my stomach lurched. I was worried someone would say something to me about why I was in the classroom first, or why I'd been off for two days right at the start of term. Octavia had told me that practising what to say in my head before I say it can sometimes help something come out, so I repeated in my head:

My brother's really ill in hospital.

My brother's really ill in hospital.

My brother's really ill in hospital.

If I managed to say that, no one would say anything horrible to me, surely. Even the Manor High psychopaths couldn't be that cruel. I could feel my face getting warm at just the thought of someone talking to me. I sank deeper into my chair and tried to hide behind my hair, while the words I'd prepared in my head collapsed like a tower of Jenga.

When the voices came into the classroom, I relaxed a little bit. It was Sian, Elsie and Michael. They were okay to me. By okay I mean they completely ignored me, but didn't join in if Maisy or Connor said stuff to me, and that was A Million Times Better than some of them.

They carried on talking even when they saw me. When you're a Nobody, no one seems to care if you overhear what they say. It's like you don't matter. Or maybe I am just literally invisible to some people. Elsie said, "I heard it's one of the Year Nine girls in the orchestra. Apparently she was annoyed about the Christmas concert thing and someone broke her flute."

Michael said, "Yeah, well, I reckon if it is then Crystal and her mates will beat her up. Crystal whacked a boy last term just for leaning on her locker."

And Sian said, "There might be another one tonight so text me if you see it before I do."

Then they started talking about maths homework, but I didn't worry about that because I couldn't quite believe what I was hearing. I tried to look extra interested in my calligraphy. Could they be talking about…?

More people came in, including Connor, who casually swept all of my stuff off the desk when he walked past like he didn't even have to think about it. As if it wouldn't cross his mind *not* to push my stuff onto the floor. I got up and picked my things up without looking at him or anyone else, feeling my face turn deep crimson like a new bruise. I wished really hard he would not do it just for one day, or at least take a day off sick or something. I made a mental note to ask God why Seb was so poorly when bullies like Connor never even caught a cold.

Mr Bryant arrived and told everyone to sit down about five times and then said, "This is the last time I am going to say it!" really loudly. But today I didn't care how long it took some people in my class to listen to Mr Bryant, because my mind was busy racing. Could they really have been talking about my blog? I needed to get to a computer so I could see how many visitors I'd had since last night. But that meant I had to wait two whole lessons until break time. In fact, it was worse than that: double science.

Because I had missed a lesson, Miss Sheldon came over to tell me everyone was working on projects for the science fair. Everybody was in pairs already except for me. We have an odd number in our class, and Miss Sheldon said the words I dread hearing at school on practically a daily basis: "Who would like to work with Rosalind?"

And the number of hands that went up was Exactly Zero.

Miss Sheldon looked at me sympathetically and glanced around at the pairs of people working together.

Oh, no, I thought, she is going to put me with a pair. She is literally going to force people to work with me. I did an emergency prayer:

Please God, don't let her do this. I would rather be burned to death in a tragic Bunsen burner accident than for Miss Sheldon to force me into an awkward trio with people who don't like me.

My heart was racing. I tried to communicate with Miss Sheldon telepathically as my throat felt like it had a massive rock in it.

Maybe she picked up on my Massive Silent Panic or maybe she noticed the other sixty eyes saying, *Please don't make us work with The Weird Girl Who Can't Speak*, because she said, "Well, for now, why don't you work on your own and decide what type of experiment you'd like to do, and then we'll see if we can find you some people to work with later." I nodded and she smiled. Clearly she was as relieved as I was that she didn't have the potentially awkward situation of every pair in the class rejecting me, because she said, "Oh, good, okay then. I'll come and have a look at your proposal in a little while." Then she walked back to her desk at the front.

Even though I was a lesson behind everyone else, glancing round the room, it didn't seem like anyone had made much progress. One thing that did seem weird was

Maisy working with Adrian, Miss Sheldon's top student. Maybe Miss Sheldon had chosen the pairs. Or maybe (more likely) Maisy had made Adrian be her partner so he would come up with a Brilliant Idea and do all the work and she could take the credit. Adrian was probably too scared to say anything.

I flicked through the textbook Miss Sheldon had put on my desk, then looked up at what she was writing on the board.

Make your project truly spectacular!

She said, "Now remember, everyone, the best projects will have a stall at the science fair where you'll present your idea to the judges. Then, the truly spectacular ones will be presented to the whole school in our Science Week assembly!"

Vinnie whispered to Connor, "What about a time machine?"

I had to think of something Completely Unspectacular for my science fair project. Presenting to the judges at the science fair and then potentially the entire school in a special science assembly sounded like a punishment to me, not a prize. There was Absolutely No Way On Earth I wanted to win.

I had to do something not good enough to get into the fair, but not bad enough to fail. I flicked through the textbook again and saw the title *Sugar Concentration in Fruit Juice*. That sounded boring enough to stay under Miss Sheldon's radar.

Then I heard Maisy say, "How about investigating why The Weirdo can't speak?" and a few people started laughing.

Miss Sheldon said, "Maisy! That's not very nice."

Maisy turned around to me and said, "Sorry," then mouthed, "Not sorry," afterwards.

I leaned my forehead on my hand and imagined Miss Nobody typing out a special message for Maisy until the angry tears went away. And for the rest of the lesson I tried to not think about Seb or notice the other horrible things Maisy mouthed at me, which wasn't exactly possible.

When the bell rang I got ready to rush out of the door but Miss Sheldon called my name and asked to see my proposal. I was dreading being in trouble as I had hardly done anything, but when I showed her she said, "Investigating sugar concentration sounds fantastic! I was hoping someone would do something like this! This is exactly the kind of science that could impress the judges at the fair!"

So either Miss Sheldon was just trying to be nice to me because it was obvious everyone in my class hated me, or the judges are Massively Boring. She said, "Well done! I'll give you some help next lesson," which I took as my opportunity to leave and I walked as fast as I could out of her lab without actually breaking into a run.

Dad told me ages ago that even if you want to, try not to actually run away from a conversation because most people will consider it Even More Weird than not talking. I asked him if it was okay just to back away slowly then and he said, "Look, Rozzie, backing away slowly might be considered a little more polite than just full-on running away from someone, but really you ought to just stick it out, however uncomfortable you find it, like the rest of us have to." Which is what I always try to do now.

I rushed straight to the library, found a computer in the corner with the screen facing the wall and logged on. The library was empty as usual, but I couldn't take the risk of anyone seeing what I was doing. I typed in my blog address and waited.

Then –

ACCESS DENIED
YOU DO NOT HAVE PERMISSION TO VIEW
THIS WEB PAGE

Which was just typical of my school. There were people being bullied everywhere and they block the one person who is trying to help them!

And that's when I noticed Mrs Goodacre's computer screen.

It seemed to be looking at me. She always went to the canteen on Friday break times to get an iced bun. I looked around for Rajit and the other library monitors, but they were nowhere to be seen. There were a few people browsing the shelves in the corner, but they wouldn't be able to see into the office.

So before I had even stopped to think about what I was doing, I was sitting on Mrs Goodacre's twirly chair logging onto my blog. I clicked the notifications button.

98 New Visitors
56 New Post Likes
51 New Follows
33 New Comments

And for the first time that morning, a small smile crept across my lips. I scrolled down.

CamillaXO is now following your blog
YumYumNomNom is now following your blog
RitaDita commented on your post
SuZiYama liked your post "I AM MISS NOBODY"
SuZiYama is now following your blog

RudyTudy7 commented on your post
HorseyG liked your post "I AM MISS NOBODY"
Adrian90 is now following your blog

And they went on. I had Likes! I had Followers! And I had a lot of them! People actually Liked Miss Nobody. People Liked what she had to say. I took a deep breath and clicked on the Comments link. Then my tummy felt like it was doing somersaults, because I read yes I want to join, and me too sick of manor high bullies!!!! and Like this ☺, and hey miss nobody, this is my life lol!! And one saying: pi = 3.14159265359 pie = nom nom. And when the bell rang I almost twirled off Mrs Goodacre's twirly chair. She would be back any moment. I quickly logged out, closed down the window and hurried out of the office.

That afternoon I spent most of the double history lesson ignoring Mr Dean's Extremely Long And Detailed Explanation Of The Geographical Significance Of Cardiff Castle and thought about the amazing comments on Miss Nobody, and what to write for her next post. I'd promised my followers I would speak up against the bullies of Manor High, and that was exactly what I had to do.

Maisy twirled her hair around her Hello Kitty pencil and gazed at her reflection in the window. She was one of the most popular girls in our whole year. But why? As far as I could tell she was made out of pure meanness, considering how much she seemed to enjoy threatening violence against innocent people by the lockers for No Actual Reason, and only ever said things that were either a) completely horrible or b) completely stupid.

Mr Dean must have noticed her gazing at the window too because he said, "Maisy, what is the capital of Wales?"

Maisy said, "England?"

"No, I said Wales, what is its capital city?"

And Maisy said, "I just told you, Mr Dean, England. England is the capital of Wales. Isn't it?" Mr Dean put his head in his hands. Then she said, "Well, I know it's definitely *in* England."

Mr Dean said maybe it was time for him to retire. Everyone else in the class was either scared of Maisy, or they must have thought her answer was reasonable because no one said anything. So that is another one of the many problems with my school to add to the list: it's possible that no one here has heard of Wales.

Mr Dean carried on his lecture, and Maisy whispered to me, "At least I can say Wales."

I realized that as much as I hated her, if I wrote a blog about Maisy, people might suspect Miss Nobody was in my year or maybe even in my class. I wasn't sure if she bullied anyone apart from me. I didn't know if she was

Whole School Famous yet. Maybe it was better if people kept thinking Miss Nobody was a girl in Year Nine. Maisy Love, unfortunately for me, would have to wait.

Later, when the bell rang for the end of the day, I felt fizzes of excitement in my stomach. Ever since I'd seen my Miss Nobody notifications, for almost every moment of the day, I'd been desperate to get online. I wanted to read the rest of the comments so badly. I couldn't wait to write another post too because (for once) people would hear what I had to say.

But when I checked my phone I had a text saying:

Still at hospital. Seb OK waiting for test results. Go to Mrs Q's. Back in time for dinner. Dad xxx

And I thought, oh great, just what Manor High's new super blogger needs: a whole evening at Mrs Quinney's. The only person in the entire world without the internet.

21

#greywords

When I knocked at Mrs Quinney's it was just starting to rain. I could smell that concretey smell as I waited for her to answer. She always took ages. Partly because she was so old, but also because she said that you should never immediately stop whatever you are doing to answer the door or the telephone. She said if something is important, people will wait. Which basically meant she believed in doing things about ten times slower than normal people. (And I mean normal *old* people.)

For example, if she was in the middle of a crossword puzzle and the telephone rang, she wouldn't just stop doing the puzzle for a minute and answer the telephone like most normal people. She would slowly fill in whichever clue she was answering, then slowly put her pen down, then slowly put the puzzle book down on the table next to her chair, then slowly get out of her chair and slowly walk out to the hall where the telephone was. By the time she reached the telephone it would almost always have stopped ringing. And then she would say, "Well, it couldn't have been very important!" Whenever it rang she would always say, "What a nuisance!" Needless to say, I never phoned Mrs Quinney. And I've spent a considerable part of my life sitting on her doorstep.

I watched the raindrops gathering in a small puddle. I wondered if any more people were following Miss Nobody by now. I chewed the sleeve of my school shirt. I wondered what the rest of the comments said. I felt a tiny smile on my lips.

Mrs Quinney made me jump when she opened the door. She had never answered the door this quickly in the entire time I had known her. She told me to come in, called me a poor thing, and for the first time in our entire relationship gave me a hug. I was so shocked I almost fainted.

Being hugged by Mrs Quinney was a bit like being wrapped in an enormous blanket. And for some reason it made me think about Seb, hooked up to the machines, waiting for test results that might say he wasn't getting better again. I definitely didn't mean to, but being hugged like that by Mrs Quinney for the first time ever made me cry. And, before I knew what was happening, I was sitting on Mrs Quinney's lap with my head resting on her massive boobs and she was saying, "There, there," and I was sobbing like a baby. It was all a bit embarrassing really.

Once I'd just about stopped crying, she made me sweet tea in my favourite Austrian teacup and gave me one of her famous currant buns. Her house felt so warm and safe compared to my house. And I knew Seb was the one who was really poorly, so he was the one who needed looking after, but it felt nice when I got looked after too. Even if it was by my crazy-cat-lady next-door neighbour.

Either Mrs Quinney just happens to know Exactly What To Do when Someone Like Me has an uncontrollable crying fit or she can definitely read minds, because as soon as I had finished eating my currant bun she said, "I'm telephoning your father to tell him you're staying for dinner. That's all right, isn't it, Mary?" who miaowed as if to say yes. (Bernard didn't seem bothered either way.)

I wanted to check my blog more than anything, but Mrs Quinney's house was like being in a hot bath; I just didn't ever want to get out. Or go home. I didn't like it when Seb wasn't there. In every room there seemed to be a big Seb-shaped hole where he was supposed to be. And Mrs Quinney's house is one of those places where you don't have to worry about anything like that because the outside world seems to fade away. It's peaceful and special and feels a bit like going back in time. Probably down to the fact it looks like she hasn't updated her wallpaper since the Victorian times.

At my house when Seb's bad, things are a bit like when you haven't tuned in the radio station properly so everything sounds fuzzy and it makes a bad noise. And even though I can speak normally, I have loads of big scary thoughts that I can't say, like:

Is he going to die?

And:

What would our family be like without Seb?

And some little thoughts like:

Will he ever stop going on about poo the whole time?

For dinner Mrs Quinney made one of my favourites, which is her home-made broccoli quiche with new potatoes, which may not sound like much but sometimes this woman makes me eat cabbage soup. She also made a salad, which I don't like that much but Mum told me that you have to eat a little bit of everything at Mrs Quinney's just to be polite. Even though I wasn't hungry and even though my eyes hurt from crying, I ate everything that Mrs Quinney put on my plate, which was a lot for me, but I hadn't eaten at lunchtime because I was too busy writing my next blog post.

By the time Mum came to pick me up from Mrs Quinney's it had stopped raining but outside still smelled cold and wet. As soon as we got through the door she gave me a hug. And it was nice, even though I could tell she'd been crying because her eyes were red and her make-up had blurred into little black splodges under her eyes. She said, "Dad's staying at the hospital tonight. I thought we could watch a film or something. Try to take our minds off everything." But she didn't say anything about Seb so it was like his name was there in this big unspoken word bubble between us.

While Mum was making us her special hot chocolate with floating marshmallows, I sat on the sofa reading the comments on Miss Nobody. They said stuff like yea happens to me, and I get called a geek all the time, it sucks, and lol true! and craig always steals my donuts!!!!

And it made the worries in my head about Seb get replaced with how Amazing it felt to be Miss Nobody.

I clicked the lock screen button when Mum came in and we put on *The BFG* DVD Seb had got me for Christmas. When it ended Mum wiped tears away from her eyes, pulled me in for a hug and said quietly, "Seb's test results weren't good, Rozzie."

And I had been wishing for ages that Mum would speak to me about Seb, but those words were sad and grey and I wished she hadn't said them. Because that night I heard them over and over again and they felt like enormous tears stuck inside my head.

22

#shoutout

Octavia's office was weirdly tidy. The books usually on the floor had been neatly stacked into a new bookcase and all the papers and folders which normally covered her desk had totally vanished. I looked around the room and said, "What happened?"

Octavia's laugh sounded like a trombone and she said, "My New Year's resolution! Now, how is your New Year's resolution going?" And I told her about speaking to Friendly Checkout Lady, that I had started writing a diary (only a Mini White Lie) and that I had practised getting words in my head in class, but so far none of them had made an actual appearance, even though I *had* managed to speak in the library. She said, "Small steps, Rosalind, you're making brilliant progress," which is what she always says to everything.

So just as my therapy was going well, Seb wasn't responding to his. He had to stay in hospital for a while so the doctors could monitor him. Dad said, "We'll bring him home as soon as we can. You'll be able to visit him after school."

But I had worries constantly swimming around in my head about Seb, and A Million Questions that I didn't dare say out loud. Mum and Dad were acting even more weird than usual. They would go really quiet when I entered the room, and I started feeling like I wasn't the only one in the family with a Special Talent for being Totally Silent.

#

The next week at school we were doing our science project experiments. Miss Sheldon was trying to tell Connor and Vinnie that Illegal Wrestling Moves wasn't a science project, and that they weren't allowed to put each other in headlocks, but I guess she must have given up because when she went back to her desk Connor shouted, "Japanese Backbreaker!" and bellyflopped onto Adrian's back.

Miss Sheldon stared wide-eyed from her desk and shouted, "Connor!" (She spent a lot of our science lessons wide-eyed and shouting, "Connor!")

Adrian said, "I'm all right, Miss," and picked up the rocket launcher he'd been making from the floor.

Miss Sheldon said, "Connor, why don't you and Vinnie go and use the computers in the library to do some research?" And before she even finished writing the permission slip they had both run out of the door like the room was on fire.

I had four different cartons of orange juice open in front of me and I was recording the results of the sugar test strips in my exercise book, when suddenly my whole desk was flooded with orange. I jumped up and saw Maisy walking off. She shouted, "OMG! Look what she's done!"

Miss Sheldon grabbed some paper towels and said, "Don't worry, accidents happen!" and Maisy slowly sat back at her desk, looking at me and smiling. I looked down at the orange juice soaking into my book, and tears started forming in my eyes. I wished and wished I could just shout out how much I hated her.

#

When Dad picked me up he said Seb was very tired and we couldn't visit him, even for a short time. So when he asked me, "How was school today?" instead of telling him about Maisy spilling my orange juice and almost ruining my experiment, I told him that it was a Really Good Day because I managed to speak a word in class. And even though it was Actually A Massive Lie, it made him look less like he was worried about everything in the world all at once.

The only thing stopping me from having another Major Emotional Meltdown On A Colossal Scale was being Miss Nobody. Because when I got home and checked my blog, I had a notification beaming out at me like an enormous smile.

1 New Message

Someone had sent me a private message. And maybe that doesn't sound like much to you, but the only people who had ever even texted me were members of my immediate family.

I clicked on the message and it opened.

From: beanzontoast

I'm in yr9 and get bullied by a boy in my year called Jamie and 2 of his mates because they think my name is funny.

They do it before and after school. I avoid them at break times because I know they hang out in the science block. I think they bully other people too. I don't know who you are but thanks. I'm gonna do something about it. My names not beanz on toast btw lol xo

And I felt like an Actual Real Life Superhero, only definitely without the muscles or costume. (I did put my coat around my shoulders like a cape once, but only in front of Seb to make him laugh so it doesn't count.)

That weekend, in between visiting Seb, I checked my blog, and wrote new posts as often as I could without making Mum and Dad suspicious. And at the hospital, while Mum and Dad were getting coffee, I showed Seb the screenshots I had taken of Miss Nobody, and his eyes practically exploded out of his head.

"Rozzie!" he said. "You are like a superhero!" I smiled because it was good to see him happy like that, and it felt nice to finally have someone to share my excitement about being Miss Nobody. He carried on flicking through the comments. "This means you must have a superpower!"

"If I did then I would swap it to make you better."

And he said, "And I would swap it for tornado wees!" then demonstrated what they would be like until Mum and Dad came back and told him to lie down.

By Sunday I had 164 visitors and more messages and comments from people at school telling Miss Nobody things that had happened to them at the hands of the Manor High bullies. It was like all of a sudden the Nobodies were speaking up, and they had a lot to say about one particular bully with bleached hair: Crystal.

So that evening, when Dad was burning something for dinner, I wrote a blog all about Manor High's verbal-bullet shooter before Dad even realized I was on the computer. Crystal and her gang were about to find out what it was like to be in Miss Nobody's firing line for a change.

QUEEN CRYSTAL AND HER CLONES

These Queen Bees of Manor High have been stinging way too many of us lately.

They are the ones who think it's Literally Impossible to go more than ten minutes without applying lipstick. They must get through more make-up and fake tan than the entire cast of TOWIE. Unfortunately, the result is less Healthy Glow and more: Do You Work For Willy Wonka?

How many of us have had our lunch money stolen by this crowd of tango tormenters? How many of us have been pushed around by these bronzed bullies?

According to the messages I've received, it's A Lot.
So Miss Nobody says: No More.

Let's not spend our school lives being ruled by Crystal
The Tangerine Queen and her army of ladies-in-faking.

Believe in yourselves, Nobodies. We can't have a dictator
with a face that looks like an orange pancake.

Let's start our own revolution by Speaking Up.

Calling timeout on Manor High tyrants.

I am Miss Nobody.

A few minutes later I was sitting at the dinner table
thinking, Mission Accomplished, when Dad presented
me with a plate of something just about recognizable as
macaroni cheese and said, "I checked my email today.
There was one from one of your teachers."

And that's how I found out my science project was
going A Lot Worse Than I Could Ever Have Anticipated:
Miss Sheldon had picked it to be in the science fair.

23

#everybodys talking aboutit

It was A Disaster On Practically A Global Scale. I could not imagine anything worse than being in the hall in front of everyone not being able to speak about the sugar concentration in orange juice. I told Dad that Miss Sheldon only chose me because everyone else in our class sucks at science, which was true but it was also probably because she knew I literally couldn't say no.

"Well, she said in her email that your project was fantastic and that she was really impressed with your effort in science."

"Then maybe she was lying."

"I don't think so, Roz. She also said that parents are

invited to come along to the fair, which is weird because you never mentioned it."

"I didn't think you were interested in science."

"Roz! I design washing machines for a living! My job is a kind of science!"

"Well, we've never studied washing machines in science lessons."

But Dad ignored me and said, "I'll see about getting a couple of hours off work so I can come to the fair."

And I wanted to face-plant my burned macaroni.

The idea of Dad coming into school and seeing me being The Weird Girl Who Can't Speak and With No Science Project Partner and With No Actual Friends whilst standing next to The Most Boring Science Project Known To Planet Earth was about as appealing to me as being hanged, drawn and quartered. But when I said this to Dad he said, "Actually you wouldn't be hanged, drawn and quartered, women were just burned at the stake, and I think only if you'd been convicted of treason." Which was still much more appealing to me than not being able to speak in front of my dad and the whole science fair.

Because even though my parents understand I can't speak in These Kind Of Situations, I still hate being Totally Silent in front of them. It makes me feel A Million Times More Weird than I do already. But it's kind of hard to argue with someone who says, "It's still one hundred per cent better than being Completely Normal!" even when it one hundred per cent definitely isn't. Plus it meant there was a chance he could find out I lied about speaking in class. So basically, I started to really not like Miss Sheldon.

I asked Dad if he was worried about being hanged, drawn and quartered for what he said about the Prime Minister at Christmas. He said, "I think the Prime Minister is probably more concerned about keeping their job at the moment." Which made me a little bit more hopeful because if someone as important as the Prime Minister could lose their job maybe there was a chance Miss Sheldon could lose her job and I wouldn't have to do the fair after all, but Dad said he thought the chances of that happening were about one in a billion.

So that night I went to bed with a sick feeling in my tummy, and it wasn't just the burned macaroni. Because I knew speaking to Dad in the hall with everyone around was going to be impossible. And if a Massive Silent Panic can happen just in front of one person at school, which it did on practically a daily basis, this feeling would be x100,000 in front of the judges at the fair, and x100,000,000 if I had to do it in front of the entire stupid school in assembly. And I thought Miss Sheldon was totally horrible for making me do it. And I know that was maybe quite a bad thought, but I thought it anyway.

# #

The next day, the only thing stopping me from stabbing myself in the head with the library letter opener was how amazingly epically brilliantly popular Miss Nobody had become. Everywhere I went people were talking about her. And, like a real superhero, I cherished my secret identity and welcomed my new Whole School Fame.

But that wasn't the only Totally Brilliant Thing about being Miss Nobody.

At lunchtime Suzi said that some of the people in the school chess club had stood in front of the arts block at break time, like a real-life line of pawns, stopping the three Year Nine bullies, Jamie and his mates, from entering. They literally could not get through the doors.

Then she said it was the same thing with Craig Bull. When he walked into the canteen, so many people laughed at him shouting, "Spider-Man pants!" that he turned around and left. "And so this morning when he told me to give him my lunch, I said, 'No thanks, Spider-Man pants!' and walked away! It was so awesome!"

I covered my mouth with my hand in case she saw the

enormous smile on my face. I couldn't wait to see Seb after school and tell him the Best News Ever: Project Meteor had taken its first casualties! Then I had the thought that probably no superhero has had ever: I have to get my notebook!

I spent the rest of lunchtime writing a blog post to upload at home later. The knowledge that Craig Bull and the three Year Nine art cupboard bullies had been stopped in their tracks meant that with every word I wrote, I was making Manor High a safer place to be a Nobody. Now maybe bullies would think twice before messing up classrooms, stealing money, throwing food in the canteen, intimidating people at lunchtime, drawing felt-tip boobs on ballerina displays, and generally making Someone Like Me feel scared all the time.

Only, I realized, when I was writing Miss Nobody, I didn't feel so afraid.

And I wasn't exactly sure what the feeling was to begin with, because it wasn't something I had really felt before. But there I was in the library with my notebook, thinking about what I could write for my next post, and I thought, I actually feel like a Somebody, only not like most of the Somebodies at my school because I wasn't a total bully.

And there I had it, my next post:

HOW TO BE A SOMEBODY AT MANOR HIGH

Have you ever wanted to not be a Nobody and be a Somebody instead?

Well, maybe you'll change your mind when I tell you what it takes to be considered a Somebody at Manor High.

The first thing is: Don't Do Any Work. That's right, Nobodies. Forget about enjoying your favourite subjects if you want to be popular at Manor High. Because Popular People Do Not Have Favourite Subjects! Forget getting good grades or any plans you might have for a future career. Because to be cool you have to do As Little Work As Possible. And obviously the last thing you want to do is homework. Unfortunately, this could mean you might get a lot of detentions. But don't worry – I think spending break times in detention might actually be considered cool for a Somebody!

Another thing that is Totally Crucial if you want to be a Somebody at Manor High is to Be Mean. That's right! Meanness is Extremely Cool And Popular with these Somebodies! Making a Nobody cry is like winning the popularity lottery for a Somebody! (You might need to practise this at home, but that's okay because of all the free time you'll get by not doing your homework.)

Basically, think the Exact Opposite of kindness and you might be getting somewhere close to #manorhighcool.

And don't you think it's time that changed?

Do you know any Somebodies at Manor High? Message me and they could be featured in my next post, The Manor High Cool List!

Exposing the truth about #manorhighcool and Speaking Up for #manorhighnobodies.

I am Miss Nobody.

As I was writing, I felt like I was speaking to Actual People. And it was a really nice feeling. Because I'd been at school for nearly five months now and I still hadn't actually spoken to anyone apart from Mrs Goodacre, who I had started liking even more than usual because she no longer checked the books I said I was mending. (Which was good for me because I wasn't mending books I was writing my blog, but probably not very good for her if she wanted to keep her job as school librarian.)

And later at home, after I uploaded my post onto Miss Nobody, and read comments like lol I'm glad I'm a geek, and boy in my class gets detentions all the time & thinks he is cool lol, and proud to be a nobody, making someone cry isn't cool ☺, I felt like maybe I was starting to make a difference. And even better than that actually, was that I felt different too. And for once not in a bad way.

24

#strange word

The next morning in form time things got even better. Unfortunately Connor was still doing his Not Very Hilarious joke of knocking all my stuff on the floor, and Mr Bryant was running late so it meant he did it even more times than usual. My cheeks felt totally boiling hot and the words **LEAVE ME ALONE** were practically deafening me because they were stuck behind lips that were superglued together, when I overheard Elsie telling everyone about what happened yesterday on the way home from school.

And it was about a boy at our school called David Gay. And I know that teachers tell us that gay means happy and I suppose it does if you live in a Jane Austen book or something, but let's face it: we Definitely Don't. And there is obviously nothing wrong with being gay, but some people at my school don't seem to get that, like they don't get most things. So going around being called David Gay when you are thirteen years old and go to Manor High is a bit like walking around with a massive sign on your back saying: Please Bully Me Relentlessly For My Entire Life. (Rufus Jelly didn't have it so easy either.) David had it really bad at our school. And he did what most people do at my school if they want to survive – absolutely nothing.

Only yesterday, on the way home, David Gay got into a fight. An actual fight. He was being pushed around by some boys in Year Nine who were calling him gay as usual, when suddenly David pushed one of them back and punched another one in the face. This was Incredible News. David was almost as quiet as me. It was a bit like hearing Mother Teresa had karate-chopped someone. It didn't seem possible. No one could believe it.

And while Elsie was talking, I thought about the first ever message Miss Nobody was sent. The words I'm gonna do something about it popped into my head. I felt my lips get unstuck and move into a smile.

When school finished Dad was waiting for me in the

car park. He said, "Hey, had a good day? Mum says Seb's feeling a lot better today. He's looking forward to seeing you." And I was so happy because it felt like ages since they had used the word "better" about Seb. I closed the car door and once we had driven out of school Dad said, "You know what is slightly more weird than usual though? Seb told Mum that you two need to have a *meeting*."

I tried to sound casual even though my heart actually stopped. I said, "He must be missing me. Mum's probably been reading him *The Secret Garden* again or something."

Dad said, "Hmmm." When Dad says "Hmmm" it means he knows something is going on but can't prove anything. Then he said, "Strange word to use, 'meeting', don't you think?" And he looked at me in a way which meant he Definitely Knew We Were Up To Something and was trying to figure out if it was a Good Something or a Bad Something.

I shrugged and said, "Strange brother."

When we got there Seb was awake and talking to Mum. He was sitting up but with lots of pillows behind him and I was expecting him to look better because of what Dad said, but actually he looked worse than he did on Sunday. But I tried not to think about that because I was happy to see him, even if he did look the most poorly

I'd ever seen. And I wondered, if this was better then what did worse look like?

It's weird when you have to see your little brother linked up to machines and with tubes connected to him. Because even though you know he is sick and the machines and tubes are helping him to get better, what you really want to do is just pick him up and carry him away from all of it. Away from the doctors and nurses and hospital with the wrong jungle-hugging animals and weird juice, to somewhere safe where he didn't get cancer in the first place.

Mum said, "Seb has been such a brave boy!" in a really cheerful way which meant that she was about to have an emotional breakdown any second, so Dad said, "Want to get a coffee and leave these two to their *meeting*?" And I tried to look normal and not suspicious in any way, but it isn't very easy to do that when you have a secret identity. I wondered how people like Clark Kent and Peter Parker had kept theirs a secret for so long because I'd only been doing it for a little while and already I practically jumped out of my skin any time anyone mentioned going online.

Once Mum and Dad had left the room and closed the door I said, "Are you okay? Dad said the medicine makes you sick."

Seb said, "I'm not sick, I'm having my software updated."

And I liked it when he said stuff like this because it meant he wasn't sad or scared. And that is what he was like all the time and why I knew he was Definitely Going To Get Better At Some Point because people who are definitely dying aren't like that; they are grey and sad and worried and serious, and I knew that because I had seen loads of them on TV in *Casualty* at Mrs Quinney's house. So I told him the latest Brilliant Things About Being Miss Nobody and he high-fived me, which was extra brilliant because people who are dying definitely do not do high fives.

Then Seb told me about the new doctor he had met today called Dr Howard who was his new favourite doctor because he'd given him a special pouch to put over his drip which had dinosaurs on it. Then he held up a picture he had drawn which was a new dinosaur he'd invented called the Pooposaurus. It was a really tiny dinosaur sitting on a massive mountain of poop and he said, "It can't move because it poops too much! When I showed it to Dr Howard he said, 'Does it need me to prescribe some anti-diarrhoea medication?'" And then Seb laughed saying, "I'm a LOLosaurus!" until he cried.

Once he had calmed down and I had given the Pooposaurus a Fear Rating of 7/10, Seb said, "Miss Nobody is getting loads of hits every day now," and I must have looked confused because then he said, "Nurse Mandy let me use her iPad this morning because I drank some medicine that tasted like fly's wee." He told me that Miss Nobody was getting hits from the same people but that it was getting new hits every day too. Which could only mean one thing: word was spreading, and fast.

This was such good news that I almost didn't notice Mum and Dad coming back down the corridor with a doctor I didn't recognize. I quickly said, "Be careful what you say to Dad, okay, he already thinks we are up to something. Remember: we need to keep it Top Secret."

Seb nodded and said, "Just one last thing: I am going to need a pay rise."

Before I could say anything Mum and Dad came in with the doctor. She was wearing a badge saying *Dr Mistry, Paediatric Oncologist*. I hadn't met her before but I liked her because she didn't ask me any questions and then she said the good news which was that Seb might be able to come home in a couple of weeks.

And I thought, that means he is Definitely Getting Better! But the only people looking happy about it were me and Seb. And the beeps from Seb's machine rang out like big red dots in the silence.

25

justask

For some Unknown Reason, Connor's morning ritual changed. Instead of knocking my pencil case off my desk, he picked it up, opened the zip and held it above the bin saying, "Say something or I'm chucking your stuff in here." People stopped their conversations and started staring at me. I sat there with my words trapped because it felt like someone really strong had their hands around my throat stopping A Million Things I Wanted To Say To Connor Mould from getting out.

Someone ran in shouting, "Mr Bryant's coming!" then Connor emptied the entire contents into the bin. I heard people laughing and someone said, "Nice one, Connor."

Just before Mr Bryant came in Maisy said, "I just don't get it! Why doesn't IT ever say anything?" which made people laugh even more. I stared down at my desk, praying for form time to be over so everyone would leave and I could go and get my stuff out of the bin without anyone staring at me or saying anything.

When I was dusting pencil sharpenings off the cat highlighters that Mary and Bernard had bought me for Christmas, Mr Bryant said he Needed To Have A Word With Me. I froze. Few things on earth felt worse than Mr Bryant talking to me and me not being able to say anything. And the words that filled up inside my head were:

Maybe he's found out about Miss Nobody.

I could feel heat creep over my skin and my heart started pounding and it is possible I actually started sweating. It turns out I was right to be worried because although he hadn't found out about Miss Nobody, what he asked me to do felt A Lot Scarier And Worse.

"We have a new girl starting in our form," he said. "And I would like you to be her buddy for a week."

I could have fainted from shock. Every tiny part of my body was screaming **No!** because it would be way too scary and actually completely impossible to talk to a Totally New Person and show them around the school. But I didn't know how to say that to Mr Bryant so what actually came out of my mouth was this:

Then to make it worse, I smiled and nodded.

Mr Bryant said, "Great! Don't worry about not being able to talk to her right away because I will explain everything. Mrs Kingsley thinks it's a great idea too." Which came as Not Exactly A Surprise.

Mr Bryant told me her name was Ailsa and she was from Edinburgh but she'd moved here because her dad had died and her mum wanted to be closer to her family. Mr Bryant said that he would normally choose someone who took the same bus, but as I was so understanding and kind he thought that I would make a great buddy for her! What he probably actually meant was that I definitely wouldn't bully her unlike some people in our class. (And possibly because he thought I was the only one likely to have heard of Edinburgh.)

And even though part of me was thrilled and amazed that there was a tiny chance I could have that rarer than stardust thing – A Friend! – mostly I was Massively Terrified.

#

That afternoon I told Octavia about it. She said a good thing for me to do when I am extremely worried about something is to Write Down My Fears because it will stop them from flying around in my head so fast. She gave me a big piece of paper and a marker pen and I wrote this then read it to her out loud:

I am worried about being Ailsa's buddy for the week because I feel like one or some or maybe all of these things might happen:

1. Everyone will laugh when Mr Bryant announces that I am going to be Ailsa's buddy and so he will immediately change his mind and pick someone else then people will tease me about it For Ever.

2. Everyone will look at me. It will totally draw attention to me and I don't like it.
3. Maisy Love will tell Ailsa that I am The Class Weirdo and Ailsa will become her buddy instead without telling Mr Bryant.
4. People will be even meaner to me than they are already and they might start to be mean to Ailsa because she is my buddy.
5. My throat will close up like it usually does so I won't be able to say anything to Ailsa, not even "Hi!" So she won't like me and she will think it's stupid Mr Bryant chose me to be her buddy when I can't even speak to her.
6. Ailsa could turn out to be a bully and might punch me in the face when Mr Bryant introduces us because I can't say "Hi".

Octavia said, "It must be really hard to do anything at all when all these worries are in your head!" I thought, actually that's only a Very Small Percentage of them because I didn't want to ask for more paper. Then she told me an important thing, which I tried really hard to remember as she was saying it and it was this:

It is okay to feel worried about things before they happen, like before you do an important job like being someone's buddy for a week, but you should give it a try to see what it is like before you decide it will definitely be a bad thing. Feeling worried is really horrible, but those feelings can't physically stop you from doing anything if you try really hard.

She also said that although she usually gives no absolute certainties, she gave me a one hundred per cent speech therapist guarantee that Ailsa wouldn't punch me in the face for not saying hi.

Then she said, "Do you think Ailsa might also be feeling a little worried about starting at a new school?"

I said, "Yes. Probably."

She said, "I mean, Ailsa may not have a long list of worries like yours, but she is probably worried. And remember, Mr Bryant has chosen you because he thinks you will be a great buddy for her, so maybe you should trust him." I didn't mention Mr Bryant's mug that says *You Put The Cool In School!* which is part of the reason I didn't one hundred per cent trust his judgement.

Then she made me do this thing where you balance bad thoughts with good ones, so next to every worry I had about being Ailsa's buddy, I had to write what I thought a positive version of it would look like, so Octavia could email Mr Bryant and Mrs Kingsley with things that might help.

So I wrote this:

1. It would be a positive situation if Mr Bryant doesn't make me stand up at the front of the class or in any way announce that I am Ailsa's buddy.
2. It would be positive if people didn't look at me.
3. It would be more positive if Maisy and Connor don't say anything about Ailsa being my buddy.
4. It would be nice if people are kind to Ailsa.
5. Maybe I will be able to say something to Ailsa once I get to know her and if I can take her to the library maybe I could try to speak to her in there.
6. It would be positive if Ailsa is a nice person and that she doesn't mind if I can't say anything to her at first.

Then while Octavia was explaining about where in the brain anxiety comes from, I added:

7. And if no one gets punched in the face.

Despite what Octavia had said, I was still Massively Worried when I got home. I tried to make Dad let me have the week off because of it. But as usual what happens in my house when I try to get any time off school even if it is for a Totally Valid Reason like having to be Ailsa's buddy for the week, Dad said things like, "But it will be so good for you!" and "It is such a good opportunity!" and "It will be fine!" and then eventually "Please stop now, Rozzie, I'm very tired."

So I kind of did take Octavia's advice to write stuff down when I am feeling worried about something. Because that night instead of reading in my room like I told Dad I was doing, I posted the latest instalment of Miss Nobody's Speaking Up At Manor High campaign. And weirdly it did make me feel a bit better.

To all the Nobodies who have messaged me: this blog is dedicated to you.

(I know what it feels like, believe me.)

THE MANOR HIGH COOL LIST

It's no secret that to be Considered Cool at Manor High is pretty hard. I mean, imagine all the work that goes into being Totally Horrible to people you don't even know! But, somehow these people make it look easy...

JACK SIMMINGTON

Jack must have a busy life being cool at Manor High, because just in the past week, he has stolen someone's trainers (while they were still wearing them), thrown someone else's bag onto the arts block roof and told a girl in Year Seven she should be on a diet. Jack, the only thing that should be on a diet around here is your Massive Mouth. But well done for hitting the Cool List Top Spot! There was A Lot of competition, believe me.

PENNY IN YEAR NINE

Already considered cool for regularly throwing people's stuff out of windows, Penny outdid herself last week when she actually hit a girl in Year Eight for the Serious Crime of "having the same bag as her". Penny, if you are going to blame anyone for that, maybe you should blame the high street.

JAMIE AND GANG

These meatheads really are pushing New Boundaries Of Cool at Manor High. Lots of you have messaged me about these boys and what can only be described as their

Science Block Boys' Toilets Phenomenon. Jamie and his gang lie in wait for Nobodies uncool enough to go to the toilets at lunchtime, ready to squash your head in the door, flush your stuff down the toilet and possibly hit you with balls of wet loo roll. Let's just hope these three toilet trolls wash their hands. (Something tells me they probably don't.)

Proving you can buy fame at Manor High, but only if your currency is Spite and Stupidity.

And I say it's about time we got some change.

I am Miss Nobody.

On Friday when I saw Seb after school he told me Miss Nobody had got more hits than ever. Then over the weekend I had even more likes, and received more messages from people about candidates for the Cool List which I added onto my blog. And it would have felt Epically Brilliant, but I also got a message from someone who probably wasn't exactly a Major Fan of Miss Nobody, because they were called me4evaC and said this:

miss nobody whoeva the hell u r u r ded

And even though it was technically a death threat, the main thing I noticed was that me4evaC couldn't spell the word *dead*, so I know they *were* threatening to kill me and everything, but this person wasn't exactly a Murdering Mega Brain. So without even realizing it, this Mystery Death Threatener confirmed exactly what I already suspected about the Cool Crowd of Manor High – they were all pretty stupid actually. Even the potential murderers.

26

#iswear

It was Monday morning – my first Official Day as a buddy – and we were running late. Dad had to get ice off the car, which took ages, then he drove in a way he said was Just Being Safe, but was actually Way Slower Than Any Other Car On The Road, which he didn't really appreciate me pointing out. When we finally got to school I had to get out in front of some people hanging around at the gates, which was scary because I couldn't even go fast in case I slipped over. Then Dad shouted out of the window, "Good luck, buddy!" which made them stare at him and then me.

As I approached the form room I felt really hot like I was

going to faint even though the building must have been about minus five degrees. Octavia had told me she would email Mr Bryant, but I was still Massively Worried he would make a big announcement about it and form time would be even more embarrassing and scary than normal and I would probably never be able to speak to Ailsa. In my head I could hear everyone laughing at me.

When I walked in most people were already in there, which I didn't like because I like getting there first so people don't see me come in, but Mr Bryant was in the classroom and I saw him talking to the new girl, who was Ailsa. And I'm telling you the complete truth – she was the nicest and most kind-looking person I had ever seen in my life. Miss Carter has a Roald Dahl poster on her classroom wall and it says:

> *If you have good thoughts they will shine out of your face like sunbeams and you will always look lovely!*

and Ailsa's face was a bit like that, only with loads and loads of freckles, like the face version of a sunset only with green eyes.

Mr Bryant signalled for me to come over. He introduced me to Ailsa and she smiled at me. I could tell from her eyes and her smile that she was nice and clever and kind, and my heart almost burst with how relieved I felt because she was practically the First Person Ever at Manor High who I could look at without feeling like they might make me cry.

Mr Bryant said, "Now, Ailsa doesn't expect you to say anything to her, so I've given her this special book so you can write things down if she has questions." And I was really pleased because that is a thoughtful thing to do for Someone Like Me. It meant me not speaking wouldn't be so bad for Ailsa and also because I like writing things down. It felt like the massive glacier of words that had frozen in my head started to melt a little bit.

Ailsa followed me to my table and sat next to me and I wrote in the special book:

Hi and Welcome!

And she smiled and then she wrote:

Thanks ☺

I showed her where to write her timetable in her new planner and she looked at mine and said, "You have really nice handwriting," and I smiled at her without looking away. And even though I felt nervous my throat didn't totally seize up and it was the best non-conversation I'd ever had. I kept my fingers crossed under the table for the whole of form time that Ailsa would stay my buddy for a week and then did a mini prayer which was:

Please God, help me say something to Ailsa this week, even if it is just one word.

Already I felt like I was in a dream, but a dream where you aren't on the edge of a massive precipice or trapped in an underground room or drowning in a flooded house. A good dream that feels warm and safe and magical.

The dream feeling carried on into our science lesson because Miss Sheldon said that Ailsa could partner up with me for the science fair. I showed Ailsa my work so far and my plans for the display and she said, "This project is really good," then her green eyes lit up and she said, "Why don't we make a giant carton of orange juice out of cardboard to be eye-catching at the fair?" So I nodded, because if I had Ailsa as my partner I thought maybe it wouldn't be so Totally Terrible if people noticed my project because she could answer the questions from the judges. (Also maybe I could hide behind the giant orange carton.)

At lunchtime I wrote in the book:

Do you want to see the library & do you like books?

And Ailsa said she loved books! I took her to the library and showed her the sign about being a library monitor. Ailsa said, "That sounds cool,"(!) so I took her to meet Mrs Goodacre, who said, "Great, Rosemary! I could do with another pair of hands!" And she told her to ignore Rajit when he said about the interview. And I actually laughed a little bit. So Ailsa was in the library committee and I had laughed in front of her and it felt like The Best Day Ever.

But good feelings like that don't last very long at my school. When we were walking out of the library I saw someone I recognized: The Girl With The Smudged Eyeliner (although her eyeliner wasn't smudged this time). She was with some of Crystal's clones. And maybe I stared a bit too long because when they walked past she pushed me so hard I fell over and my knee skidded against the icy concrete. It ripped my tights and my knee stung and bled a little bit. Ailsa shouted, "Hey!" as they ran off laughing. She said should she get Mrs Goodacre, but I shook my head and pretended I was fine and that it didn't hurt. But that wasn't Actually True. It did hurt, but not so much in my knee as in my head and in my heart because more than anything I didn't want Ailsa to see how much people at school hated me in case she didn't want to be my buddy any more.

But Ailsa said, "People like that are just stupid." Then she told me that there were people like that at her old school. She said, "I know you can't speak at school, but I think you should tell someone if people do stuff like that. I could tell Mr Bryant if you want me to?" But I just shook my head.

I didn't want her to say anything to Mr Bryant or to anybody. I got out the notebook and wrote:

Please don't say anything. They just do that to everyone!

But inside my head, I swore to myself that if my school was going to keep barfing up bullies like that who would push me and make me cut my knee in front of my First And Only Ever Buddy and The Nicest Person Ever to come to Manor High, then maybe Miss Nobody would have to give out an extra dose of medicine.

# #

When I got home Mum asked what happened to my tights and I said I'd slipped on some steps. She gave me a hug and said, "Poor thing!" And even though I felt like crying I didn't. Because instead I closed my eyes really tight and thought about all the things I wanted to say to the stupid clones who pushed me over. And all these words started forming like massive angry tears inside my head, then I went upstairs and logged onto Miss Nobody and wrote a new blog post.

CAUTION: CLONES CAN BE HAZARDOUS TO YOUR HEALTH

Have you experienced any of the following symptoms brought on by contact with Crystal's genetically modified gang members?

Getting pushed over/tripped up/squashed into a wall.

Having your stuff stolen.

Being called names.

Getting ganged up on.

Having to hide at school.

If so, you may be suffering from a terrible virus sweeping Manor High known as Clone Contamination. The virus is Highly Contagious and the symptoms are Serious.

It turns out these worker bees are just as deadly as the Queen.

Do everything you can to avoid contact with Crystal's Clones. And Spread the Word.

If you see anyone suffering from their sickness, Please Help.

Fighting the bullying infection at Manor High.

I am Miss Nobody.

And I totally ignored the message I got later telling me:

when I find out who u r u r ded btw

27

#whatdoyou think

A Brilliant Thing was happening, because Ailsa had been my buddy for four whole days without being stolen, or not liking me or punching me in the face, which meant that (although I didn't want to ruin things by being too pleased with myself) there was the tiniest possibility that An Actual Massive Miracle had happened and Ailsa was My First And Only Proper Friend (only a little bit by force, and not counting Mrs Quinney or cats or Mrs Goodacre or family members or therapists).

She sat next to me in every class, even history, because Mrs Kingsley had emailed all the teachers and told them to let me sit with Ailsa. And it kind of was special treatment, which I usually don't like, but this time it was special in a good way. And even though Maisy whispered, "Good! I'm so glad I don't have to sit next to The Mute-ant any more!" I didn't feel as scared as I normally did. Having Ailsa next to me made everything at school feel A Million Times Better Than Normal.

At break time I didn't worry so much about getting things from my locker because even though my locker wasn't in the same section as hers, Ailsa came with me to get my things and I went with her to get hers. We stayed together at lunchtime, which meant that I didn't have to hide in the English block toilets or the library to eat my lunch. It was freezing, but Ailsa said she was used to the cold, so we ate our sandwiches on the benches in the quad outside the library. And even though she didn't say it, I think she suggested eating there because we had gone into the canteen and a girl had barged me and said, "Move, weirdo!" And I wanted so much to say something back, but all my words disappeared into some kind of black hole inside my head, and when we sat down I couldn't nod when Ailsa asked me if I wanted a biscuit, but she gave me one anyway, only I couldn't move my mouth to eat.

Ailsa didn't seem to mind that I hadn't spoken yet, but I really wanted to say something to her. And the only place I felt I could do that in school was the library.

The next day, Ailsa said how she was really excited about our science fair project, and that her mum could get us loads of cool materials for our stand, so I wrote in the book during our art lesson:

Do you want to work on it in the library at lunch?

And she wrote back:

Yes!! ☺

(She always did a smiley face when she wrote back.)

So that lunchtime we went to the library with our science books and sat at a table near the corner. Rajit was doing a sudoku and Mrs Goodacre was in her office and a few other people were reading by the windows. I took a massive deep breath. I felt my feet on the floor and hummed a little bit which was what Octavia had told me to do, then I quietly said, "What do we need for the stall?"

And I felt a sort of crash, like the enormous thundercloud that had been stuck in my head all week saying

 had finally been silenced.

And Ailsa smiled and her eyes lit up then she said, "Definitely orange juice!"

Then Ailsa asked if I wanted to go to her house one Saturday to work on our project. The idea of going to someone's house that wasn't Mrs Quinney's was so Amazing and Exciting I think my cheeks went a little bit red when I nodded and said, "Yes!" but Ailsa was too nice to say anything. She must be The Only Person In The World who doesn't think my SM makes me too weird to be friends with.

Ailsa asked for my phone, then she tapped her number into it and didn't even say anything about it not being a very expensive one. She handed it back to me and said, "Call me so I have your number, okay? And I'll text you later once I've spoken to my mum. It might have to be in a couple of weekends' time. We're still unpacking so the place is a bit of a mess at the moment."

I said, "My house is like the Exact Opposite of that. My dad's obsessed with cleaning."

And she said, "My dad was obsessed with making stuff! He made me this." And she showed me a necklace with a silvery-blue jewel dangling from it. "It's a crystal. If you look closely you can see my name. He wrote it on a special kind of paper. Can you see?" She held it up to the light. I leaned closer and could just make out really tiny writing inside.

I read it out loud, "Ailsa."

"I wear it all the time now. As a good-luck charm," she said, and she wiped away the sparkles of tiny tears in her eyes. "Anyway, hopefully it will bring us luck with our project. I won the science prize at my primary school so let's just say, I sort of know what I'm doing." And she smiled a big smile and wrote Make an awesome stall! ☺ on our *Stuff To Do* list.

But also that day, it was like Maisy Love had turned her hatred towards me up a few notches. In French when we were supposed to be practising conversations she said, "What's that noise? Oh, nothing – it's Mute-ant!" and in art when Katie walked past me Maisy said, "Watch out – you'll catch the Mute-ant disease." Plus now she had a nickname for me, other people in the class started using it. Like in science, Vinnie said, "Mute-ant, can I borrow a felt tip?" and he used it until it ran out making a poster for their so-called science project: Illegal Wrestling Moves. In history Connor knocked all the stuff off my desk and said, "Look at Mute-ant, she's bright red!" And even though I didn't want it to, it hurt quite a lot.

And the next day they started saying things to Ailsa too. Like, "Why are you friends with a Mute-ant?" and "What's the point of having a friend who doesn't even talk to you?" And I couldn't say anything, but Ailsa would say things like, "I don't care what you think," and "If you don't like us, why don't you just leave us alone?" And part of my heart was full of tears because they were picking on Ailsa because of me, and part of it felt Totally Amazed she could stand up to them. But mostly I just felt Really Bad that she even had to.

Then at lunchtime, while me and Ailsa were sitting in the library working on our science project, a Seriously Bad Thing happened, which made me feel even worse.

We were sitting at one of the tables by the windows overlooking the quad when suddenly a big crowd of people started gathering outside. Crystal and her clones were at the front of it. Ailsa noticed it too because she said, "What's going on?" and stood up.

I couldn't see very much because there was a crowd of people in the way, but what I found out later from basically everyone in class talking about it was this.

Crystal and her gang surrounded a girl in Year Eight called Holly and beat her up. Holly's friends wanted to stop them but they were too scared to do anything so they went to get a teacher, who broke it up. Afterwards Holly had a black eye and a big cut on her lip.

Only I couldn't listen to the rest of it because Katie said something that got stuck in my head and it was all I could hear over and over and over again:

"It's because they found out Holly is Miss Nobody."
"It's because they found out Holly is Miss Nobody."
"It's because they found out Holly is Miss Nobody."
"It's because they found out Holly is Miss Nobody."
"It's because they found out Holly is Miss Nobody."
"It's because they found out Holly is Miss Nobody."
"It's because they found out Holly is Miss Nobody."
"It's because they found out Holly is Miss Nobody."
"It's because they found out Holly is Miss Nobody."
"It's because they found out Holly is Miss Nobody."

28

#waiting tohear

On Monday everything outside was frozen again and I was really scared about walking through the school gates. Only this time I wasn't scared about slipping over as much as I was scared that Seb's imaginary forcefield wouldn't protect me from Crystal's actual fists. Or how bad I was still feeling about Holly.

Words were flashing in my head the whole day like a neon sign saying

I am Miss Nobody

And I could barely speak at all to Ailsa at lunchtime in case I accidentally blurted it out even though, actually, I hadn't been Miss Nobody all weekend.

In history Mr Dean was talking about these punishments in the medieval times where they made people carry a red-hot iron bar around, or chopped their hands off, and just thinking about it made my hands go funny and I felt sick. Ailsa whispered, "Are you okay?" and even though I Definitely Wasn't, I nodded. Later in the lesson I overheard Katie saying that Crystal had been excluded for three days for what she did to Holly. And part of me was Massively Relieved because I still had the big neon sign in my head, and part of me thought, Crystal is actually quite lucky she wasn't born in medieval times.

After school I was at Mrs Quinney's, waiting to hear if Seb was coming home or not, and Bernard was purring at my feet because I'd given him some cream from the cake we were making. Mrs Quinney was telling me about the story of the Good Samaritan (which I already knew as she'd told it to me so many times) in between telling me which ingredients to put in and how to use the wooden spoon correctly. And while she was talking I was thinking about Holly and Crystal and Miss Nobody and what I decided was this.

I actually had two Quite Major Things on my side:

1. Seb had made sure no one could trace Miss Nobody back to me. No one in the entire world knew I was Miss Nobody apart from me and Seb, and we Definitely Wouldn't Tell Anyone.

2. Miss Nobody was actually the only person speaking up about people like Crystal, and she would be back at school in only three days. So I couldn't exactly stop now, could I?

It was like a real-life version of the witch hunts. Crystal and her gang were on a mission to track down Miss Nobody and so obviously it was Totally Possible that some people would be falsely accused. Especially if they were like Holly and told people they were Miss Nobody in their sports lesson, which she did apparently.

Even though Holly had technically been beaten up because of Miss Nobody, how many people had actually been *saved* from getting beaten up? Because if it's a numbers game then I was probably definitely winning. Somebody had to speak up for the Nobodies at Manor High, and that somebody was me.

And that night, while Mrs Quinney was praying long enough to set a new Guinness World Record, I got a text from Ailsa saying:

Mum says next sat is ok to come over ☺☺☺

And I felt Brilliant until Dad came to get me and told

me Seb couldn't come home yet. I went straight upstairs, logged onto Miss Nobody and wrote:

MIND GAMES FOR THE MINDLESS

Did you witness the Brutal Bullying of one of my followers last week by the Queen Bee and her vicious swarm?

It seems like writing my blog has become a little bit dangerous actually.

The Manor High Meanness Mafia are fighting back.

They don't want Miss Nobody to Speak Up.

They don't want any of us to Speak Up.

The thing is, they've hurt totally the wrong person. Not that they probably even care. But I do. I don't want anyone else to get hurt. That's why I'm Miss Nobody and why I'm saying this (because we can't keep being silent for ever):

Nothing will stop me Naming And Shaming the bullies of

Manor High. Nothing will stop me Speaking Up for Nobodies. Nothing will stop me FULL STOP.

Miss Nobody is afraid of nobody.

And even though my heart was pounding, I clicked Publish a few times just to be sure.

29

#telling
stories

That whole week I wasn't allowed to visit Seb. He was having lots of tests apparently and wasn't feeling well enough, and Mum and Dad wanted to talk to the doctors on their own. And I had the feeling Something Bad was happening, but I wasn't exactly sure what. I didn't understand why he still wasn't home yet. My tummy had this weird feeling in it, a bit like the one you get before you have to do a test. And it was made even worse by everyone at school talking about who the real Miss Nobody could be. Maisy said Crystal and her clones had been asking people on the bus what they knew. And the whole time she was talking, I sat there with a big silent bubble in my head saying **GUILTY.**

After school on Friday I had to go straight to Mrs Quinney's. When I got there she sat me down on the sofa. The cats were sleeping on the footstool. Mrs Quinney said, "Hurry up, dear. I'm about to read Mary and Bernard the story of the lost sheep!" I don't actually mind this story because it is quite short compared to some of the other Bible stories and ends with rejoicing (which is like an old-fashioned way of being really glad). And when I asked if I could do some calligraphy while I was listening, she nodded.

I always like her Bible stories that end with rejoicing because it means we both get one of her famous currant buns. Some stories end with the opposite of rejoicing which is repenting. Mrs Quinney says that is when you have to be really sorry to God otherwise you will get a terrible punishment, like all your crops will die or you will get weird dreams for ever. And after those stories we don't have a currant bun because Mrs Quinney has to pray for ages. But it's better than being at my house when the grey silence is everywhere.

Anyway, Mrs Quinney must have realized I was feeling worried because she gave me a currant bun with an extra

226

big dollop of jam and said, "Don't worry, dear, Seb will be home before you know it." And I felt bad that I'd been worrying about being beaten up by Crystal and her clones instead of Seb.

After she'd finished telling the lost sheep story, I asked, "Do bad things happen even if you're on The Right Path?"

Mrs Quinney said, "Yes, dear! Sometimes The Right Path can be a little rocky." Then she tutted and said, "Just look at Mary." Mary was sitting up, watching a bird outside the window. "She's not paid attention to a word I've said all day!" She turned back to me and said, "You'll know you are on The Right Path because God will be smiling down on you, dear." And that's when she told me about moral compasses.

In your heart there is a sort of tiny compass which tells you when you are doing something right or doing something wrong. When you are doing something right, like helping others or saying kind things, your moral compass will make you feel good and tell you: This is Totally The Right Thing To Do. If you do something wrong like steal or say mean things to someone for no reason, or break a promise, your moral compass will make you Feel Really Bad. That way we always know in our hearts whether something is the right thing to do or not.

Mrs Quinney said that everyone is born with a moral

compass, except a few people lose it along the way. But I wondered if that could actually be true. Unless by some weird twist of fate the few people in the world with lost moral compasses all ended up going to my school.

I'm one hundred per cent sure Crystal and Maisy and Connor and Lucas Merry do not have moral compasses. In fact, Maisy has probably never even heard of a normal compass.

Mrs Quinney got up to look at the calligraphy I had done and said, "Dear, I know you are on The Right Path, because you have the hands of a little angel."

And although talking to Mrs Quinney isn't exactly like talking to God, she is kind of the nearest thing I've got. So without even realizing it Mrs Quinney had given me the green light to carry on being Miss Nobody. No Matter What.

30

#lookwhos talking

When I woke up the next morning I felt two things: Massively Excited about going to Ailsa's house for the first time, and also A Horrible Sick Feeling in my stomach in case I wouldn't be able to speak there. Ailsa texted me saying:

We have so much cool stuff!! See u soon ☺

and I wished and wished I could be a better friend to her by just being Completely Normal.

"Ailsa is actually amazing at science. She won the science prize at her last school – that is how good she is. Her dad was some kind of science engineer and they used to do experiments for fun in their garage! She's got a special type of crystal necklace that he made with her name written on a tiny piece of paper inside. She knows all of the chemical symbols, even the hard ones, and she knows about loads of famous scientists you've probably never even heard of who made really important scientific breakthroughs that basically changed the world. And I'm not just talking about Einstein."

And that was about everything I could say about Ailsa in the car on the way to her house before Dad said, "Wow. She sounds like the perfect partner for a science project then. I don't think I've ever heard you say that much about anyone. Let's just hope she likes orange juice!"

"She does, Dad. Ailsa being Totally Amazing At Science is the reason our stall is probably going to be one of the best at the fair."

"Right. And you're looking at me like that's a bad thing because…?"

"Because I was hoping not to have to do the assembly!"

"Of course. Well, maybe Ailsa could do the speaking part and you could just stand there."

"Just stand there?"

"We all have to start somewhere!" And he laughed and gave my hand a squeeze. "It will be fine, don't worry." Which is what he always says whenever I have to do something I really don't want to. I wondered if Just

Standing There in front of the entire school would even be physically possible for me.

"Okay, Apple Tree House. Here it is." Dad stopped the car.

There were two huge trees planted in the pavement and the drive was made of little red tiles and the house was covered in ivy and next to it was a double garage with bright yellow doors. I thought, this is one of those streets where people say "Hello!" to you all the time. I checked no one was coming before I got out.

Dad came up to the front door with me and said, "Ready?" And even though I nodded, in my head there was a massive question mark because I wasn't sure if I would be able to speak in front of Ailsa's mum or not, and I really, really wanted to.

Dad rang the bell and I could see someone coming through the bubbly glass. She opened the door and she had a freckly face that was warm like a sunset exactly like Ailsa's. And even though I didn't say anything, I didn't feel like my lips were superglued together either. She said, "Helloooo!" in a really cheerful voice and then, "Come in, come in! I'm Jen." And when we walked in there were two big boxes in the hall and she said, "Sorry, still some unpacking to do! I don't even know what's in there!"

Ailsa came downstairs and my dad had a cup of tea in

the kitchen while Ailsa showed me the huge bag of things her mum had bought us like cardboard, string, paint, coloured paper, glue, glitter, tissue paper and loads of other cool stuff for decorating our science fair stand. There were even some ping-pong balls Ailsa's mum said we could paint to look like tiny oranges.

And I said, "Wow!" because it was Amazing. And I felt my heart smile because that meant my words definitely weren't hiding.

Dad squeezed my shoulder and said, "Try not to make too much of a mess!"

But Ailsa's mum said, "Oh, it's fine to make a mess in the name of scientific progress!"

Dad said he would pick me up later and gave me a hug. And I didn't even mind him hugging me in front of Ailsa because the massive

?

in my head had been replaced by a big

☺

And I tried not to feel too pleased with myself just for saying one word at Ailsa's house, but when you are

Someone Like Me, saying one word feels like a million miles away from Total Silence, and that's a really nice place to be.

We made the backdrop for our stall first and Ailsa's mum brought us some lemonade because she said, "You are probably sick of the sight of orange juice!" Which I definitely was. "Now, do you need any help painting anything?"

Ailsa said, "Mum's an artist."

But she said, "Not a very good one, I'm afraid! That's why most of my paintings are hanging on these walls! Anyway, it's been such a long time since I've painted, I'm not sure I can even be called an artist any more!" But I thought that all her paintings were really nice. There were massive canvases all around the room of things like fuzzy meadows and hills and skies with big silver clouds and suns painted in gold and orange. And I could see why Ailsa was such a kind person, having a mum like hers. She is one of those mums who tries to make you feel special, like they are glad to have you at their house, and like everything (even the science fair) is going to be all right. My mum used to be like that before Seb got ill, but now her eyes look sad and Dad says she is fine but I'm not so sure.

Ailsa and her mum talked about her dad quite a lot which is like the Exact Opposite of my house because

Mum and Dad had hardly even mentioned Seb recently, and he was only ill. While we were painting the ping-pong balls they told me about a time when Ailsa was little when her dad made a talking clock which said, "Ailsa, it's time for bed!" But the voice he recorded kept getting distorted and it ended up sounding really scary and it frightened Ailsa one time when it went off in the middle of the night. Her mum did an impression of it like a crazy robot going, "Tiiiiime forrrrr beeeed!"

Ailsa's mum helped us paint the giant orange carton, and she made it look exactly like a real one, only massive. Then we made pretend chemical equipment out of cardboard, glitter and tissue paper. It was the first time I had worked on a project with someone else when I didn't feel like my throat was being totally squashed and my words had vanished. I could speak. And it felt like the enormous dark cloud of my SM, that usually followed me around everywhere stopping my words from coming out, didn't make it inside Ailsa's house. And it felt Amazing.

When it was time to go I had a huge smile on my face that Dad noticed because he said, "You look like you've had fun!"

In the car on the way home I told him, "I'm actually not even feeling that nervous about the fair any more!"

It was like the happiness and enthusiasm at Apple Tree House were catching and I started to feel like maybe the fair would actually be okay.

Which considering what happened was a pretty stupid way to feel.

31

#dontaskme

The next week at school it seemed like me and Ailsa being actual proper friends annoyed Maisy even more than when she just was my buddy, because she spent most lessons saying things like, "It must totally suck to have a friend who can't even *talk* to you!" and "Ailsa must be so *boring* to be friends with the Mute-ant!" and Connor and Vinnie joined in too. I wished I could just tell them all to **SHUT UP!** But my stupid throat always closed up and my face got too hot and the words stayed inside my head.

Ailsa would say, "Just leave us alone, Maisy," and "It's got nothing to do with you," and "Miss, can you ask Connor to stop talking, please?" and other stuff that made me realize

Ailsa was Totally Amazing and I was Definitely Not.

And she wrote stuff in the notebook we still shared like:

Science fair is going to be so cool! ☺

and

Library at lunch? ☺

Like she didn't care at all about what anyone said, and wanted to be my friend anyway. And even though the stuff Maisy said made me feel sad, having Ailsa there made me feel happy, so it kind of cancelled it out. A bit like when you mix blue and yellow it makes green.

Each night when I got home Seb still wasn't back from hospital. And when I asked Dad what was happening, he would say, "We're just waiting for some test results," and "He'll be home soon, don't worry." Only not worrying that your brother might be dying is Literally Impossible.

I stayed up late most nights blogging. Miss Nobody had 504 visitors and I got messages that said stuff like: Yesssss Miss Nobody!!! and Lucas always bullies people on the bus!!! and girl in y9 pushed me today ☹, and comments that said: lol yep bullies suuuuuuck. And someone called Rita_Kuri put can someone help me??? craig & his mates shout stuff at me by the gates, and someone called Dragon_Lair_Boy wrote back yep ok no probs.

So being Miss Nobody online was working out a lot better than being Actual Me in real life. Apart from another message from me4evaC, which said:

ur gonna pay for this NOBODY loser

And when I read it I felt a bit weird, like when you suddenly wake up from having a bad dream and it takes you a while to realize it's not real and they can't hurt you, but you still feel a bit scared anyway.

By the time we broke up for half-term I was really excited about visiting Seb, because it felt like ages since I'd seen him. Only on the way to the hospital Dad said, "You might need to prepare yourself for how Seb is, Rozzie. He might not quite be his usual self so, just…" But he never finished the sentence so I wasn't really sure what I was supposed to do.

When I saw Seb his face was puffy and his skin was a weird colour and he didn't seem to be properly awake even though his eyes were open a bit. Mum held my hand and said, "He wants to come home, so we just have to wait for him to feel a little stronger."

Dad said, "He's had to take really strong painkillers, so

he's a bit zoned out. He might wake up a bit more later."
Only he didn't.

One of the nurses gave me a brown sweet that tasted really weird, like minty butter, and I didn't like it but I had to eat it in case she thought I was being rude, and it lasted for ages and made me feel a bit sick. So it wasn't a good visit because of that, and because I couldn't say anything to Seb and he didn't say anything the whole time I was there either. So I listened to Mum reading *The Secret Garden*, and Seb breathing, and Dad tapping his foot on the chair, and the nurse checking machines that made beeping noises, wishing and wishing for some words to come into my head that I could actually say for once.

A few days later I went to Ailsa's to finish off everything for our stall because it was the science fair on Monday. Jen said, "Helloooo!" when she answered the door and invited my mum in for a cup of tea. Ailsa showed me some plastic test tubes they'd bought because she'd had a Brilliant Idea for getting more people to come to our stall. Mum looked at me when she said that and gave me one of her It Will Be Okay smiles.

Only maybe she was lying because it definitely didn't turn out okay at all.

#

On Monday morning Dad came into my room while it was still dark. "Sorry, Roz. I have to get into work extra early this morning. I need to make up my hours. Will you be okay getting the bus?" I groaned. "I'm sorry. But I should be able to make it to the science fair later." He gave me a quick kiss on my head and left. And I groaned again.

Mum was sitting at the kitchen table not eating her toast and looking like she was going to cry any moment so I didn't ask her for a lift. She gave me a hug and said, "Good luck today, I wish I could be there, but I don't want to leave Seb for too long." Only I was actually really glad she couldn't make it. I hate not being able to speak in front of Mum. It always reminds me of being little and hiding behind her legs while random people said, "Oh, are you shy?" to me, like that would be a question I could even answer, and Mum saying, "Yes, she's very shy, she'll grow out of it soon!" only obviously I never did. (I did manage to stop hiding behind Mum's legs eventually.)

It was raining a little bit when I left the house. I was nervous about getting the bus because I hadn't got it for ages, but glad that Ailsa was taking most of the stuff for our stall in, so I only had one extra bag to carry. I had my hood up and in my head I was telling the bus to **HURRY UP** because Lucas Merry was splashing me with puddle water and I was worried it would go on the decorations.

When the bus came, I had to squash the bag past all the seats then sit with it on my knee. The girl next to me said, "What's all that for?" only I couldn't say anything because it was like my words had Disappeared Completely, so I spent the whole journey watching the rain run down the windows, listening to Lucas shouting "Weirdo!" at me, wishing I could be invisible as usual.

When I got into school, the sun was shining on the concrete giving the puddles a sort of oily glimmer. I took deep breaths of cold air that smelled of rain and thought to myself, I will say one word in here today. Only when I opened the door to the hall it was really busy and loud and all the one-word sentences I knew started popping into my head really fast over and over again and they got in a Massive Muddle. I couldn't see Ailsa anywhere.

Everyone around me was moving really fast and speaking loudly and I felt like I was stuck in a silent bubble that might burst at any moment. I couldn't move my legs to walk forward so I was stuck there by the door and people kept coming in past me and brushing against my massive bag.

Then I felt a hand clutch mine and it was Ailsa. "Come on, our table is over here!" And she took the bag off me and led me through the crowd to our table and then said, "It is going to look so awesome!"

By the time we had finished and all the bags were empty, my Massive Silent Panic had calmed and our stand looked like an orange-juice-shop window display crossed with Dr Frankenstein's laboratory. Ailsa put out samples of different orange juices in test tubes for people to taste, which was a really clever idea because it made lots of people want to come to our stand to try it. But even though I was really proud of how our stand looked, what I actually wanted was for Exactly No One to come over and see it.

The hall filled up with even more people and I kept telling myself that everything would be okay. Even though inside I was wishing something would happen to stop the fair, like we could get raided by thieves or the school could suddenly become infested with killer ants or the fire alarm could get stuck going off, so we all definitely had to go home immediately. And maybe to you those scenarios sound a lot worse than just doing the science fair, but to me they seem A Million Times Better than any scenario where I have to talk to people and I can't.

Adrian and Maisy's stall was next to ours, and it was already the most popular by miles. Maisy's mum had got them bright pink T-shirts saying *How high can a bottle rocket go?* They were about to go outside to do their bottle-rocket launch in front of the judges and I could see Adrian setting it all up while Maisy took selfies.

Ailsa said, "Oh, there's my mum! I'll be back in a minute." So then I was on my own feeling totally lost, praying no one would ask me about orange juice or anything else I definitely couldn't tell them.

Suddenly I spotted Dad making his way over to me. A horrible sick feeling came into my stomach because I knew I wouldn't be able to speak to him. He came over and said, "Wow, Rozzie, this looks great! Very, um, orange! Are you feeling okay?" I nodded and tried to look like my words weren't Frozen Completely even though they were.

Suddenly a big "Oooh!" came from the crowd watching the bottle rocket go off outside and it made me jump. I couldn't have been the only one because a crash came from the *How much glue is needed to make papier mâché?* stand behind us. A papier mâché head slowly rolled across the floor and stopped in front of a pair of very shiny shoes. Mr Endeby leaned down, picked up the dented head and gave it a smile. Then he headed over to our stand with Miss Sheldon and two other teachers I didn't know, all holding clipboards, Mr Endeby still with the papier mâché head under his arm, which now looked as if it was staring at me.

I wished it had been my head rolling off because there was Literally Zero chance of me saying anything. The papier mâché head had more chance of speaking to the judges than me. I did a quick emergency prayer for the floor to collapse or a lightning bolt to strike Mr Endeby and I could hear Dad saying, "Roz, are you okay?" when suddenly Ailsa appeared with her mum.

Mr Endeby said, "Extraordinary!" and, "Well done! Lots of creativity here!" I was so scared he would ask me something I couldn't even move my face into a smile. My heart was pounding so loudly I couldn't hear the questions properly or Ailsa answering them. I stared at my shoes on the wooden floor, wishing time would speed up so the whole thing would be over.

Miss Sheldon said, "Well, thank you, girls! Great stand!" and they started heading to the papier mâché table. Ailsa's mum said, "Well done!" and hugged Ailsa. Then one of the teachers I didn't know came back and said to me, "Why did you choose orange juice by the way?"

I wanted more than anything to answer his question because he was looking right at me. I tried and tried but my heart was going too fast and my lips were stuck together and the part of my brain where the answer should have been was like an enormous page with no words on it. Dad was looking at me probably wondering how he was related to such a Total Weirdo and that made it all feel Ten Million Times Worse. And even though silence has no colour or shape it felt like my silence was the biggest and most obvious thing ever.

Then Dad put his arm around me and said, "Just because everyone drinks orange juice, right, Roz?"

And I just about moved my head into a tiny nod.

Later, when we were packing up and I was still feeling like A Science Fair And Family Member Failure, Miss Sheldon came over to deliver even worse news.

We had made it through to the assembly.

The only thing stopping me from climbing into the giant orange carton and never coming out was Ailsa. She was so happy and excited that I couldn't help but feel bad for not wanting to do it. I could hear Miss Sheldon's voice saying how our experiment was brilliant and our stall looked amazing and that we should be really proud, and that she would help us prepare for the assembly. And Ailsa was saying how brilliant it was we had been chosen, and how all our hard work had paid off. And I was thinking this:

I would literally rather drown in an enormous ocean of orange juice than win the non-prize of standing in front of the entire school not being able to speak.

Later at home, while Mum was upstairs getting ready to go back to the hospital, I logged onto Miss Nobody and wrote this:

QUICK QUIZ

Question: What makes Lucas Merry?
Answer: Being totally stupid, picking on people half his size, and generally acting like a Total Gorilla, even though that is probably an insult to gorillas.

Next time you see this beast picking on an innocent Nobody, please tell him to return to the zoo.

Speaking Up against Manor High's most vicious animals.

I am Miss Nobody.

Because if there was anything that could make me feel less like I was stuck being A Totally Silent Failure for ever, it was being Miss Nobody.

Suddenly I heard Dad's car pulling up outside. I quickly pressed Publish and shut down the computer. I grabbed the *Encyclopedia Britannica*, and put my face as far as I could into it without my eyeballs actually touching the page.

Dad opened the door and said, "Hi, Rozzie! That's a lovely sight to come home to!" He took off his coat and said the words I'd been dreading, "Want to talk about what happened today at the fair?"

I said, "Not really," because Dad seeing me not being able to speak is one of the Worst Feelings In The World. (Talking to Dad about it is The Next Worst Feeling In The World.)

Only clearly it was one of those annoying questions parents ask that don't need an answer, because he carried on talking anyway. But instead of saying You Are So Much Weirder Than I Even Realized (which was sort of what I'd been expecting) he said, "You did really well. I'm really proud of you."

And I said, "Thanks." But I wasn't one hundred per cent sure if he was lying or not.

32

#thatsyour
cue

Wednesday started as one of those days where you wake up before your alarm even goes off, and everything is absolutely fine for about three seconds. Then you suddenly remember it is about to be The Worst Day Of Your Entire Life: the Science Week assembly.

We were due to go on second, after Maisy and Adrian's rocket presentation. This was The Worst Possible Situation because Adrian is the best in our class at science and his experiment was A Million Times Better than ours and definitely had The Wow Factor. Plus Maisy was really confident and part of the Manor High Cool Crowd. Unlike me.

I couldn't eat my breakfast because I was feeling so sick with nerves. Dad sat next to me and said, "Come on, Rozzie, try to eat something, or at least drink your orange juice!" Which kind of made me want to tip it over his head. Then he said, "Why don't we do one of these positive exercise things you do with Octodoc?"

I shrugged and said, "Okay."

He said, "Right, so what are some positive things that could happen today?"

I thought for a minute then said, "We could be involved in a non-fatal road accident and get to school too late to do the assembly."

Dad said, "Okay, let's try to imagine a scenario that doesn't involve us having a car accident, please."

"An outbreak of a deadly disease?"

But he said, "No diseases allowed in a positivity exercise."

So I said, "An earthquake?"

"Unlikely."

I put my head in my hands and said, "Then I give up."

He put his arm around me and said, "It's just an assembly, Roz. It's not such a big deal. You're going to go up there, hold that giant juice carton high, and if you feel you can speak, then say your line, if you can't then Ailsa will say it for you like you practised with Miss Sheldon.

And everyone will sit there listening, totally flabbergasted and, before you know it, it's done! And you've saved your entire school from a lifetime of drinking sugary orange juice."

I said through my hands, "How likely do you think it is for the school roof to collapse?" Dad just sighed, so I added, "With no casualties?"

And he said, "Want me to drive you in extra early today if you're ready? I can't promise we'll have a non-fatal road collision, but you never know your luck."

And I think I just about managed a small smile.

I texted Ailsa saying I would be in school early and she replied:

Ok me too!! Meet u in library ☺

Dad kissed the top of my head and said, "I wasn't going to tell you this until later, once you'd got the assembly over and done with, but the doctors have said Seb can come home tomorrow."

And that was literally the only thing that made me get up and leave the house.

Ailsa was already in the library when I got there. I sat down and quietly said my One And Only Line over and over again, while Ailsa recited all of hers perfectly. I wish I'd just told her then that I couldn't go onstage, but this weird thing had happened to me since having An Actual

Friend like Ailsa: I would rather walk through fire than make her think I was any more weird than she probably thought already. Like if I couldn't stand next to her in assembly, then maybe I didn't deserve her at all.

I really wanted to hide in the library toilets for ever (even with the possibility of being beaten up) but I really, really didn't want Ailsa to do the assembly on her own. So when she asked me if I was feeling okay I said, "I can do it." And we had time for a final practice before we went to the hall.

As I was waiting at the side of the stage with Ailsa, I felt the air drop out of my lungs and my face felt like it was on fire. I couldn't breathe properly. The dusty air was clogging up my throat but I didn't dare cough. Ailsa squeezed my hand and whispered, "Good luck! It will be okay!" And I wanted to tell her I definitely couldn't say my line so we have to go with Plan B which was basically Me Just Standing There Holding The Orange Juice Carton Looking Totally Silent And Stupid, but I couldn't even say that, because the only word in my head was a massive

HELP!

I wanted to walk straight out of the fire exit, go home and get back into bed. And if I had then maybe everything would have been okay. But what I've learned about having a friend is that sometimes you have to do things for them, even if for you it turns out to be The Worst Thing Ever.

We waited for the clapping to stop after Adrian's presentation. Maisy was smiling and pointing at the *How high can a bottle rocket go?* slogan on her T-shirt. Then we walked into the middle of the stage. And even though the spotlight wasn't switched on, I could feel it beaming down on me like the brightest light ever, showing everyone how Totally Petrified And Weird I was.

It was like I had arrived in An Actual Horror Movie. But a horror movie where the entire school was watching me do a science presentation in assembly. I held the giant orange carton in my shaking hands, feeling my heart throbbing against my ribcage. I could hear the blood pumping around inside my head. Then, just as Ailsa was about to say her first line, I dropped it.

The carton made a huge bang on the floor and I could hear everyone laughing. I couldn't bend down to pick it up because I was frozen like a rabbit trapped in the headlights, only worse, like a rabbit that had just been squashed by someone's tyres.

And as Ailsa picked up the carton and said, "Good morning, everyone!" someone shouted out, "She can't speak!" and then people laughed again. Then someone else shouted, "Freak!" and then, "Mute-ant!"

Miss Sheldon and another teacher stood up and tried to get everyone to be quiet but it seemed to take about twenty years.

Ailsa whispered to me, "Don't worry." Then she said loudly, "How does the sugar concentration vary in different brands of orange juice?" Tears formed in my eyes and I wanted to run off the stage, but it was like my feet were superglued to the floor.

I heard Miss Sheldon and some other teachers saying, "Sssssshh!" and "Be quiet!" And even though Ailsa must have been explaining our experiment, all I could hear were the words flying around inside my head:

FREAK FREAK
FREAK FREAK
FREAK   and

HA HA HA
HA HA!

and my whole body went into some kind of Major Lockdown so there was nothing I could do to escape.

Ailsa said, "So, that was our experiment!"

And I thought, this might be the moment Ailsa realizes that I am actually a Really Bad Friend to have because everyone in the whole school hates me.

But what she actually did was this.

She took a bow and said, "Thank you to *most* of you for listening!" Then she took my hand and led me off the stage and out of the hall the back way and outside into the fresh air where I could finally take a breath.

We sat on the damp concrete steps underneath the pillars and she said, "Don't cry over them," and "Our experiment was really good!" and "Who cares what they think anyway? People at the front were listening and I could tell they liked it and Miss Sheldon was smiling." She put her arm around my shoulders. I felt Anxious and Sad and Frightened and More Silent than I had for a long time. But also I was overwhelmed with happiness that she was still there and still wanted to be my friend. I was pretty impressed she had managed to carry out the giant orange carton under her arm too.

Of all the possible things that I had imagined happening in the Science Week assembly, the one thing I had prayed not to happen was this: for it to be so Totally Obvious that I am unable to talk in front of everyone in my entire school. So I don't know what happened; maybe God misheard me or something. And the tears that came into my eyes were worse than ever before because they felt doubly sad and doubly never-ending.

33

#heart
toheart

The rest of the day passed in a kind of daze because I couldn't stop crying. Ailsa took me to Mrs Kingsley's office and told her what had happened. Mrs Kingsley said, "Can you write down what you think is the best thing to do now, Rosalind?"

So I wrote:

Go home.

But she said she thought it was important for me to stay at school, which was something to add to the new list forming in my head: Reasons I Do Not Like Mrs Kingsley. She said. "I tell you what, why don't you sit in the library for the rest of the morning? I'm sure you did a lot better than you think!"

So I spent the rest of the morning not reading the same page of *Jane Eyre*. At lunchtime Ailsa brought me some sandwiches and we sat on the floor next to the two tallest aisles of books. She told me about a time at primary school when she played the wizard in *The Wizard of Oz*, and when they pulled down the sheet to reveal her at the end, she wasn't ready. She fell backwards off the stage and had to be taken to hospital to have six stitches in her head. She parted her hair to show me the scar. I whispered, "I wish that had happened to me today." And then we laughed even though inside I still felt like crying.

After school I had to go to Mrs Quinney's because Dad was working late and Mum was still at the hospital. I didn't tell Mrs Quinney the whole story, just about dropping the orange carton and she said, "There, there, dear!" and gave me an unexpected hug, also known as me face-planting her boobs. She said, "Bernard's having a difficult day too, dear," and we both looked down at Bernard rolling around with one of her fluffy slippers. She tutted, shook her head and said, "He's sex-mad, that cat. I'll get you one of my currant buns, dear." And she disappeared into the kitchen.

And even though I was feeling like The Worst Person In The World, at least I was better off than Bernard.

When she came back in she said, "I've been having a bit of a sort-out today, dear. Let me show you those old photographs from my time in Africa." She took out an old biscuit tin from the cupboard, removed the lid and placed it on my lap. "Now," she said and took out a photograph of a beautiful young woman with long brown hair tied back with a ribbon and an enormous smile, sitting in a field with children playing in the background. "Don't tell me you don't recognize your own Mrs Quinney!"

And no joke, I almost choked to death on my currant bun.

We drank sweet tea from the Austrian cups and she told me all about teaching little children to read and write and telling them Bible stories like the ones she told me (only slightly shorter, less confusing versions I hoped). And I don't know if she planned it this way or if her and God were in this together, but I started feeling happier and the horrible words that had been flying around in my head all day seemed to disappear.

Just before I went home, Mrs Quinney showed me one last photograph. "Ah, here he is," and she gazed at a kind-faced man wearing a shirt and neckerchief standing in front of a little white chapel. On the back in perfect calligraphy was:

Henry O'Kelly, Botswana 1963

She looked like she was about to say something, but then she shook her head and said, "We mustn't dwell on the past, dear."

And I was transported back to the present with a bump.

34

#newsflash

Mum picked me up from Mrs Quinney's and took me home. But instead of asking me the question I'd been dreading – which was *How did the assembly go?* – what she actually said could have been the title of the horror movie I felt like I was starring in earlier:

I KNOW WHAT HAPPENED IN ASSEMBLY

Ailsa's mum Jen had phoned my dad. "She was worried about you. Ailsa told her you got upset. I'm sorry, Roz,

I really wish I was here when you got home. The school should have called me. Or you could have texted me." And she gave me one of those mum hugs which even though it's nice, it makes you cry. "You're lovely. And you've got such a wonderful new friend in Ailsa. And you've got a wonderful little brother who's coming home tomorrow!" I nodded and she wiped the tears from my eyes. "And *he's* been calling you a *superhero*!"

My heart stopped. Because that's what he always said about Miss Nobody.

"So there are a few Reasons To Be Cheerful as Mrs Quinney says. Now, what shall we have for dinner?"

And my heart started again so I said, "Not burned macaroni."

"Okay, not burned macaroni coming up."

While she was cooking, I sat at the kitchen table and made Seb a welcome-home sign in my best calligraphy which said:

Welcome Home, Seb 2.0!!!

and drew pictures of robots on it.

And while I was drawing I wondered if I told Mum how I was really feeling about going into school tomorrow, maybe she wouldn't make me go. Maybe she would never make me go back to Manor High ever again. Maybe she would let me be homeschooled and everything would be okay.

But when your little brother's coming home from hospital the next day and he thinks you are actually a superhero, and your mum seems something close to happy for the first time in ages, it's kind of impossible to say anything like the truth. Which was that actually: I'm not a superhero, I'm a Freak and a Weirdo and a Mute-ant and everyone in school knows and tomorrow feels like a fate worse than getting an arrow in your eye in the middle of the Battle of Hastings like whoever that happened to (not Anne of Cleves).

So I did what any Possibly Not Very Normal Person would do in this situation: I ate not burned macaroni, told Mum about Ailsa's *The Wizard of Oz* stage accident and pretended my Manor High stage debut was not so bad compared to that.

After dinner Mum said Jen had mentioned a Cardiff Castle trip that she didn't remember getting a letter about. (Which she wouldn't because I had put it at the bottom of the recycling bin ages ago, because going on a school trip with my entire year was one hundred per cent Not My Idea Of A Fun Day Out.) She said, "Jen's invited you to stay at theirs the night before as it's an early start, and she'll take you into school together if you want?"

And I immediately changed my mind. "Yes! Okay! I've always wanted to visit a real castle actually!"

And later, under the pretence of trying to find the letter about the Cardiff Castle trip I knew probably wasn't on the school website, I changed all the confusion and fear and anger and sadness I'd felt that day into words. And I put those words online.

NEWSFLASH!

Urgent news just in – some of Manor High's beasts have escaped!

Well-known gorilla (Lucas Merry) has been witnessed harassing Year Seven girls again. We may need a tranquillizer dart for this one.

Connor Mould, an Unknown Species, was last spotted near the biology pond. He may have decided to hide out there because the pond creatures are on the same level as him intellectually.

Crystal is back at school and has been seen roaming the quad looking for new victims. *Approach with caution!*

If you see any other wild beasts roaming Manor High searching for prey – Speak Up. It's time we defended our habitat.

Taming Manor High's most dangerous animals.

I am Miss Nobody.

35

#tellyou later

The next morning it took all the willpower I had not to beg Mum and Dad to let me stay at home. Over breakfast I wanted more than anything to tell them I was Seriously Ill, Possibly In Danger Of Actual Death, but they were going to the hospital to bring Seb home, so I didn't say anything. Plus, when I'd checked my blog I'd seen Miss Nobody had got 691 visitors, which was more than Year Seven and Year Eight put together! So I would be able to have a secret Project Meteor celebration with Seb later.

In the car on the way to school I thought: compared to what Seb has gone through, what is the worst the Manor High meatheads can really do to me? And I tried to keep that thought in my head, even when all the other Million Bad Thoughts About What Might Happen That Day came in to attack it.

By the time I got to school I was expecting the worst. Let's face it – thanks to Miss Sheldon I was no longer just the class weirdo, I was now The Weirdo Of The Entire School, so I was expecting people to laugh, say stuff and maybe even push me around a bit. But I wasn't really prepared for this.

As soon as I walked into the classroom I saw it. A drawing on the whiteboard of a stick person with bright red cheeks and puke coming out of its mouth and what I suppose was meant to be wee going down its legs, standing next to an orange juice carton. At the top there was a massive speech bubble saying *Nothin!!!! LOL!!!!* in big black letters and underneath were the words *FREAK!!!* and *MUTE-ANT!!!!* a few times in different-coloured pen.

My heart was beating so fast that I'm actually quite amazed I didn't just have a massive heart attack right then and there, which would at least have meant I could've left the room. I went to my seat, opened my planner and put my head down so no one could see how scared and silent and stupid I felt. Some people were laughing and Adrian was saying, "Hey, that's not very nice." And, "Are you okay?" to me. But I couldn't look up because in my head I was saying:

Don't cry!
Don't cry!
Don't cry!

And I wished Ailsa was there but she wasn't.

Just then Mr Bryant came in and said, "What is this? Who did this?" But I couldn't see properly because tears were in my eyes and no one owned up anyway. It was the first time our class was Totally Silent. Mr Bryant wiped the board and said, "I do not want to hear anyone speak for the rest of form time."

Connor shouted, "Not a problem for her, sir!"

And for the first time ever Mr Bryant said, "Get out!" to Connor, who looked just as surprised as I was.

Connor walked slowly out of the door looking more confused than when we have to do equations, just as Ailsa and some others came in. They stopped talking as soon as they noticed the Totally Awkward Silence we were all in. Marcus said, "Sorry, sir. Our bus was late."

Mr Bryant nodded, "Fine. Sit down without talking, please." So they went to their seats looking confused as

Mr Bryant was never usually like this. Ailsa sat down next to me and put her hand on my arm. She mouthed, "What's happened?" and I just shook my head because I couldn't even open my lips to mouth something to her. Then she wrote on her hand, Tell me later? And I nodded. No one said anything about the picture or about me until later because on the way to geography everyone was talking about Connor being sent out.

I didn't know for sure who did the picture, but I knew whose fault it all was.

Miss Sheldon's.

Miss Stupid Science Week Sheldon. It was her idea to put me onstage in the first place. And what was going through my mind all morning was this:

1. Miss Sheldon literally forced me to do the fair.
2. And the stupid assembly.
3. When people shouted out she didn't do anything to help me when I was up there.
4. She knew I couldn't even speak in class so why did she think I would be able to stand up in front of the whole entire school?
5. She must know everyone hates me and still she literally *forced* me to go up onstage. All to make her stupid Science Week look good.

But it gets worse. I was also thinking this:

6. She cannot even control our class.
7. She is also not even that good at science, because once she wasn't able to tell us why Pluto wasn't a planet and even Seb knows that and he's eight.
8. She is the one who started this whole Science Week Assembly Total Nightmare.
9. All of this is her fault.
10. I actually hate Miss Sheldon.

In geography, when Ms Bhatt went out to get some paper, Connor came up to me holding a pen in his hand like it was a microphone saying, "Here I am with The Mute-ant, what is it like being such a freak?" and "What does a Mute-ant eat for breakfast? ORANGE JUICE!" and shoved the pretend microphone in my face.

Ailsa said, "Leave us alone, Connor," and he did, for like ten minutes, but then he whispered to her, "What's it like being BFFs with a Mute-ant?"

Ailsa said to me, "Just ignore him," so we did and even though on the outside I probably looked like I was ignoring him, on the inside I had A Million Angry Words flying around in my head, about school, the assembly, and my SM, and Seb, and everything. They all built up into this Massive Muddle that felt painful because I needed to speak them and I couldn't.

The next time Connor whispered something to her, Ailsa

put her hand up and said, "Ms Bhatt, Connor keeps whispering horrible things to us." And when Ms Bhatt made him move seats I just wrote: ☺ in my notebook to Ailsa. Because it's not very easy to write that your head is hurting because it's so full up of words about anger and sadness and fear and worry. And I didn't know an emoji for that.

On the way to the library at break time some boys laughed at me and shouted, "Mute-ant!" and some others pointed and some people whispered, "There's That Girl Who Can't Speak!"

And if you want to know what it feels like being Whole School Famous, it's like this: I was used to the feeling of wanting the ground to swallow me up, but this was even worse than that. I wanted to Disappear Totally so I didn't even exist any more.

Only two things got me through that day:

1. Ailsa stayed with me all day, which makes her actually the best friend I have ever heard of.
2. Seb would be there when I got home.

I didn't cry the whole day maybe by some kind of Sympathetic Act Of God. But when I got home I burst into tears as soon as I walked through the door. Only there was a doctor standing in the hallway I didn't know who smiled awkwardly and said, "Don't worry, I often have this effect on people!"

Dad hugged me and said, "It's okay, just an emotional day for all of us!" He carried me upstairs (which he honestly hasn't done for ages) and when we got to my room he said, "Seb's doing okay. Don't worry. He just needs lots of rest. He's home now, we've brought him home. He's not going back to the hospital. It's okay." Which is definitely what Mrs Quinney would call A Reason To Be Cheerful and what I would call Maybe A Reason To Not Have An Emotional Breakdown Any More.

After dinner I went into Seb's room. He was fast asleep and his glow-in-the-dark ceiling stars made everything look green. He looked pale and small and I wondered if the doctors could see what I could see, because he definitely did not look okay. I didn't want to wake him up so I said really quietly, "Welcome home, Super Seb. I really missed you, little bro."

Before I went to sleep, I prayed so hard I could feel a pounding beat inside my head.

God – if you are up there, please make Seb get better. Because Dad said he's okay, but he doesn't look very okay to me. And, if you are listening, please turn me into somebody else. Please let me go to sleep and wake up as somebody else. Please, please, please don't make me have to be me ever again. Or (because I'd learned by this point it might be good to give God a few alternatives) *please make Manor High not exist. Or if you can't manage that, could you make some kind of Major Miracle Happen At Manor High and please, please let me be able to speak up.*

36

#promise

So I had two choices.

1. Go to school and be trapped in a silent bubble made worse by people constantly calling you names while you constantly wish your life had some kind of escape button.

Or 2. Convince your parents you are too sick to go to school so you can stay at home where it's safe and normal(ish).

Only those two choices were significantly reduced due to my parents having no sympathy whatsoever for Genuine Pretend Illnesses.

On Monday, I mashed up a banana in a bucket and

made loud retching noises. I showed it to Mum so she would think I'd puked up, but she said, "Are we eating bananas out of buckets for breakfast in this family now?"

On Tuesday, I stood in the garden in my pyjamas for half an hour before Dad got up for work and until my fingers felt like they might fall off. I told him I was freezing and might be dying of Extreme Coldness. But he said, "Well, what do you expect if you go outside in your pyjamas and bare feet? What *were* you doing?"

And when I answered, "I don't even know, that is how ill I am," he told me to get dressed and Put A Jumper On. (Which he said was Dad's Miracle Cure for feeling cold.)

On Wednesday, I covered my face with talcum powder until I looked deathly pale. I told Mum I didn't feel well and that I was On The Verge Of Death, but she just said, "More like On The Verge Of Becoming A Goth. Wash your face and get dressed."

It didn't seem to matter what I did, every day they said the same words: "You'd better get ready for school." Either I'm not very brilliant at faking illnesses or they have no sympathy for anyone ever. How Seb got them to take him to hospital is a mystery to me. They never believe anyone is ill.

So on Thursday, I lay in bed under the covers praying for a Minor Miracle that my parents would just forget about me today. But Seb came in and said, "Rozzie, get up! Mum says I can make pancakes today!" And it had been ages since I'd seen Seb excited like that, so suddenly eating Seb's pancakes seemed more important than staying under the duvet with too many words in my head.

As the kitchen filled up with the smell of banana pancakes, I realized why none of my attempts at avoiding school had worked. Dad put his arm around me and said, "You can spend the whole weekend with Seb, you know. The last thing he wants is for you to miss school because of him." Which wasn't true at all so I know Dad definitely didn't ask him. But I didn't say anything, just put my books in my bag, hoping I might get Exceptionally Lucky one day and actually get ill for real.

Being friends with Ailsa was the only thing that protected me from the constant whisperings and shouts. She told me, "Don't worry, they'll get bored with it soon," and "It's not your fault, they're just stupid," and "It will get better, I promise." And other things that Possibly Weren't True but made me feel like I had someone on my side. (I also spent most days praying for someone with a non-fatal disease to sneeze on me.)

On Friday in English Miss Carter gave us an extract from a book about zombies to read and told us to highlight words associated with danger. And as me and Ailsa were highlighting words like *cracked* and *burning* and *cobwebs* and *snaked*, words like *freak* and *weird* and *mute-ant* and *HAHAHAHAHA* were all getting highlighted in my head.

At lunchtime, on the way to the library, a boy shouted "FREAK!" in my face at a hundred decibels. And it felt like there was this enormous stopper in my throat and all the words I wanted to say were getting stuck behind it. And the pressure was building up and building up, but even when I started crying no sound would come out.

Ailsa took me into the library toilets and I splashed my face with water. She said, "I think we should tell someone. Maybe we should see Mr Bryant about it? Maybe he could help. Or we could speak to Mrs Goodacre?"

I shook my head, "It's not that bad. It will probably stop soon." But she didn't look convinced so I said a Mini White Lie: "Okay, if it carries on next week then maybe."

Then she said, "What about messaging Miss Nobody? I can get her page up on my phone."

My heartbeat got louder and louder and louder. And without really meaning to I nodded my head, and said, "Okay."

And as I was writing

Hi Miss Nobody, there are some bullies at our school who say stuff to me. A lot of stuff. They make me feel totally small and worthless. Like in Alice in

Wonderland when she shrinks down really tiny, only not in a good way. And I can't say anything back.

I wondered, is messaging Miss Nobody about Miss Nobody technically lying?

But when I pressed Send and Ailsa said, "Hopefully she will help us!" I decided that unfortunately it probably kind of was.

37

#idontknow whattosay

On Saturday Dad took Obsessively Cleaning The House to a whole new level so Seb started calling him The Housebot. Dad said, "We all need to be on constant germ patrol!"

And Seb said, "That puts an end to the game of bogie tennis I had planned."

Mum said, "What about playing Top Trumps?"

Seb said, "Only if Dad promises not to actually trump this time." But Mum said she thought that might be Asking The Impossible.

And Seb said, "Can we do chalk pictures on the drive again?"

But Mum said, "Maybe tomorrow. It's getting a bit late."

Seb's skin was a funny colour, and he had little blue bruises on his arm, which Mum said was because of the new treatment they'd tried, but Seb said was because he was turning radioactive. Mum said, "In that case, maybe I should report you to the germ patrol unit." And it was the first time in ages it felt like our house had gone back to being normal. Which in our house was: Dad being surgically attached to a packet of anti-bacterial wipes and freezing anytime anyone looked like they were about to sneeze; Seb coming up with disgusting versions of games then showing us how a Tyrannosaurus rex would eat a human being starting with their bum, and Mum hysterically crying every ten minutes, sometimes with laughter, sometimes with sadness. But still, it was A Million Times Better than all the weird grey silences.

When it was bedtime, Seb asked me to read him a story. That week I had borrowed a book from Octavia to practise reading out loud called *The Velveteen Rabbit*, which was really for reading at Christmas, according to her, but I thought Seb wouldn't mind. Dad insisted on giving the book a thorough wipe, and I'm not sure if it was because I told him ages ago that Octavia was seriously messy or if he was just starting yet another major wipe-down of Literally Everything In The House. He said, "If it doesn't breathe, I'm cleaning it!"

Mum came up to tuck Seb in. "Ten minutes then lights out, and a Sweet Dreams Kiss, okay?" Which meant she was in a happy mood because when she was really sad she would just say lights out and would forget about the Sweet Dreams Kiss bit. I liked it when she said it, because Seb rolled his eyes and clutched his stomach and pretended like he was going to be sick, but really I knew he liked it.

I started reading the story but Seb said, "Are you going to write a blog tonight?"

I shrugged. I hadn't told him about the Science Week assembly. Because even though he would probably make me feel better about it, telling him about that would mean telling him about people calling me Mute-ant, and whispering stuff, and feeling like everyone was staring and pointing at me the whole time. And I wanted a weekend of no one feeling sad. (Apart from me.)

I said, "I've been really busy with schoolwork." Which wasn't exactly A Total Lie because I did have some homework to do.

Seb said, "But you're getting so many hits! Project Meteor is massive! People like you, Rozzie."

And it was weird because I hadn't really thought about it like that before. Because even though people liked Miss

Nobody, it felt like, apart from Ailsa, nobody at school liked Actual Me at all. (Librarians and library monitors don't count.)

Then he said, "Probably because they're Mega Geeks like you!" laughed and said, "Maybe they read it and get mega-LOLs!" Then he couldn't stop laughing in between saying, "Now I got mega-LOLs!" and begged me not to give him tickle torture, which he only says when he really wants me to tickle him, but he looked weak, like tickle torture might break him, so I didn't.

When Seb finally stopped mega-LOL-ing he said, "Dr Howard told me they can't make me get better." And for the first time around Seb I didn't have any words, but not in an SM way because it felt different, like I just didn't have any words that could make him feel better. Because unfortunately words aren't magic. Words can't make someone not die. Words can't make Actual Miracles happen. Sometimes words just don't do anything at all. Sometimes they don't even matter. I stayed quiet and held him close, and tried to stop my tears from rolling onto his face.

"If I don't get better, will you mummify me?"

And I said, "Yes, definitely, if it's allowed."

"Okay, awesome! And what about getting one of Mrs Quinney's cats and mummifying it too as an act of worship?"

Dad came in and said, "I'm not sure I like the sound of that, what about the hygiene issues?"

Mum stood next to him smiling a proper smile for the first time in ages and said to Seb, "Come on, my little baby, time for sleep." She put her arms around me and kissed my head and said, "You too, my big baby."

Seb pointed at Dad and said, "That makes Dad your supersize baby!"

So Seb did get his tickle torture in the end.

I didn't want to think about Seb not getting better, so in my room I took out my notebook and thought about all the things I wanted to say to people at Manor High. Since the Science Assembly Disaster, my life at school had been worse than ever. Everyone now knew me as The Weird Girl Who Can't Speak, and made me feel A Million Times Worse about it than I did already. I had even lied to Ailsa. Science Week had basically ruined my entire life.

Then I had a Brilliant Idea.

I stayed up writing until Mum came into my room. She said, "Ten minutes then lights out," then gave me a Sweet Dreams Kiss. I was really glad she did because I needed it, plus it reminded me to up the number of prayers I was doing for Seb, just in case he was serious about mummifying Mary or Bernard.

Once Mum had closed my door, I typed out my

Brilliant Idea onto Miss Nobody and hit Publish. I got into bed, but I couldn't sleep at all. The moral compass bit of my heart was going off like a car alarm. Which made me think, maybe that Brilliant Idea wasn't so brilliant after all. So I switched my phone back on and deleted my post.

I'm not sure if it was Mum's Sweet Dreams Kiss working its magic, but I slept really well that night. It was the first night I didn't have bad dreams for ages. I just wish and wish that Mum had a magic kiss called Stopping Your Daughter From Making A Terrible Mistake, but it turns out she definitely hasn't.

38

#tellthe
truth

The next day I went to Ailsa's house to Just Hang Out, which was something I hadn't properly done before. She asked me to show her how to do calligraphy, so I taught her in exactly the same way Mrs Quinney taught me: starting with sitting in the correct position, then holding the pen in the correct way, then practising loops and swirls. It was fun teaching Ailsa because she listened and copied carefully and even though she didn't do it totally perfectly I made sure I didn't say what Mrs Quinney used to always say to me which was: "Now, dear, I don't think Our Lord Jesus would be very impressed with that odd little squiggle!" I told her how poorly Seb was, and about

Octavia, and how much I wanted to speak at school. She told me how funny her dad was, and about what it's like in Edinburgh, and how she would help me speak at school if she could.

And while I was there I felt like a girl who was Quirky Not Weird and Ailsa was a girl who was An Amazing Best Friend, a bit like being in one of those American films about high school. Only maybe in films they don't exactly spend their time doing calligraphy.

While Ailsa was practising her loops and I was making a sign for Book Week, she said, "I felt really scared on my first day at Manor High, you know."

And I said, "Me too!" I wanted to also say I'd been scared pretty much every day since, but I didn't because I was worried she might think it was stupid to feel scared so much.

But she said, "I feel scared now too sometimes." And I was just about to say *me too*, but then I froze because she said, "But it's like Miss Nobody says, it's the bullies who should feel bad, not us. Shall we read her blog?"

And I nodded because my mind was going into a Total Panic Overload Meltdown and all I could do was stay Totally Silent. She scrolled down and read some of what I'd written a couple of days before.

FEELING SMALL?

Nobodies – do the bullies at Manor High make you feel a bit like Alice after she drank the bottle marked DRINK ME and shrank down really tiny? So small she hardly even feels like a real person.

Because someone messaged me recently, and said that's how they felt.

Ailsa smiled at me when she read that bit and said, "See? She read your message!"

And it's kind of how I feel at school sometimes too.

Only I've been thinking. Why should WE be the ones to feel small like that?

It's the bullies who should feel bad, Not Us.

Why should WE spend our whole lives wishing we could disappear down a rabbit hole?

The only people who should be disappearing from Manor High are the people on Team Mean.

I stared at the paper I'd been writing on. I could feel my face burning and my hands sweating. Which of all the things I could have done was probably the thing that made me look really guilty, but I couldn't control it. If Ailsa had just taken one look at me she probably would have seen the truth, because I felt like I had a big sign in my eyes saying

IT'S ME BY THE WAY!

that I needed to hide.

Luckily I'd had a lot of practice at hiding my face in my notebook. But still, if I could rewind time and do this bit over again, I would have told you the truth right then and there, Ailsa. I promise.

39

#shutup

A few days later I had Every Reason To Hope that things would get better for me at school. People had gone back to totally ignoring me again, and Connor seemed to have got bored with hassling me and Ailsa so much. I think Mr Bryant had spoken to him about it, because he kept him behind after form time and Connor was quiet for once in our English lesson.

Lucas still said stuff to me on the bus home and sometimes people pointed at me as I walked through school, but in general I got left alone. Thankfully Whole School Fame doesn't seem to last that long at Manor High. But then there was what happened with the brass band.

This sums up what my school is like: if you are talented at a musical instrument and join the brass band, it is an extremely fast way to becoming a Nobody.

Every Tuesday they rehearse in the music block which is right next to where loads of people in Year Nine hang out, so obviously I never go there. But every week as soon as they start playing, Craig Bull and his friends tell them to shut up. They bang on the windows, shout stuff at them, go in and take their instruments, and basically scare them so much they stop rehearsing. (Which might explain why the Christmas concert wasn't so great, even before the TUNE! interruption.)

But on the way to science, Adrian was talking about something that happened at lunchtime: the brass band didn't stop playing. Even though the Year Nines threatened to beat them up, break their instruments (one of them did have his flute thrown across the field), and said they would wait for them outside the gates after school, *they still did not stop playing*. And he had a huge smile on his face.

But that wasn't all.

Michael said he knew some people who were going to tell their form tutor about Crystal and her clones stealing their lunch money. And Sian said some Year Eights had stuck up for a boy in our year at the bus stop who was getting pushed around.

Now, I know that Miss Nobody can't take one hundred per cent credit for this whole geeks-fighting-back thing, because Nobodies like me had been unhappy at Manor High for ages, so maybe I just happened to start my blog at the right time.

But what I do know is this.

Before Miss Nobody started blogging, the tiny, quiet, invisible people had never stood up for themselves, the chess club had never stood up for the Year Sevens, David Gay had never even considered punching someone, and the brass band had never got to the end of their lunchtime rehearsal.

And that's what finally gave me the confidence to use my word cards.

Everyone had been talking about how great it was that people didn't feel as scared, and that Nobodies were sticking up for each other. So when a supply teacher came in at the start of our science lesson saying Miss Sheldon was off sick and he would be taking the lesson, I thought, okay, now feels like the right time. So I showed a card to Ailsa and her eyes lit up and she said, "Yes!"

I walked up to the front desk and showed the supply teacher the card Mrs Kingsley had made me which said:

I'm Rosalind Banks, Form 7A. Sometimes I find it

very difficult to speak. Please do not ask me to speak,
and allow me to write down my answers.

I tried to hide my hands while he was reading it because they were shaking and my stomach was doing somersaults. But he smiled at me and said gently, "Okay, Rosalind. Thank you. I understand. If you have a question maybe you could write it down for me."

And when he said that I felt a huge wave of relief come over me like An Actual Miracle had happened because I had finally used my word cards. They had been in my bag since September! And I thought, maybe I've finally arrived at the end of my settling in period after seven long months, maybe things will get better from now on. Maybe everything is going to be okay.

But I should have realized that would have been a Dream Come True, and dreams don't exactly come true at Manor High. They should make that the school motto or something. Because the next day Ailsa was off sick, so I was sitting on my own, and Maisy made a sign which said:

I CAN'T SPEAK! VICTIM OF
MUTE-ANT DISEASE!! ☹

And she held it up any time the teacher's back was

turned. It lasted all morning, which surprised me as I didn't think Maisy could go for that long without speaking. It seemed like almost everyone found it funny when she held it up. Every single time.

And maybe I would put up with that, but Miss Nobody definitely wouldn't.

I mean, here I was, speaking up against Manor High's biggest bullies, when actually Maisy Love was my biggest problem! Miss Nobody could show Maisy for the horrible moral compassless person she was, and maybe *then* things would start getting better for me at school. Because if I couldn't even use my cards in class then I would never be able to say a word.

And that afternoon in the library I got another one of those Signs From God that Mrs Quinney had told me about.

Mrs Goodacre asked me to fill up the printer paper and photocopy the sign I had made for Book Week while she went to a meeting. And she left her computer screen there staring at me. I looked up at her noticeboard. A note was taped up in Rajit's handwriting saying Book Week, Mrs G!! We need a bigger budget!! And at the bottom it said:

Sometimes you have to risk all of your lives to slay the dragon!!!

And that's exactly what I decided to do. So, now that

I think about it, God, that was a Pretty Bad Sign to give someone like me, actually.

GUESS WHO

Okay, geeks, gamers, techies and brainiacs, let's do a quiz...

Question: Who is one of the cruellest creatures at Manor High?

Who has fangs more poisonous than a snake, a deadlier bite than a killer ant, and a sting more annoying than a wasp? (Only with slightly fewer brain cells.)

She gets good grades because she copies from people who do actually work hard and she thinks Steven Spielberg invented earthquakes. She also thinks lipgloss is the Best Invention Ever.

And this Big-Bully-in-Training is only in Year Seven!

Answer: Maisy Love.

Maisy Love is an A* Bully, and she needs to be stopped in her tracks.

I think it's about time we stood up to her and said:

No more #maisyhate.

I am Miss Nobody.

And now, looking back, that hashtag was probably a Massive Mistake.

40

#saywhat

Next week in assembly, Mr Endeby stood at the front looking Extremely Serious, like he does when people are in trouble. As soon as he said the word "bullying" I could feel my cheeks getting hot. I turned my head away from him and noticed Mr Bryant fiddling with a folded piece of paper. And this would have been the most Uninteresting Piece Of News Ever, only every time he folded down the corner I could see part of Seb's Miss Nobody picture. And if I thought it was bad in assembly when Maisy was kicking my chair, it was nothing compared to how it felt seeing Mr Bryant with one of my Miss Nobody posters.

Mr Endeby put the school rules on the screen and

went on about how bullying will be taken seriously and how people need to come forward to report it. And how he wouldn't tolerate anyone becoming a vigilante, which is someone who takes the law into their own hands (I looked it up on Google as soon as I got home).

That afternoon Octavia told me that sometimes just words can change the world. We were reading famous speeches and I'd agreed to have another therapist called Simon in listening which was a Massive Step for me. I didn't lose my breath that much, and I only stumbled on my words a few times. Octavia told me, "That is some Major Progress!" And her necklaces all jangled together like they were clapping. I said it must be nice to be able to speak words like that to so many people, and she said, "So imagine if you *could* stand up and say something. What do you think you might say?" I thought about it, then shrugged. Because even though Miss Nobody had been speaking to everyone, the idea of actually speaking out loud to lots of people was too much like An Actual Nightmare to imagine it like a Dream Come True. "Well, think about it." And she tapped the speeches book. "That's what all these people did. Sometimes just standing up and saying what you think can make waves throughout history."

When I got home I told Seb the teachers had found out about Miss Nobody. He said, "I can do another forcefield of protection, only this time try to get you invisibility!" So I decided Seb wasn't exactly a Brilliant Person to ask for advice In Most If Not All Situations. Every time I thought about Miss Nobody my heart started racing, and I had to remind myself that no one at school knew Miss Nobody was me. (I was only a little bit worried the school might have a way of detecting fingerprints on posters.)

The next day I realized Octavia was right about words causing waves, because my blog about Maisy seemed to be causing a full-on tidal wave at school. My post had started trending. In a big way. And even though being Miss Nobody had mostly felt like a Really Good Thing, it wasn't long before I started wishing that Miss Nobody wasn't actually me at all.

The first thing was when I walked into form time and saw Maisy crying. Her friends were sat around her and Katie said, "Don't worry, Maisy. We'll tell Mr Bryant and he will get it taken down."

Maisy said, "But it's everywhere!"

And it was a shock seeing Maisy so upset. I thought it would feel better than it did. I thought it would make me happy seeing her having a tiny taste of the hurt she had caused me. But actually, it sort of made me feel the Exact Opposite.

When I went to the toilet that morning I found out what Maisy and her friends had been talking about. Because right there in permanent black marker pen was some brand-new graffiti on the wall that said:

WE HATE #MAISYHATE

(I know it was permanent because I tried to wipe it off.)

And on the way to geography I saw it again on the wall, and again on one of the windows, and a few more times on the way up the stairs. And each time I saw it I felt like there was a tidal wave in my stomach. Maisy was still crying when we got to the classroom, so Ms Bhatt took her outside and talked to her for ages. The whole time Katie and Ella were whispering to each other but I couldn't hear what they were saying. And when Ailsa asked me if I knew what was going on, I just shook my head and looked away.

The next day in form time Maisy didn't say a word. So actually, I was Massively Glad About That. Because even though I mostly didn't think the graffiti about Maisy was very nice, maybe a Very Tiny part of me thought she might have deserved it. And I did think it was a little bit weird that some of my followers had graffitied the school, but I decided that clearly I wasn't the only person in the world who hated Maisy, and if David Gay could punch someone in the face, maybe some people in chess club or the brass band could vandalize school property? I watched Adrian whistling and cleaning his glasses, then sorting out his colouring pencils from lightest to darkest. It seemed unlikely, but Definitely Not Impossible.

Later in English, Ailsa was showing me some calligraphy she had done, but all I could see was Maisy. Her eyes were shining like they were full of tears. And the moral compass bit of my heart didn't exactly feel good about it, but it also reminded me of all the times my eyes had looked like that. And Maisy had definitely said worse things to me than anything the graffiti said.

When I got home I wanted to talk to Seb about the #maisyhate stuff, but when I went up to his bedroom a nurse was there who I didn't know. She said, "Hello!" cheerfully and my face froze in a half smile. My heart sank because I really wanted to speak to Seb, but all the words got jammed up in my throat and none of them would come out.

Seb said, "This is my sister, Rozzie. She might not speak to you, but it's not because she doesn't like you."

The nurse stayed there the whole evening and a different one was there the next morning. And then every time I tried to speak to him over the weekend, Mum and Dad were there. And it was Massively Annoying because I wanted to tell Seb what was happening with #maisyhate, but all I could do was laugh at his jokes and play Xbox and pretend I hadn't accidentally started some kind of graffiti outbreak at school.

On Monday, Maisy wasn't in form time and there was a weird atmosphere in our class. I could hear people whispering about the #maisyhate stuff, but I didn't understand how it could have got any worse over the weekend. No one was even in school. Katie was looking at her phone under her desk the whole day, and whispering things to people. I wondered if Maisy was at home texting her about how horrible it was when people at school don't like you. And I wondered if it was a good thing or a bad thing that Maisy was experiencing what can only be described as A Taste Of Miss Nobody's Medicine.

Only later that day I realized it wasn't Miss Nobody's medicine she was tasting.

At lunchtime I went into the library toilets just as some of Crystal's clones were coming out. My heart was beating really fast and the words in my head started feeling foggy. One of them pushed past me, and as I looked down at my shoes I noticed something in her hand. A marker pen. And when I went into the toilets the walls were covered with

WE HATE #MAISYHATE

That's when it hit me that something was going Very Wrong. Because Crystal's clones definitely weren't Miss Nobody followers. They were the people Miss Nobody was writing about in the first place. It didn't make any sense. Why had the clones hijacked my post?

Only it didn't stop there.

The next morning Mr Bryant came in looking serious. He said he had to talk to us about Something Very Important. He started speaking about what bullying is and how important it is to report any incidents. He said that some people in our school had been victims of bullying and cyberbullying. And he went on for ages about what it was even though Mr Endeby had already told us in assembly.

And while he was talking I thought, finally! He finally realizes what it's like for people like me. I mean, I couldn't even remember a day recently when I *didn't* have something shouted at me, or something thrown at me, or my stuff thrown into the bin (usually by Connor), or get laughed at or pushed out of the way or Just Totally Ignored.

He said bullying made people scared of coming to school. And I thought, Yes! That is exactly what it is like for People Like Me. The Nobodies. It is scary to be bullied so badly that even if you could speak up you wouldn't dare, and you don't want anyone to even look at you, and you wish you could just be homeschooled or get a terrible illness rather than come to school. Finally Mr Bryant gets it! That people like Maisy use their popularity to bully people. That people feel intimidated by her, like me and Adrian and maybe even her friends. That we feel frightened when she's around. That sometimes even at home we still feel totally worthless. And that she enjoys doing it, and makes stupid signs. And that maybe this graffiti thing about her wasn't exactly nice, but it seemed like it was the bullies who were doing that anyway!

Mr Bryant talked about lots of things before I realized which bully he was actually talking about. And it wasn't Maisy, or Connor or The Girl With The Smudged Eyeliner or Crystal, or the Year Nine Cupboard Squashers. Or even the clones writing #maisyhate on toilet walls. He wasn't talking about any of them. And a sick feeling started in my stomach.

"So, if you are smart, like I know you all are, you won't visit any of the social media pages set up by this Miss Nobody, because the school is monitoring them all and…"

Only I didn't hear the rest of what he said because thoughts were rushing through my head like speeding trains.

He's talking about Miss Nobody?
About VICTIMS of Miss Nobody?
People are afraid of Miss Nobody?

Only that meant he wasn't talking about Miss Nobody. *He was talking about me.*

And my blood ran so cold it felt like ice. Miss Nobody didn't have any social media pages. I hadn't set any up.

So if it wasn't my Miss Nobody, who was it?

And that's probably when I realized things had started to get quite serious actually.

41

#peptalk

As soon as I got home I went upstairs and shut my bedroom door. I took out my phone, typed in the website everybody had been whispering about after Mr Bryant's talk, and searched for #maisyhate. And afterwards wished I hadn't. Because there were lots of pages about Maisy, only I'm one hundred per cent sure they weren't ones she'd set up herself.

Unless Maisy had taken selfies then added horrible words and arrows pointing at her face, and then added loads of nasty comments. I clicked through a few more, then stopped. Staring back at me from the screen was a photo of Maisy with a skull drawn over her face and

RIP underneath. And I had two thoughts:

1. This is actually way more horrible than the toilet graffiti.
2. Maisy's death threatener is definitely a lot worse than mine.

The next day it seemed like anywhere I went there was a reminder of what I'd done in the form of #maisyhate written in permanent marker pen. Maisy still wasn't in school. And although technically I still hated Maisy, seeing all the stuff online about her did make me feel really bad actually.

But I told myself that:

1. Maisy had been really horrible to me which was the only reason I wrote about her in the first place. Plus Miss Nobody was trying to *stop* people like Maisy being horrible.
2. It wasn't me who did any of the graffiti at school or any of the stuff on the social media sites. And I was pretty certain it was Crystal and her clones doing the graffiti, and they were actually supposed to be friends with Maisy. So it just proves Miss Nobody was totally right about them.
3. There was still a small chance I could be struck down with a terrible illness and have to be homeschooled.
4. I was pretty sure it was either Mrs Quinney or actual

God who had told me to start Miss Nobody in the first place.

5. It is obviously way easier to persuade Maisy's parents to let you take time off school than mine.

In art everybody was talking about it. Only they weren't talking about my blog any more. Katie said Miss Nobody was sending Maisy horrible texts. Michael said most of the stuff online had been closed down, but he'd seen a new page called Miss Nobody HATES Maisy that none of the teachers knew about. Ailsa turned to me and whispered, "Have you seen it?" and I shook my head. And though that was Definitely Not The Actual Truth, I did my best to make it look like it was. Because The Actual Truth was I'd spent most of the night before looking at it. And it was so bad it made the RIP skull photo of Maisy look actually quite flattering.

That night, while Mum and Dad were watching TV, I told Seb how Project Meteor had gone so far off course it was practically in a different solar system. He suggested writing a blog telling people to stop being mean to Maisy. His skin was paler than usual, and when he spoke it was like he was losing his breath. I logged onto Miss Nobody and clicked New Post, only each time I tried to write, I couldn't think of what to say. And anyway, I was worried it was all a bit too late.

The next day Mr Bryant told us Mr Endeby was investigating the cyberbullying that had been happening recently, and if we knew anything then to speak to him at break time or put an anonymous note in the messages box outside the staffroom. He said, "Someone in here must know something." And he glared at us, saying it was A Serious Matter and we should Do The Right Thing.

I thought all morning about writing an anonymous note to Mr Bryant, but I didn't know what to put. I already thought I had been doing The Right Thing when all of this started. And I didn't even know what The Right Thing was any more.

People talked about nothing else all day even though they were told not to. And all day I was listening. Katie said Maisy was changing schools. Sian said teachers were looking at everyone's social media pages, because apparently people had been putting stuff on Maisy's profile during lessons. Elsie said she wondered if Miss Nobody would write another blog.

And all the time I said nothing, but this is what I was thinking:

1. God moves in mysterious ways so maybe I should just Trust Him On This One.

2. I did write the blog about Maisy, but I definitely didn't do any of the really horrible things like nasty

face swaps or putting horrible comments on her selfies or sending her online messages during lessons. (This was literally the only time I was glad my phone didn't have 3G.)

3. It could all simply be a case of Maisy getting A Taste Of Her Own Medicine.

4. I had better double-check with Seb that no one can trace Miss Nobody back to me.

5. Maybe I should just stop being Miss Nobody altogether.

6. But then, the #maisyhate stuff would probably stop now if people were getting into Serious Trouble, and Maisy was changing schools anyway. So maybe Miss Nobody had sort of done The Right Thing because Maisy wasn't at our school bullying People Like Me any more, so although not exactly a Total Success, it wasn't one hundred per cent Totally Bad! Maybe now Maisy would change her ways. In a weird way I might have actually done her a favour!

Then I thought:

7. If Miss Nobody carries on like this, Manor High could be completely bully-free by the time I finish Year Seven. Maybe even sooner!

And just as I had convinced myself that I should

definitely carry on – that it was a bit like those moral crusades Mrs Quinney told me about and there are obviously going to be a few Minor Mistakes along The Right Path – I saw something I had been waiting for this whole time:

An Actual Sign From God.

Only this time it wasn't so good.

42

#toolateto apologize

I was hurrying for the bus because I'd stopped at the library to pick up some coloured paper to make decorations for Book Week that had a note from Rajit on saying GIRLS!! TAKE HOME!! I was dreading the bus ride as usual and Lucas Merry shouting in a voice like a sports commentator out of the window, "Here she comes, the weirdo that never speaks! Is she about to break into a run?" seriously did not help.

I put my head down but I could feel my stupid cheeks giving me away by going bright red and I wanted to tell him to JUST SHUT UP! but my words were muddling as usual. The last couple of people were getting on, and that's when I noticed it, The Biggest Actual Sign From God Ever: Miss Sheldon and Ms Cox, the head of science, cleaning a car in the school car park.

At first I thought, that is A Bit Weird considering a) teachers never seem to care about what their cars look like, except that one PE teacher who wears really short shorts and fake tan, and b) why would they wash their car at school?

Miss Sheldon saw me and smiled, but she looked like she'd been crying. I got on the bus and quickly sat down in the seat nearest the driver (and furthest away from Lucas, who was still shouting things).

But I didn't hear exactly what Lucas was saying, because I was too busy trying to pretend I hadn't seen Miss Sheldon or the car or the letters sprayed on the side saying *BIE!!!* which I thought could maybe be a misspelling of *Bye*. And in a funny way that was kind of not a massively horrible thing to say to someone at the end of the day.

But deep down, the moral compass area in my heart was screaming

ZOMBIE!
ZOMBIE!
ZOMBIE!

And it was a bit like when I saw the #maisyhate graffiti for the first time. Only when I saw that I thought, okay it's pretty bad but Maisy probably one hundred per cent deserves it. But this time, when I saw Miss Sheldon's car, I thought:

Someone saw that blog post before I deleted it.

Then I thought:

This is so much worse than the one about Maisy.

Because instead of going straight to sleep that night when Mum gave me a Sweet Dreams Kiss, all these horrible words were knotted up inside my head and I had to get them out.

So I'd written a blog post about Miss Sheldon.

Lucas's voice was still shouting things at me, but I could hardly hear it because the words I wrote that night kept scrolling in my head.

MAJOR PROBLEM AT MANOR HIGH

But this time I am not talking about the bullies.

This time I'm talking about the people who ignore People Like Us – the bullied, the terrified, the victims of Manor High's Team Mean.

There are some sick people in our school and it's about time Miss Nobody gave them some medicine. Yes, that's right. I am talking about our teachers.

The people who walk around Totally Ignoring our suffering. Who never seem to be around when we need them.

And this teacher is one of the worst at Manor High (which is really saying something) – Miss Sheldon.

Lucas's voice shouted something at me in the background. But then I heard another voice too. Someone was saying the words to Lucas which had been trapped inside my head for months. "Shut up, Lucas!"

Then someone else said, "Yeah, just leave her alone, Lucas."

And it was a Really Weird feeling, because suddenly there were other voices sticking up for me too, and it should have made being me feel Amazing, but the words I wrote about Miss Sheldon kept flooding into my head. And I just kept feeling worse and worse.

Despite being one of the few teachers at Manor High whose breath doesn't smell like a dog dying of a coffee overdose, Miss Sheldon's combination of perfume and hairspray in a science lab must at least be a Major Fire Hazard.

Not that she probably even knows how to turn on a Bunsen burner.

I'm actually wondering if she even knows what H_2O is.

This so-called scientist doesn't even react when people are being dangerous in her lab!

Maybe she needs some better science goggles.

Or maybe she has a black hole where her brain is supposed to be.

Has anyone checked Miss Sheldon isn't actually a zombie or something?

And if I could unwrite anything then that post would be it. Because when the bus finally pulled off, and I watched Miss Sheldon cleaning the last letter off her car, what I wanted to do more than anything in the world was something I knew I definitely couldn't, which was to say:

It's all my fault.

I'm Miss Nobody and I'm sorry.

315

43

#badjoke

I got home and went straight upstairs to see Seb and without even meaning to I started crying. And to Seb it must have seemed A Little Bit Weird but to Mum it must have seemed Quite A Lot Weird. So I had No Choice but to say it was because of what Lucas had said to me on the bus. Because whatever lies I had to tell it was one hundred per cent better than Being Completely Honest and telling them the truth about Being Miss Nobody. Because I really didn't want to be her any more.

When Dad got back from work Mum made me tell him what happened on the bus, and after that everything kind of roller-coastered. Dad said he was going into school in the morning and he emailed Mrs Kingsley and Mr Bryant, which took him ages. He even said he was going to speak to Octavia although I'm not exactly sure why considering she didn't even know who Lucas Merry was.

Then Dad started giving me a Massively Long Lecture about talking to him and Mum more. I tried telling them that people had stood up for me, but they didn't seem to think that was The Most Amazing News Ever. And maybe deep down, my heart didn't think so either. Because the whole time Dad was talking I kept thinking about the word on Miss Sheldon's car, and the words I had deleted too late from my blog. And I felt sick.

So that night, I made a Major Decision. I was going to stop being Miss Nobody for good. And my moral compass felt pretty relieved. Because instead of feeling invincible like I did when I first started it, I actually just felt really scared. (And not just that everyone would find out it was me, although I was Honestly Really Scared About That.)

I just didn't know how everything had got so far out of control.

The next morning Dad came into school with me. I had to sit in Mrs Kingsley's stuffy office while Dad told her everything I had told him about what Lucas said to me on the bus. I stared down at the beige carpet wishing it would turn magical like that one in *Aladdin* and carry me away, only not to a whole new world, just home so I could hide under my duvet.

Mrs Kingsley said, "I see," and "Oh dear," and "Leave this with me," and "We do take bullying very seriously." And the word my dad kept saying exploded in my head like a giant piece of popping candy:

Later in history Mr Dean reminded us For The Millionth Time about taking a packed lunch on the Cardiff Castle trip, which he had started calling The Cardiff Castle Which Is In Wales Trip. Ailsa wrote in my notebook

Do you like peanut butter? ☺

I could hear Sian and Elsie saying they were going to report some new Miss Nobody pages to Mr Bryant because they were Really Bad. And while I was writing

Yep! ☺

inside I was feeling the Exact Opposite of a smiley face, which was Extremely Worried it might be all my fault.

Because it wasn't just Miss Sheldon's car someone had written ZOMBIE on. The next day at lunchtime me, Ailsa and Suzi were tidying up the tall bookshelves at the back of the library, trying to avoid Rajit because we hadn't finished the Book Week decorations yet. Suzi said, "Did you see the graffiti on Miss Sheldon's classroom door?"

Ailsa said, "No, but someone smashed the plants in her classroom too. People were talking about it on the bus yesterday."

But I didn't see The Full Picture until I was at Ailsa's the night before the The Cardiff Castle Which Is In Wales Trip.

I was half Massively Excited about my first ever sleepover (sleepovers at Mrs Quinney's when you're faking illness don't count) but half Seriously Worried something terrible was about to happen to me. And I'm not just talking about being on a coach with Connor Mould for four hours. I was worried someone would find out I was Miss Nobody.

And if you combine that worry and multiply it by About A Million then that was how I was feeling about Seb. Because when I'd popped in to say goodbye to him, he had barely opened his eyes.

When Dad dropped me off at Ailsa's, the moon was already out and the sky was grey but with a dark pink sweep across the horizon which reminded me of the big painting in Ailsa's kitchen. Dad switched off the engine and said, "Here we are. Listen, I'm certain Mrs Kingsley will make sure it doesn't happen again, you know, on the bus."

I said, "Yep, or Lucas will just actually kill me."

Dad laughed. "I really hope not!" He tapped the steering wheel and looked like he was about to say something then changed his mind. "Well, this is it! My first ever sleepover!"

And I said, "Oh my God, Dad, you're not staying over at Ailsa's with me!"

He said, "No! I mean, my first sleepover as a dad. As your dad. It's just I didn't expect to feel…well, I mean, it's like you're leaving home or something, that's all. I'll miss you."

"It's one night, Dad."

"I know. But still…" And he kissed my head and told me not to stay up all night talking which I said was literally the last thing that would ever happen.

And what I wanted to say but didn't was this: *I'm really worried about leaving Seb, because he hasn't seemed like himself for days, and please, please don't make me go on The Cardiff Castle Which Is In Wales Trip tomorrow because I want to stay at home and make sure Seb is okay.*

And of all the words I never said in my whole life,

which let's face it is Quite A Lot, those are probably the ones I wish I'd said the most.

But for me to say stuff like that I have to be feeling brave, and I wasn't. So I just said, "Bye," and reminded him what time to pick me up.

Ailsa's mum opened the door and said, "Helloooo!"

And Ailsa said, "Come in!"

Their house smelled of cooking and the windows were all steamed up. It felt a bit like when I go to Mrs Quinney's house because I felt like myself and I could speak normally there, only it didn't smell like they were making cabbage soup luckily. Me and Ailsa helped make dinner, which was fun because her mum had a special silver machine that made really long spaghetti.

After dinner her mum said she wanted to work on a new painting and would we be okay entertaining ourselves.

Ailsa said, "Can we use your laptop?"

And she said, "Yes, of course," without even asking why, which would just Totally Never Happen in my house.

Ailsa said, "She's started painting again." And I smiled because that was Definitely A Good Sign she wasn't still sad, according to Ailsa. Then she said, "Do you want to see the Miss Nobody stuff everyone's been talking about?" Because she knew about my dad's Computers Are Really Bad For Your Health Unlike The Encyclopedia incorrect theory, and maybe because I'd lied to her about not seeing it.

I was one hundred per cent sure I didn't want to look at it in front of Ailsa, but I said, "Okay," anyway.

Ailsa clicked through a few pages and then there it was. Blinking out at me: A Massive Miss Nobody Profile Of Hate. And it was like the Exact Opposite of one of her mum's paintings because it wasn't gold and orange and meadows and suns, it felt more like storms and chaos and darkness and like there was Nothing At All I could do to fix it.

I stared at the screen as Ailsa scrolled down. And I can't really describe how it felt, but it was like someone had stolen Miss Nobody's identity and turned her evil. And they had done it Big Style. There were horrible posts, memes about teachers, a list of people to get beaten up called Miss Nobody's Face Beats, photos of people from school with their faces swapped with animals, and not exactly very nice captions. It was an online hate-a-thon, and it had Miss Nobody's name written all over it.

"I don't understand," I said, which wasn't even A Lie.

"Me neither," said Ailsa. "It's like Miss Nobody has turned nasty."

"But…"

And that was all I could say. Because I wanted to tell Ailsa the truth – that I was Miss Nobody and I didn't write any of it, and that I didn't mean for any of this to happen – but I didn't have any words to say it. And not in an SM way as if they were hiding, but because they just wouldn't come into my head to begin with.

Then I noticed Miss Nobody's Face Beats said:

THAT ANNOYING Y9 LIBRARY GEEK WITH
A BRIEFCASE AND WRIST BANDAGES.

So instead of revealing my secret identity to Ailsa like I wanted, I suggested we did an emergency prayer for Rajit.

That night the sick feeling I had got worse the closer it got to six a.m. Each time I rolled over and tried to sleep, the words on the laptop appeared in my head, flashing silently at me in bold text. No matter which way I turned, or how tightly I shut my eyes, or how many times I told myself It Wasn't Me, the words

**I am
Miss Nobody**

kept flashing bigger and brighter and more silently.

It was still dark outside as I got ready. All I could think about was telling Ailsa the truth, but every time I thought about what to say, the words Disappeared Completely. And it made everything I did say sound like A Massive Lie. When I said I wanted cereal for breakfast and thank you for my packed lunch and thank you for having me, all I could hear was this Massive Silence where the truth should have been.

Ailsa's mum dropped us at school just as the sun was coming up, and we walked to reception where everyone was waiting for the coaches. People were milling around in groups and Mr Dean was carrying a clipboard and Connor was drinking a massive green can of ENERGIZE. I thought, great, just what I need when I'm already feeling sick – four hours in a confined space with a fully ENERGIZEd Connor Mould.

We stood with our class and Connor came straight over to us. He said, "Will it talk? Will it talk?" over and over again in between sips. His eyes were wide open and his lips were bright green.

Mr Dean looked up from his clipboard and said, "Connor, come here! Leave those girls alone!" Then Connor took his passport out of his pocket and handed it to him. Mr Dean said, "What is this? We're only going to Wales!"

"But you said it wasn't in England, sir."

Mr Dean let out a long sigh. "I give up. They're a lost generation."

The coaches arrived and me and Ailsa got pushed to the back of the queue while everyone else had a big squash for the back seat. Which actually turned out pretty well because we sat in the only double seat left, directly behind Mr Dean and another history teacher I didn't know. If it meant not being teased by Connor Mould, I was more than prepared to listen to Mr Dean's Interesting Things You Didn't Know About The Normans for four hours.

Ailsa fell asleep about an hour in, but all that time listening to Mrs Quinney must have given me some kind of anti-boredom staying power, because I spent the whole journey there and back learning way more about the Normans than probably the Normans themselves ever knew.

Anyway, the reason I am telling you about this trip is not because of Mr Dean's The Normans Were Incredible And That's A Fact! lecture or because when the tour guide said, "Don't worry, there is no such thing as a stupid question!" she obviously hadn't had someone like Connor on her tour before because he asked, "What was the date of the fort *erection* again, miss?" about fifty times. Or because Cardiff Castle really does have a wall of stone animals that Seb had told me about, or that we actually got to see a real live joust.

I am telling you about it because this happened.

After the joust show we were allowed to eat our packed

lunches before we had to get back on the coach. Everyone sat on the grass and as is Totally Normal For Our School, a few people started throwing food like they do sometimes in the canteen. Mr Dean told them to stop and sit down, but some people were still running around and two boys were pretending to joust each other with baguettes.

Me and Ailsa sat down away from everyone so I could talk, but mainly we wanted to eat without feeling like someone would attempt to smash our heads off with French bread. We found a grassy bit that wasn't too muddy. I took my coat off and put it on the ground so we could sit on it. I had so much spinning around in my head that I think I just forgot where we were, because suddenly I saw something flying through the air about to hit Ailsa. Before I knew what was happening I shouted, "Ailsa!" and quickly moved her out of the way.

Then everyone including me just stopped.

Because I had just heard what everyone else had just heard for the first time ever. Something I thought Might Never Be Possible: me speaking in front of people.

44

#emergency

The whole way back on the coach I felt like I was in a bubble. Octavia told me later it's called Having A Massive Shock. I know to most people saying literally one word like that is so not A Big Deal, but to Someone Like Me it felt like kind of A Big Deal. Kind of a Massive Deal actually.

Usually when these first-time talks happen, my voice comes out in a tiny scared whisper, but this time it was loud. And it sounded like my actual normal voice. That's why one word can feel like a major breakthrough for Someone Like Me. I also think it blew Connor's mind. He'd been trying to get me to speak for so long and all it took was for someone to throw half a cheese baguette at Ailsa.

The whole way back I was expecting him to double his teasing now he knew for sure I could speak, but actually he left me alone. I'm not sure if it was because he was so stunned I spoke or because he was experiencing some kind of massive sugar crash from all the cans of ENERGIZE, but he spent the whole journey passed out on the back seat with his bright green mouth wide open and his head on Vinnie's shoulder.

But anyway, it wasn't long before Connor Mould and my massive one-word breakthrough and all the rest of my problems became totally irrelevant to me.

When we got back to school I couldn't see my dad's car, which was weird because he was always on time for stuff like this because he knew I would panic if he wasn't there. And for my first school trip I knew he would definitely be there. Then I saw Ailsa's mum coming towards me. But she wasn't smiling like usual. She came up to us and put her arm around me, but she didn't say "Helloooo!" like she did last time. She said she was going to take me home because Seb had taken a turn for the worse and my parents couldn't leave him.

And when she said those words I stopped feeling pleased about my one-word speaking breakthrough because the only word filling up my head a million times over was:

Seb Seb Seb Seb Seb Seb Seb Seb Seb
Seb Seb Seb Seb Seb Seb Seb Seb Seb Seb
Seb Seb Seb Seb Seb Seb Seb Seb Seb Seb
Seb Seb Seb Seb Seb Seb Seb Seb Seb Seb
Seb Seb Seb Seb Seb Seb Seb Seb Seb Seb Seb
Seb Seb Seb Seb Seb Seb Seb Seb Seb Seb
Seb Seb Seb Seb Seb Seb Seb Seb

And everything else inside and outside my head went Totally Silent.

I don't know how many times I'd had a one-sided conversation with God, but I prayed as hard as I could the whole way home.

God, Mrs Quinney says you are Definitely Up There and listening to me, so please, please, please let Seb be okay. I know I have probably messed up majorly, but I need my little brother. Please, please let him be okay.

And I know it wasn't exactly the best prayer in the world or anything, but it turned out to be the last time I spoke to God anyway.

When we got to my house Ailsa and her mum came with me to the front door and Dad opened it before I even got to the first step. He pulled me into his arms and started crying, and said, "He's still here, Seb's still here. He's been holding on for you."

When I opened the door to his room, a nurse was sitting in the corner. Mum was holding Seb's hand, and even though she didn't sound like she was crying there were tears rolling down her face. When I came in Seb only smiled a tiny bit, not big like he usually did. He lifted his hand up to reach out for me, but he didn't really seem like my Seb at all.

Dad held my hand and said quietly, "He hasn't got long left now, Rozzie, he's not in any pain."

And I didn't understand what Dad meant at first, but then all of a sudden it sank in that I was losing him. And it felt like being suddenly plunged into really deep water, only worse because when you finally come up for air you don't have Seb any more and you can't breathe and the entire world has changed for ever.

45

#timetosay goodbye

I spent the morning of Seb's funeral wishing I had another brother or sister because when your heart and head are all broken up, it would probably be nice to have someone else who felt that way too. But instead it was Just Me and the sound of Mum crying because she didn't have the right shoes on, and for not putting better directions on the email they sent out to people, and because she couldn't find the necklace she wanted to wear, and how no one was answering the phone. But Dad said she was really upset because there was nothing she could have done to stop Seb from dying. And then I knew how she felt, because I felt like that too.

It had been eight days since Seb died, and my house felt a bit like it was underwater. People who had come round spoke quietly. No one laughed, and all the voices and noises seemed to blur together like *sorry* and *loss* and *tragic* and noises of teacups and crying and silences that were the bad kind.

Only that morning no one came round apart from Auntie Marie, who was the only person so far who still spoke in her normal voice. She was wearing all black apart from white lace gloves. She had a furry coat wrapped around her shoulders and a silver unicorn brooch pinned to her dress. She gave me a minty kiss on the cheek and said, "Now, don't you worry about speaking. I'm only here to give hugs." She poured what seemed like non-stop cups of tea for Mum, who only took a few tiny sips then left them on the side.

The whole time we were in the kitchen that morning waiting for the cars to take us to church, Auntie Marie never stopped talking; Mum held my hand really tightly and stroked my hair; Dad stared out of the window. And everything seemed to take a really, really long time.

Then suddenly Dad said, "They're here."

And everything speeded up.

The last thing on earth I wanted to do was leave the house and say goodbye to Seb for ever. But Auntie Marie took my hand and told me that unicorns have special powers that can protect us. She took the brooch from her dress and pinned it onto my cardigan. Then she squeezed my hand and said, "I'm right here. If you want anything at all today just come and squeeze my hand like this." She showed me a notepad and pen she had in her handbag and said, "Then write it in here, okay?" which strangely enough did make me feel strong enough to stand up and go outside, even though I didn't think I would ever be able to.

I knew it was going to be a really bad day, not just because pretty much my whole life Seb had been one of the few people in the universe I could talk to without feeling like I would lose any words, but because like everyone kept saying, he was a truly special person. I missed him more than anything. And A Million Times More than I could ever say, even if I could speak normally. Which I knew today I definitely couldn't.

In the car the sun was shining so brightly it hurt my eyes and Auntie Marie said, "He's shining down on us," and even though I wasn't one hundred per cent sure if she was talking about Seb or God, it made me feel a little bit better.

When we got there, Mrs Quinney came over to give me one of her hugs only it lasted even longer than normal.

She said, "Sometimes God takes back the really good ones so He can keep them as angels." And I thought Seb would like that because he was always going on about getting a brilliant job *and* wishing he had a superpower, so maybe now he had both. Although I did worry a little bit Seb might have asked God for tornado wees. Then she told me, "Funerals are so we can say goodbye, but Seb's already in heaven, so you can still talk to him any time you want." Only since he died I hadn't been able to speak to anyone, even God.

All my words were locked up inside my head and part of me was worried they would never come out, and part of me didn't want to let them go. I was glad Auntie Marie had given me the unicorn brooch because I needed all the protection I could get; even an actual real live unicorn probably wouldn't have felt like enough.

In church I tried really hard to not look at the huge photograph of Seb smiling, because what I was trying really hard to do was just breathe. Which it turns out isn't easy at all in Weird Situations Like This One, and the last thing I wanted to do was collapse and die at my brother's funeral for obvious reasons. Dad spoke about Seb and told everyone about his obsession with the pharaohs and how he had wanted to be mummified and everyone laughed even though they were sad, including me.

When we went back outside it was cold even though the sun was still really bright. I held onto Mum's hand and looked down at my black shoes on the concrete. She bent down and hugged me really tight and said, "You are so brave." Only I wasn't sure if that was true, but maybe she didn't notice all the tears in my eyes.

There were already people in my house when we got back. I recognized most of them even though I hadn't seen them for ages. Mum and Dad stopped inviting people I couldn't speak in front of years ago. I saw Brain and Mrs Long and Dr Howard and Nurse Mandy, and some of the people who lived on our street. And it felt like the house was underwater again because all the voices merged together, apart from Auntie Marie's telling people to eat the buffet and another one I knew, which was Ailsa's mum.

Ailsa was sitting next to her and looked sad until she saw me and then her green eyes lit up. She didn't say anything, just moved up so I could sit next to her. She put her arm around me and it made me feel less like I was alone (and less like I wanted to face-plant the buffet table). I didn't actually say anything to her that day, but I didn't feel so much like my entire brain was on lockdown either.

After she left Dad said, "You don't have to stay here with everyone if it's too much, Rozzie. If you want to go upstairs that's okay. Or Mrs Quinney said she can take you next door if you like, or you could go on the computer or something. People won't stay that late." Which wasn't Totally Weird because since Seb died Dad kept saying it was okay to do whatever I wanted, even go on the computer for hours. Like if I *had* suddenly face-planted the buffet table he would just say, "Don't worry, it's okay to face-plant buffets."

I did want to go to Mrs Quinney's, because there were still people in the house, but for some reason I decided to go onto the computer to check my blog first. And let me tell you, it is not a good idea at all to check your blog on the day of your brother's funeral, because what might happen is that you get a message which says this:

miss nobody u r DED

And after that it's possible the only thing that will make you feel better is one of Mrs Quinney's enormous-boob hugs, and luckily one was waiting for me next door.

46

#youshould
havetoldme

Mrs Quinney put a new set of calligraphy pens for me on the kitchen table and said, "To take your mind off it all, dear." I sat down and she held my hand with her eyes closed for ages (which is what she does when she is talking Directly To God) but I didn't close my eyes because I was still angry with Him for wanting Seb to be His angel instead of letting him stay on earth and be my little brother like what was supposed to happen.

Mrs Quinney took out her tin of photographs again and said, "I'm going to tell you something now, dear, that maybe I should have told you a long time ago. My name isn't Mrs Quinney." And it was like one of those dramatic

Casualty episodes and I thought, Oh My God! She is going to tell me she is really my mother and I am going to have to live with her for ever. But it wasn't.

She told me that she was a Quinney but not a Mrs like everyone thought, she was really a *Miss* Quinney.

Then she told me this story about the beautiful woman called Ida Quinney and the kind-looking man in the shirt and neckerchief called Henry O'Kelly, who I had seen in that old photograph.

In 1958 Ida Quinney met a man at her church called Henry O'Kelly. He had an incredible singing voice and she loved listening to him belting out the Praise God songs they always sang every Sunday. She had never seen a man like Henry before. He listened to Vicar Fernie's speeches with a huge smile on his face and she would always get to church early so she could sit in the exact same seat where she knew she could watch him (even though she was definitely primarily there to Praise God).

One day Henry asked her if she would like to take a walk beside the river because it was another glorious day on God's earth, and of course she nodded because she had been in love with him this whole time and never even spoken to him yet (which is what happened sometimes in the olden days). Henry had moved here from a place called Limerick with nothing more than a handful of luck and a pound note in his back pocket. Henry was just as obsessed with God as Ida and it wasn't long before they made the decision to go and do God's Work together.

They worked in many different countries and, no matter where they were or what time they finished work, they would always have supper together. Henry would say Grace and he would always end it by blessing the sick and needy children they were helping and right at the end he would say, "And please, Lord, bless Ida too." And when he said this, Ida would also secretly pray that Henry didn't notice her going bright red or how it took her heart ages to stop pounding or how she could barely speak. Because Ida was shy like me.

They worked right beside each other for nearly five years when one evening, just as they were eating their supper, Henry said he was going to move to America. He took Ida's hand and said, "Would you come with me as my wife, Ida?" But Ida was so shocked and scared about the hand touching and the proposal that she couldn't speak. Then Henry said, "Do you love me, Ida?" But she said nothing. And Henry left the next day and she never saw him ever again.

Miss Quinney wiped a tear from her eye, gave me a kiss on the head, patted my knee and told me, "Dear, there's a time for being quiet, and there's a time for speaking up."

#

I waited until I got a text from Dad saying everyone had gone before I went back home. I suppose I must have felt slightly worried about the latest death threat, but because I was so sad about Seb, no other feelings came anywhere close. Because since he'd died I'd had a really bad feeling in my stomach, a bit like before you go down a roller coaster but not in a This Is Scary But Exciting And What A Brilliant Ride! way, but more like This Is Too Scary And Not Fun At All And It Is Never Going To Stop And I Feel Like I Am Definitely Going To Die! So maybe that's why someone threatening to kill me didn't really have that much impact.

I went upstairs and saw Mum in Seb's room. She was lying down on his bed holding his pyjamas, staring at the glow-in-the-dark galaxy on the ceiling. I wanted to go in there and stare up at Seb's stars too, but I didn't know if that would make her more or less upset, so I just went straight to my room. Because what people don't tell you is when you lose that one super special person in your family, you also kind of lose the other people as well.

I got into bed worrying that maybe no one in my family would ever feel happy and I would never be able to speak ever again, and that I would end up spending my entire life living in Absolute Silence only not as a nun, but at home, not staring at Seb's ceiling stars and occasionally going next door to Miss Quinney's to eat cabbage soup, practise calligraphy and get enormous-boob hugs.

When I did finally fall asleep, I had bad dreams about Seb being trapped somewhere in the house but I couldn't find him to help get him out. I kept calling out for somebody to help but no one could hear me because my voice was so quiet and I woke myself up crying.

Mum came in not saying anything apart from, "Shh," but not in a Be Quiet way like teachers did in assembly. In a I Love You And Want You To Not Be Sad And Scared Any More sort of way, which made me feel like maybe I wasn't going to be Totally Alone And Silent for ever. She held me while the bad dream went away and a few minutes later Dad came in with hot chocolates. He didn't say anything either. But for the first time in ages it wasn't a rain-cloud-grey-silence, more like a rain-cloud-grey-with-some-sunlight-behind-it silence. Because I felt my words, that had been all scrunched up for days, slowly start to unfold.

After Mum and Dad went back to their room I got out of bed, opened my curtains and leaned on my window sill. I could feel the night air on my arms. I could only make out a few stars and the moon was half-covered by silvery clouds. I thought about God, and Seb maybe being up there somewhere in heaven. But at that exact moment, heaven seemed millions and millions of miles away from Byron Hill.

Then the clouds in front of the moon drifted away and as I looked down into the street below I could just make out the words

SUPER SEB

written in faded chalk near a puddle at the end of our drive.

Tears came into my eyes and for the first time since he died, I felt like my little brother was close to me. Like he had somehow died and gone to heaven, but at the same time stayed inside my heart. And it was Painful and Sad and Beautiful and Happy and Scary and Safe all at the same time.

I opened my mouth and said, "I love you, Seb." And I didn't even have to think about speaking because the words just came out by themselves. All that night, even when I fell asleep, I felt like Seb was watching over me. Then in the morning as soon as I woke up, I knew exactly what it was I had to do.

47

#letstalk

That morning I did what every girl has to do sometimes: I spoke to my dad about it. Obviously I didn't tell him The Whole Exact Truth; if he ever found out I had written a horrible blog post about Miss Sheldon he would probably have a massive heart attack from shock. And maybe it's Just Me, but I really didn't want to risk losing another family member.

So I said, "Dad, say you'd hurt someone by accident, what should you do?"

And Dad said, "Well, it depends. I suppose you should start by saying you're sorry."

I said, "But what if you can't?"

And he said, "Ah, I see. Well maybe you could *do* something to show you are sorry, like that time your mum was pregnant with Seb and I said she was starting to look quite big, which I meant as a compliment by the way, but she got upset, so I bought her some flowers, and a Take That album. And now that always does the trick when your mum has overreacted to something."

"I can hear you, by the way!" Mum shouted, and popped her head into the kitchen. "What actually happened was we had a fancy-dress party to go to and Dad said maybe I could go as Moby Dick!" And when I looked at her blankly she said, "Moby Dick is a *whale*. And by the way don't think I've forgiven you." And we all laughed for the first time in what felt like a hundred years. And I thought: for once Dad might actually Be On To Something.

Later that morning I sat in my bedroom with my phone in front of me, and the poem I'd written about Seb on the way back from the Space Centre, which seemed like a million years ago, in my hand. I looked down at Miss Carter's words at the bottom: *I hope you are able to read it to me one day*. I took a deep breath and waited until I was sure that tears were definitely not on their way, and pressed record.

Once I'd finished, I went onto the Manor High website, clicked on the English link, and found Miss

Carter's email address. I thought about what Octavia was always telling me about small steps, but as the Sent icon popped up and my phone made a whoosh sound, it felt like a pretty massive step forward actually.

That afternoon we went to the garden centre to buy a tree to plant in the park in Memory Of Seb. As we pulled into the car park, I asked Dad if I could get some plants for Miss Sheldon for helping me so much with my science fair project and he looked at me a bit strangely but Mum said, "What a lovely idea, Rozzie! Of course you can. You can have whatever you want!" I think they were so relieved I was talking again that they would have agreed to buy the naked statue by the entrance if I'd asked.

Mum chose a little silver birch tree sapling and I picked out three small indoor plants, then after we left we went straight to the park at the bottom of Clare Street. Mum picked a place near the corner to plant the tree and said, "It will be nice to come here and sit under it and think about Seb. He used to love playing here."

Dad said, "We were thinking about donating the money from Seb's holiday fund to the children's hospital. What do you think?"

I nodded, and I felt glad about it because they were nice to him there and anyway I didn't want to go to Egypt any more if Seb wasn't going. But there was something else I wanted to do with the money too.

After we planted the tree Mum said how much she loved Seb and that he would be in her heart for ever. Dad talked about how he would never forget the time Seb said his birthday wish was to live in a house made entirely out of jelly. And when it came to my turn there were some people walking past and Dad said, "Don't worry, Roz, you don't have to say anything."

But I took out my phone, tapped the recording I did earlier, and pressed play. When it had finished, I looked up to where I thought heaven might be and said really quietly, "Seb, you were a brilliant little brother. And a brilliant friend. And I love you." And in my head I added, *Please don't ask God for tornado wees.*

And when we got home Mum and Dad sat in front of the computer while I googled my idea for some of the holiday fund: Name A Star. Mum had tears in her eyes the whole time, and Dad kept asking me to go back so he could read all the links properly, but eventually we chose a supernova, the brightest star in the constellation, and named it Super Seb. Mum said, "He'll always be our lucky star," and Dad said he would set up the telescope so we could look at it later. And I didn't feel so much like Seb wasn't there any more.

#

I went back to school on the Friday after the Easter holidays. Mum said a Friday would be easier as it was just one day then the weekend. Dad said the best thing for us all to do was to carry on with our normal routines as much as possible because it was What Seb Would Have Wanted. Considering Seb said he wanted to live in a jelly house, I wasn't totally convinced. But I didn't complain or fake illnesses or even wish I didn't have to go, because this time I had stuff I wanted to do.

Dad drove me into school early, and I put my things in my locker then carried the little box of plants to the science block. I knocked on the science office door. I wanted to ask the technician lady Mrs Peterson if it would be okay to put the plants in science beakers for Miss Sheldon. I'd been practising what I was going to say, but when she opened the door she looked at me suspiciously and said, "What do you want?" I started taking a deep breath like I had practised, only before I was ready she said, "Come on! Are you messing about? I haven't got all day, what is it? Spit it out!"

And instead of coming out, my words got in a Massive Muddle. I tried to open my mouth but I couldn't even do that. I was trembling and the box of plants was shaking and then she did a massive loud sigh like people do when they want to let you know they are really annoyed and said, "What have you got those for?" And I knew I couldn't answer her so I just shrugged and looked at the floor. Then she said, "Honestly, you kids!" And the door closed.

And normally in this situation I would Totally Give Up On The Whole Idea. But today was different. Because I'd made a promise I couldn't break.

So I got out my word card and wrote in my notebook, then I knocked on the door again. This time when she answered she said, "You again!"

I nodded and handed her the card that said:

I'm Rosalind Banks, Form 7A. Sometimes I find it very difficult to speak. Please do not ask me to speak, and allow me to write down my answers.

While she was reading the card and the note I had written asking for the beakers, I mouthed a tiny, "Please," that hardly made any noise at all, but felt like the most giant loudest PLEASE that had ever existed anywhere.

And she said, "All right, but I'll check you gave them to Miss Sheldon later. God knows what you kids will do next!" And when I smiled I didn't look down but when I took the beakers I could feel my hands were still shaking.

I looked through the window of Miss Sheldon's classroom. She had her head down staring into a book.

I knocked on the door and went in. She glanced up and saw me with the plants then looked like she was about to cry, which wasn't really the reaction I was expecting. She said, "Rosalind! Oh my goodness! I'm so glad you're back! Are those for me? Thank you! That is so sweet of you! That has really cheered me up!" And half of me was Really Happy that I had made her feel cheered up, and half of me still felt Really Bad And Really Scared because I was the person who wrote the horrible stuff about her in the first place.

Miss Sheldon told me the Latin names for the plants and where they liked to grow, how they seeded and why she liked them and everything and I thought, whoops, she is really clever at science actually.

While she was talking I took deep breaths and my lips started to move. I tried to say "Miss Sheldon" only I kept stumbling over the M and I felt like my breath was running out. Then suddenly Mrs Peterson poked her head around the door and made me jump. She said loudly, "Just checking you've got the beakers, Miss Sheldon."

Miss Sheldon said, "Yes I have, Mrs Peterson, thanks. You don't need to worry about this student." And she looked at me and said, "She is one of the good ones!"

Then Mrs Peterson closed the door and I felt like I was falling from a great height because my tummy was flipping

over and over and over and my head was spinning. But I
thought, there's a time for being quiet and there's a time
for speaking up.

Deep breath. And Just Say It.

48

#canyou hearme

Mr Bryant must have told people in my class about Seb or something, because no one whispered *Mute-ant* or laughed when I walked into the classroom. Even Connor went past my desk without pushing all my stuff onto the floor. It was like I was no longer The Weird Girl Who Can't Speak, now I was The Weird Girl With A Dead Brother, which I suppose was a social step up in a funny kind of way.

The only person not acting weird around me in form time was Ailsa. And that's another Brilliant Thing about having a best friend. When they hug you it feels like they are wrapping a huge safety blanket around you and it gives you the feeling that everything is going to be okay, even if there is Quite A Big Chance it isn't.

At lunchtime we went to the library and when we got there Mrs Goodacre said, "You just come down here any time you need to, Rosemary. We've got Book Week starting on Monday, so that will cheer you up, I'm sure."

Rajit patted me on the back and said, "You've done some great work here, just let me know if you need some time off, after Book Week obviously."

William came over holding the *Guinness World Records* book and whispered, "Do you want to see a picture of Mrs Goodacre when she found out Rajit ordered a disco ball for Book Week?" And he showed me a picture of a woman with the world record for the poppiest out eyeballs.

Suzi took out a big biscuit tin and said, "I have some home-made cookies if you want some?"

And I smiled at the library squad without straight away looking at my shoes. That lunchtime I ate cookies and thought about how this whole time I'd been writing about how horrible everyone is at Manor High, but maybe I didn't really mean *everyone*. Because through some kind of Weird Silent Miracle that I didn't exactly notice, the library squad had actually been my friends all along.

We were allowed to miss lessons in the afternoon to

help get everything ready for Book Week. We moved tables and got new books out of boxes and put signs up, blew up balloons, and put stickers and badges out.

Rajit said, "I'm managing the whole event now by the way." He was wearing sunglasses, and had a T-shirt on under his blazer that said *On My Day Off I Slay Dragons*. He had a walkie-talkie in his hand which he kept tapping and saying, "Mrs G, do you read me? Over." But I think Mrs Goodacre must have switched her end off.

While we were hanging up the final decorations I asked Ailsa, "So did Rajit get beaten up after that Face Beat thing we saw?"

Ailsa said, "No, he's been wearing those sunglasses all week. Mrs Goodacre keeps telling him to take them off."

Suzi said, "I don't think anyone would Face Beat Rajit." And when me and Ailsa looked confused, she said, "Since he's not been allowed to play World of Warcraft, he's been watching all these cage-fighting videos."

We all looked over at Rajit tapping the walkie-talkie and repeating, "Come in, Mrs G! We need paperclips, over!"

Suzi said, "He practises the moves on the bus! No one dares go near him. Anyway those pages have all been taken down now."

Ailsa nodded. "I heard it was a girl in Year Nine. She's called, um, Chrissie or something like that, I think."

And without even thinking I said, "Crystal?"

Ailsa pulled out a string of coloured pom-poms. "Yeah, Crystal, that's it. Do you know who she is?"

Before I could answer Suzi said, "Crystal's been permanently excluded. She made all those horrible pages about Maisy, and she was sending her nasty texts too, pretending to be Miss Nobody apparently, to get back at her for the stuff she wrote on her blog. She thought Miss Nobody would get the blame. She'd even been sending Miss Nobody death threats apparently. Mr Endeby interviewed all of her clones, and some of them told him. People in my class think Miss Nobody was actually one of Crystal's clones – maybe one of them didn't like her very much."

And I said, "It wasn't."

Ailsa and Suzi both looked at me and Suzi said, "Oh, so who was it?"

And I did what Octavia told me to do which was this: Breathe. Wait. *Say* It.

"It was me."

49

#lastwords

That was yesterday, and now here I am, in the park on my own, sitting next to Seb's tree. The park is empty apart from a few people walking their dogs. And this is where my story sort of ends and where it sort of begins.

I have a brand-new calligraphy notebook that Mum bought me, and it sort of feels like a brand-new start for me too. And even though I'm technically an only child now, I don't really feel like one.

I put my headphones in and listen to one of the playlists I made for Seb ages ago, the first time he had to stay in hospital. And as it plays, I think about him. And the part of my heart I thought would have a massive gap in it after he died fills up with all the stuff I loved about him. And you can't feel sad all the time when one of the things your heart's filled up with is poo jokes.

The last time I saw Octavia, her keys were jangling around her neck. I said I wished she had a magic key to unlock my words. She said people don't come with magic keys, but that everything I had done so far was unlocking my words, little by little. And that I would carry on feeling less nervous and less afraid and less jumbled up. And that I could do it. In small steps.

And I think, maybe she's right.

(Maybe.)

I open my notebook at the first page and start writing. And as I write I say the words quietly. There's a man walking his dog nearby who can probably hear me, but I can't hear my voice over the music anyway, so I don't mind so much. (I don't care about the dog hearing me.) And this is what I write:

THE REAL MISS NOBODY

It seems like there has been a Major Case of mistaken identity at Manor High. And I'm not the sort of person who can leave a case like this unsolved.

So here goes.

When I started this blog I wasn't sure if anyone would read it. Most of you hadn't even noticed me before, so I didn't exactly expect to become one of the most famous girls in school. Only now people know Miss Nobody for all the wrong reasons.

And that's Just Not Right.

So, let me get a few things straight, because even if there isn't exactly a Happy Ending for me, at least there will be a truthful one for Miss Nobody.

The only place I've written anything about people at Manor High is right here, on this blog. Nowhere else.

This is the only place online you will find the real Miss Nobody.

Only Miss Nobody isn't going to be online any more.

So if you want to hear my Final Blog Post, live (and find out who I really am) come to the library at lunchtime on Monday.

I put my hand on the nearest branch of Seb's tree and say, "You'd better be there too, super little brother."

Miss Nobody only has one thing left to say. And it is definitely going to be the hardest.

50

#ablastfrom
thepast

One thing I didn't think would happen was this:

There are only 382 people named Henry O'Kelly living in America.

And only eight of them are aged over sixty-five.

So it didn't take me long at all to find the one Henry O'Kelly I was looking for.

But then, I've always known God is a bit like that.

What also made it easy was that that particular Henry O'Kelly had been searching for Miss Ida Quinney for years. (And he has his own YouTube channel.)

He has an online group for old people who want to get fit and get into God, called *Henry OK, You OK!* He posts video Bible talks that also give you health tips, like *Reach Up To The Sky For Ten And Pray!* and *Juice For Jesus!* and *Staying Holy With Guacamole!*

And this morning, when I open my email, I see this:

HEY THERE, ROSALIND!

You don't know how happy it has made me to get your email! I have been trying to find Ida Quinney for the past two years almost! I'm so thankful to you for getting in touch with me. Please tell Ida I think about her often, all the good work we did, all the wonderful suppers she cooked me! And my goodness, she used to bake me the most incredible currant buns! It all seems so long ago now. I guess it was – over fifty years! I've changed a little since the photograph you sent! I would love to speak to Ida, maybe we can set up a video chat for this week sometime?? That's if you can get her in front of a computer! Crazy she doesn't have email! I cannot tell you how happy I am to have found her again.

Written with the greatest respect and thanks to you,

Henry OK

And even Dad had to agree this is an example of Google being so much better than the *Encyclopedia Britannica*.

51

#beingquiet
andspeaking
up

Auntie Marie told me to keep the unicorn brooch she gave me at Seb's funeral. So I keep it in a special box on the chest of drawers in my bedroom and every time I look at it I think it is Totally Heartbreaking and Totally Magical at the same time. This morning, I pin it onto my blazer, and say a mini prayer asking for its magical forcefield to surround and protect me, hoping that unicorn forcefields work a bit better than pooperhero ones. Believe me, today I am going to need some magic.

Because today is my first and last day being Miss Nobody.

Dad drives me to school extra early, and before I get

out of the car he says, "I'm so proud of you, Rozzie," then he kisses me on the forehead. "Me and Mum are so lucky to have you."

And I just hope he remembers that if this all goes horribly wrong.

At lunchtime I go straight to the library, feeling like I am riding some kind of roller coaster, but one where you can't even see the end. Mrs Goodacre is pinning up the *Book Week!* banner Ailsa and her mum made over the weekend. It's decorated all around the edges with tiny book pages. Mrs Goodacre says, "Doesn't it look amazing, Rosemary!" and for the first time ever she is wearing lipstick. Book Week must be the librarian equivalent of being invited out for dinner or something.

I nod and then Rajit appears, wearing sunglasses and some sort of microphone headset. He's holding a clipboard and asks Mrs Goodacre to check the guest list but she says, "For the millionth time, Rajit – there is no guest list, everyone is invited!" Then she looks at his clipboard and says, "There isn't a VIP area either." Rajit smiles awkwardly and nods towards the tables in the corner that are roped off. Mrs Goodacre says, "My goodness!" and rolls her eyes, then makes her way over to the corner, with Rajit following, trying to persuade her to at least let him keep Gareth and Gus, the twins from his class, on the door as Security.

Ailsa asks me if I'm feeling okay and I say, "I think so," even though I'm not. I feel like when it's sunny but you look out of the window and see dark clouds in the distance only you're not sure if they will come this way or not.

I've done a lot of things over the past few months that I'm pretty proud of, and some that I am Definitely Not. But I want to make a Totally Fresh Start really badly, so I have to do it. Besides, I made a promise. Plus Octavia gave me one of her one hundred per cent guarantees that even if The Worst Possible Thing Happens (everybody in the school punches me in the face) I will still feel so much better for Just Saying It. And even though she is technically a therapist and everything, I trust her. Anyway, if it all does go totally wrong and I get excluded, my parents will *have* to agree to homeschool me.

There's a small stage set up by the windows for a local author to do a talk. It starts raining and Mrs Goodacre says, "Oh good! That should make a few more people come." Which isn't exactly what I want to hear, and as I look up at the grey sky I wonder if God is trying to tell me something, but I'm not quite sure what it is. And I'm not supposed to be looking for Signs From God any more.

People start coming in and William directs them to sit down in front of the stage. A man with a beard makes his way over to Mrs Goodacre and says, "So sorry I'm late, but I had some problems getting through your security." Rajit suddenly pretends his phone is ringing.

My hands are sweating and I can feel my throat getting drier and drier. As more and more people sit down I can hear whispers going around about Miss Nobody. That she is here somewhere. People are looking around as if they expect her to suddenly appear in a puff of smoke like some kind of blogging magician. And considering how I feel about magicians, that obviously isn't going to happen. Anyway, Mrs Goodacre had already said no to Rajit's request for a smoke machine.

My legs feel weak so I do a few deep breaths. Then I spot Miss Sheldon. She smiles and gives me the thumbs up. And whatever strength I have (or don't have) right now, I suddenly feel sure that God In All His Holy Glory and Miss Sheldon, Plant Expert And Nicest Teacher Ever, are on my side.

There are so many words going through my mind. They start tumbling and twisting like they are getting into a Massive Muddle as usual and I won't be able to say any of them. But this time I'm expecting it. And I'm ready. I take out the cards from my pocket I wrote in my best calligraphy yesterday and look down at them. And they say this:

From Octavia: Breathe. Never underestimate the importance of your breath. You can live without food for weeks and without water for days, but without breathing you would only survive a few minutes. Respect how powerful it can be Just To Breathe. Breathe, and the words will come when they are ready. People will wait. Take a deep breath. And Just Say It.

From Miss Sheldon: If I held it against someone anytime they made a mistake I don't think I could be a teacher! Don't feel bad for making a mistake, particularly when you've been brave enough to say you're sorry. It's okay. (Thumbs Up.)

From Mum: If the words you want to say are important for people to hear, then you have to try to say them, even if trying is really, really hard. And: I love you whatever happens.

From Dad: People say to imagine the audience naked, but in your situation I don't think that would be totally appropriate, so maybe imagine them in their pyjamas or something. Or you could imagine that you're just talking to us. No one else. Just me and Mum.

From Ailsa: Of course I'm still your friend! We'll be friends for ever. (And that's how it feels to have The Holy Grail Of Friendships: A Friend For Life.)

From Miss Quinney: There's a time for being quiet and there's a time for Speaking Up.

And I think back to the last ever time I saw Seb, the day after I got back from Cardiff.

We'd been sitting with him all night, and the sun was just starting to come up. I could hear the birds singing outside, but no one opened the curtains, and his room was filled with a pale orange glow. Seb was lying on his bed and he was so weak he could hardly move. He said in a quiet voice, "By the way, I've changed my mind about going to see the pyramids." Even on his deathbed he could still make me laugh. Then he said, "If I do still get a Dream Come True wish, it's for you to be able to speak whenever you want, Rozzie, because I think what you say is pretty cool." And my heart felt Totally Full Up, then he said, "Well, either that or space travel." And laughed quietly saying, "LOLcano!" He held my hand and said, "You know you thought your superpower was being weird. Well, I think it's being a brilliant sister." And before I thought that when it comes to having friends, brothers don't count. But brothers do count, they count pretty Big Time actually. And even though Mum and Dad and Nurse Mandy were there, some of the truth about being Miss Nobody came tumbling out without me even trying to say anything.

Afterwards Seb told me that one of the reasons he felt so happy all the time was because of me and the things I said to him, and how if I could make him feel better about having poo-kaemia then I could definitely tell the truth about Miss Nobody, even if I only said it once. Then he told me about one of his favourite astronauts called Chris Hadfield, who is afraid of heights but became an astronaut anyway because it was his Dream Come True, so now he's been higher than anyone on earth, even though he still felt afraid. Then Seb made me promise I would try to make my Dream Come True by speaking up. And promises to brothers definitely count.

So I turn to the next card I wrote last night and on it is this:

From Seb, my Super Little Brother and Best Friend: Promise me you will try to speak. Even it feels really scary. And: you do have a superpower because it's being my sister.

Mrs Goodacre is setting up the microphone and Ailsa gives my hand a squeeze. "You can do it!" she whispers, "And me and Suzi are here with cookies whatever happens."

I take a really deep breath, smile and whisper, "Thanks." I touch the unicorn brooch, which feels cold against my hands because they are so hot. And I think about my super little brother. And his star being up there somewhere, shining really brightly, even though I can't see it. And I think about the words I want to say. And all the words I haven't. And I breathe. And I feel really, really scared.

Then I step up.

I say to Mrs Goodacre, "Please can I just say something first?" And she looks confused and surprised but nods. I hear a few people saying, "It's That Girl Who Can't Speak!" and then Connor shouts, "Shut up! That's not true, she can speak!" And I think: maybe Connor Mould has a moral compass after all.

Then I think, he's right actually. I can speak.

And this is what I say:

"My name is Rosalind Banks. And I'm Miss Nobody. Only I'm not a Nobody. And neither are you."

If you have been affected by the
issues raised in this book, you can find
help by calling Childline on
0800 1111

Or by visiting their website at
Childline.org.uk

The
story behind
BEING
MISS NOBODY

author
interview

*Like Rosalind, **Faith Jackson** is a huge fan of books – despite spending her earliest primary school years struggling to read, by the time she was eleven she was reading 1,151 books in a year. Not quite a teenager yet, she still reads A LOT, and tweets about all the books she loves at **@272BookFaith**. So she's the perfect person to ask amazing author **Tamsin Winter** all about* **Being Miss Nobody***…*

Faith: I adored this book. It was heartbreaking at the end but it's still brilliant. I really like the idea of Miss Nobody and OBVIOUSLY I loved the books and the library! It's so interesting to hear a story from the perspective of someone who can't talk. What, or who, gave you the idea for *Being Miss Nobody*?

Tamsin: I had been trying to think of a book idea for a while, and I was just daydreaming, like I often do, when quite suddenly a very strong image came into my mind. It was of a dark-haired girl sitting in a classroom with her head down, being ignored by everybody, totally silent, with all these words inside her head, but unable to speak any of them. That girl was Rosalind Banks. And I knew immediately that I had to write her story.

Faith: How did you come up with the characters' names?

Tamsin: Rosalind has always been one of my favourite names, and it's the name of a family friend who actually shares my birthday. Mrs Quinney's name just popped into my head when I was imagining her – I wanted something quite old-fashioned sounding. The rest of the characters' names just seemed to come as I imagined what they looked like and how they acted. I do spend a lot of time googling names sometimes!

Faith: Is it hard writing from a child's perspective?

Tamsin: I can remember very vividly what it felt like to be a child and a teenager. I've worked with young people for the past fifteen years, so I've heard their voices a lot!

Rosalind's voice was very distinctive to me, so writing from her perspective felt very natural. I wrote a lot of the book "out loud", so I was speaking her voice and the voices of the other characters. I find this a really good way of writing, but it does make people look at you strangely in cafes.

Faith: Are any of the things in this book based on your own experiences, or those of someone you know?

Tamsin: A lot of Rosalind's anxieties and fears are quite close to my own experiences growing up, although for very different reasons. The magician memory from Rosalind's childhood at the beginning of the book is similar to something I experienced as a child, along with someone criticizing me for being "too sensitive". Little moments like that can shape your understanding of the world. I think most of us are a little more vulnerable than we show.

Faith: Who is your favourite character?

Tamsin: Very tough question! It's a bit like asking which person in your family you like the best! The characters all feel very real to me, probably because I've had so many imaginary conversations with them. Rosalind, as the main character, will always be very special to me. Her brother, Seb, is a little ray of sunshine despite his illness, and is so close to Rosalind, it made writing the later chapters very difficult. I loved writing the back story for Mrs Quinney; she has a lot more to her than we see at the beginning. The character who made me laugh the most while I was writing was probably Rajit. His outrageous plans for Book Week just crack me up.

Faith: Which character is most like you?

Tamsin: I suppose I'm a mixture of a few different characters. I have a lot of insecurities and worries sometimes, and my thoughts always go straight to the "worst-case scenario" like Rosalind, and I have quite a dark sense of humour, although I am much more outgoing and talkative, like Octavia. I've probably got a little bit of Mrs Quinney in me too. I've been known to put bonnets on cats. That's all I'm saying.

Faith: When and where did you write *Being Miss Nobody*?

Tamsin: I began writing *Being Miss Nobody* a few years ago. I've written parts of it in the UK, in Switzerland, in

Italy and even in Dubai, so quite a lot of different places for one book really! I wrote some of it while out for long country walks, just putting pieces of the story together in my head and deciding how to describe certain scenes. A lot of it I wrote very late at night. I finally wrote *The End* at about 3 a.m. one morning, which was too late to celebrate or even tell anyone I'd finished. The good thing about writing is you can do it anywhere. That's also the bad thing about writing. My brain never switches off.

Faith: Is there anything that helps you to write?

Tamsin: There are times when I have so many ideas I can't type quickly enough, but other days I can barely get to the end of a page. Playing the scene out like a film in my head is something that really helps me. I go out and observe the world very closely, trying to notice interesting little details. I'm kind to myself on bad writing days. I tell myself I can do it. Books are very hard things to write. I eat a lot of peanut-butter sandwiches. I find they also help.

Faith: Is there a particular message you wanted to send through Rosalind's story?

Tamsin: I think the biggest message of the story is the importance of speaking up – of not being afraid to stand up in front of people and tell them what you think, or being afraid but doing it anyway. It's something I found incredibly difficult as a young person. I also wanted the book to show how you can lose someone close to you, but keep them at the same time, and the absolute million per cent importance of having a friend. And a library!

Faith: Do you think social media is a good or a bad thing?

Tamsin: As a teacher, I have seen the negative effects of social media on young people: cyberbullying, the lack of privacy, how addictive it is, how it can lead to low self-esteem, and how false it can all be. But I've also seen how amazing social media can be in connecting like-minded people, in creating a positive force for change, and enabling people to speak up, so I wanted to explore that in *Being Miss Nobody*. I'm glad social media didn't exist when I was a teenager. I was too naïve. I thought a perm was a good idea, for example.

Faith: Do you think you will write any more books like this one?

Tamsin: I'm currently writing my second novel, which will be coming out in 2018. It's not related to *Being Miss Nobody* as it's about a whole new character. She's funny and quirky and sweet, but definitely has more of an attitude than Rosalind. Her family is also completely different – a lot more dysfunctional! There's a little bit of magic in it too, although most of it goes wrong. I think part of being human is everything going a bit wrong, and figuring out how to get things right again. It's how we grow.

For more from Tamsin and Faith,
follow them on Twitter:

@MsWinterTweets
@272BookFaith
#beingmissnobody

Look out for another
incredible book
from Tamsin Winter
in 2018...

Jemima Small isn't happy.

She's the opposite of what she thinks
a twelve-year-old girl should be.

Firstly, she's not small, she's big. Then there's
her school report, AKA the worst school report her
dad has ever seen in his life. And finally she's not happy
about her mum, who disappeared from her life before
Jemima can even remember her being in it.

So Jemima has decided she wants to become
someone else: the perfect girl she'd be if she could just
be better at basically everything. And so she makes a
list of all the things she needs to change:
The "If Girl" list...

Find out more at
tamsinwinter.com

Acknowledgements

Firstly, I would like to thank my agent, Luigi Bonomi. You were the first person to read *Being Miss Nobody*, and the first person to believe it would make it this far. Thank you, Luigi, and everyone at LBA Books, for starting me on this rather incredible journey.

I also owe an enormous thank you – actually thank yous aren't really big enough to cover your enthusiasm, support, and all the LOLs, OMGs and tears in all the right places! – to my brilliant editor, Rebecca Hill – I feel incredibly lucky to have you.

Thank you to Sarah Stewart and Amy Dobson, and the brilliantly hard-working and talented team at Usborne, who have led me down a path of, quite frankly, debilitating fear and anxiety! But with kindness, friendship and love. Thank you for being such awesome people.

I would also like to take this opportunity to thank Dr Joseph Vilanova, for recognizing this as one of my not-so-crazy ideas, and making me believe I could do it. Thank you to Becky Pinney for your valuable medical insight.

I also want to say a huge thank you to my family – your constant support, belief, encouragement, wisdom (and babysitting) has helped make this dream come true, and feel even more awesome than I imagined; thank you for not being normal.

A huge thank you to my friends, especially to Laura and Mhairi – BFFs just don't come better than you.

The biggest thank you I want to say is to Felix, for filling my heart up with love, wonder and silliness. You are my lucky star.

And finally, to my readers, thank you for choosing *Being Miss Nobody* amongst all the thousands of other books you actually still have time to read.

Tamsin Winter grew up in a tiny village in Northamptonshire where there was nothing to do. Subsequently, she spent her childhood reading books and writing stories, mostly about cats. She has a degree in English literature and creative writing, and has been teaching, travelling the world and daydreaming for most of her adult life. She currently lives in Leicestershire with her son. *Being Miss Nobody* is her first book.

www.tamsinwinter.com

 tamsinwinterbooks

@MsWinterTweets

 @tamsinwinterauthor